茅盾

# Spring Silkworms

## and Other Stories

by
### Mao Tun

**Fredonia Books**
**Amsterdam, The Netherlands**

Spring Silkworms and Other Stories

by
Mao Tun

ISBN: 1-4101-0219-X

Reprinted from the 1979 edition

Fredonia Books
Amsterdam, The Netherlands
http://www.fredoniabooks.com

# CONTENTS

# CONTENTS

# EDITOR'S NOTE

The thirteen short stories presented in this book were written between 1932 and 1943 by Mao Tun, one of China's foremost living authors. With the exception of *Great Marsh District,* which is based on a historical tale, and *Frustration,* with the War of Resistance Against Japan (1937-45) as its background, the stories describe the changes in Chinese society during the turbulent years between 1927 and 1936.

That period found China in the midst of the Second Revolutionary Civil War. Chiang Kai-shek and the Kuomintang, having betrayed the revolution with the support of the imperialist powers, particularly the United States of America, imposed a fascist rule of terror. Chiang Kai-shek and his gang ruthlessly oppressed the Chinese people and waged a civil war against the Communists in an attempt to end the revolutionary movement once and for all. At the same time, the imperialists intensified their political and economic aggression and there were endless battles among the various warlord groupings of the Kuomintang. As a result, workers and peasants in Kuomintang-controlled areas were increasingly hard put.

All over China the imperialist powers expanded their "spheres of influence." In 1931 Japan decided the time was ripe for a military adventure and invaded China's Northeast provinces. The Chinese Communist Party was the first to call upon the people to fight back. The entire nation was aroused. But the Chiang Kai-shek regime was more interested in its unpopular war against the Communists and adopted a non-resistance policy towards the Japanese. The whole of China's Northeast soon fell into the hands of the aggressor. In 1932 the Japanese attacked Shanghai. Inspired by the nationwide anti-Japanese movement, the 19th Route Army of the Kuomintang offered a partial resistance which collapsed, however, due to the policy of surrender pursued by Chiang Kai-shek.

In 1933 the Communist Party proposed that the Kuomintang end the civil war and institute democratic reforms as a basis for a united effort against the invaders. In 1935 the Party called for the establishment of a national united front and led the students in Peking in a huge demonstration which demanded resistance against Japan to save the nation. Throughout the land the people's fighting spirit was stimulated by the efforts of the Communist Party and the programme it advocated.

Finally, in 1936, Chiang Kai-shek was compelled to end the civil war. In consequence, under the leadership of the Communist Party, the people were able to fight back resolutely when Japan, using the Lukouchiao (Marco Polo Bridge) Incident as a pretext, began its all-out war against China in 1937.

The book is divided into four parts, according to the time or content of the stories. In the first part, *Spring Silkworms*, *Autumn Harvest* and *Winter Ruin* comprise a trilogy depicting the collapse of China's rural economy under the combined depredations of imperialism and feudalism. They date shortly before the Japanese attack on Shanghai in 1932. *Epitome* introduces the unlovely family of a small town despot who, quite typically, combines the activities of official and racketeer.

The second part contains four stories. They reflect the impact of Japanese imperialism on people of different occupations. *The Shop of the Lin Family* inevitably collapses, crushed by war, the bankrupt countryside and grafting Kuomintang officials. *Wartime* contrasts the attitudes of two classes of individuals in 1932 during the Japanese invasion of Shanghai — the fighting worker and the vacillating petty bourgeois intellectual. *Big Nose* represents the millions of homeless waifs who wandered through the streets of China's cities, cast-offs of a rapacious society. In *Second Generation* youngsters are already following in the footsteps of their fathers and mothers to join the political demonstrations for a free and democratic China.

There are three stories in part three, each portraying a different type of Chinese capitalist. *The Bewilderment of Mr. Chao* is a tale of a petty operator in the Stock Exchange, a little fish in the process of being eaten by the big. *A True Chinese Patriot* lampoons China's comprador bourgeoisie — agents for foreign monopolies — who waxed fat and pompous at the people's expense. *Frustration*, besides twitting a lady of leisure, depicts the disillusionment of small industrialists who moved their plants to the interior in the naive belief that Chiang Kai-shek's Kuomintang was going to build up national industry.

The fourth part contains two stories. *First Morning at the Office* gives a devastating picture of the fatuousness of Shanghai's commercial offices and the humiliations a woman white-collar worker had to endure. *Great Marsh District*, an imaginative account of the first peasant uprising in ancient China, is one of the many stories from history and folk tales which Mao Tun has written.

Mao Tun wields his acid-dipped pen skilfully and with vigour. Mercilessly flaying the sins of China's old society, he suffers and strives with the oppressed and exploited and thunderously calls them to action. In the stirring days between 1927 and 1936, the revolutionary forces fought on in spite of imperialist intervention and Chiang Kai-shek's reign of terror. Mao Tun, as an active participant in the struggle, knew every level and corner of Chinese society. Here, in this cross-section of his best short stories, we find a remarkable introduction to the awakening of the Chinese people.

# SPRING SILKWORMS

Old Tung Pao sat on a rock beside the road that skirted the canal, his long-stemmed pipe lying on the ground next to him. Though it was only a few days after "Clear and Bright Festival" the April sun was already very strong. It scorched Old Tung Pao's spine like a basin of fire. Straining down the road, the men towing the fast junk wore only thin tunics, open in front. They were bent far forward, pulling, pulling, pulling, great beads of sweat dripping from their brows.

The sight of others toiling strenuously made Old Tung Pao feel even warmer; he began to itch. He was still wearing the tattered padded jacket in which he had passed the winter. His unlined jacket had not yet been redeemed from the pawn shop. Who would have believed it could get so hot right after "Clear and Bright"?

Even the weather's not what it used to be, Old Tung Pao said to himself, and spat emphatically.

Before him, the water of the canal was green and shiny. Occasional passing boats broke the mirror-smooth surface into ripples and eddies, turning the reflection of the earthen bank and the long line of mulberry trees flanking it into a dancing grey blur. But not for long! Gradually the trees reappeared, twisting and weaving drunkenly. Another few minutes, and they were again standing still, reflected as clearly as before. On the gnarled fists of the mulberry branches, little fingers of tender green buds were already bursting forth. Crowded close together, the trees along the canal seemed to march endlessly into the distance. The unplanted fields as yet were only cracked clods of dry earth; the mulberry trees reigned supreme here this time of the year! Behind Old Tung Pao's back was another great stretch of mulberry trees, squat, silent. The little buds seemed to be growing bigger every second in the hot sunlight.

Not far from where Old Tung Pao was sitting, a grey two-storey building crouched beside the road. That was the silk filature, where the delicate fibres were removed from the cocoons. Two weeks ago it was occupied by troops; a few short trenches still scarred the fields around it. Everyone had said that the Japanese soldiers were attacking in this direction. The rich people in the market town had all run away. Now the troops were gone and the silk filature stood empty and locked as before. There would be no noise and excitement in it again until cocoon selling time.

Old Tung Pao had heard Young Master Chen — son of the Master Chen who lived in town — say that Shanghai was seething with unrest, that all the silk weaving factories had closed their doors, that the silk filatures here probably wouldn't open either. But he couldn't believe it. He had been through many periods of turmoil and strife in his sixty years, yet he had never seen a time when the shiny green mulberry leaves had been allowed to wither on the branches and become fodder for the sheep. Of course if the silkworm eggs shouldn't ripen, that would be different. Such matters were all in the hands of the Old Lord of the Sky. Who could foretell His will?

"Only just after Clear and Bright and so hot already!" marvelled Old Tung Pao, gazing at the small green mulberry leaves. He was happy as well as surprised. He could remember only one year when it was too hot for padded clothes at Clear and Bright. He was in his twenties then, and the silkworm eggs had hatched "two hundred per cent"! That was the year he got married. His family was flourishing in those days. His father was like an experienced plough ox — there was nothing he didn't understand, nothing he wasn't willing to try. Even his old grandfather — the one who had first started the family on the road to prosperity — seemed to be growing more hearty with age, in spite of the hard time he was said to have had during the years he was a prisoner of the "Long Hairs."*

Old Master Chen was still alive then. His son, the present Master Chen, hadn't begun smoking opium yet, and the "House of Chen" hadn't become the bad lot it was today. Moreover, even though the House of Chen was of the rich gentry and his own family only ordinary tillers of the land, Old Tung Pao had felt that the destinies of the two families were linked together. Years ago, "Long Hairs" campaigning through the countryside had captured Tung Pao's grandfather and Old Master Chen and kept them working as prisoners for nearly seven years in the same camp. They had escaped together, taking a lot of the "Long Hairs'" gold with them — people still talk about it to this day. What's more, at the same time Old Master Chen's silk trade began to prosper, the cocoon raising of Tung Pao's family grew successful too. Within ten years grandfather had earned enough to buy three acres of rice paddy, two acres of mulberry grove, and build a modest house. Tung Pao's family was the envy of the people of East Village, just as the House of Chen ranked among the first families in the market town.

But afterwards, both families had declined. Today, Old Tung Pao had no land of his own, in fact he was over three hundred silver dollars in debt. The House of Chen was finished too. People said the spirit of the dead "Long Hairs" had sued the Chens in the underworld, and because the King of Hell had decreed that the Chens repay the fortune they had amassed on the stolen gold, the family had gone down financially very quickly. Old Tung Pao was rather inclined to believe this. If it hadn't been for the influence of devils, why would a decent

---

* In the middle of the 19th century, China's oppressed peasants rose against the feudal Ching dynasty in one of the longest (1851-64) and bitterest revolutions in history. Known as the Taiping Revolution, it was defeated only with the assistance of the interventionist forces of England, France and the United States of America

The Ching rulers hated and feared the "Long Hairs," as they slanderously called the Taiping Army men, and fabricated all sorts of lies about them in a vain attempt to discredit them with the people.

Old Tung Pao, although steadily deteriorating economically, was typical of the rich peasants Like others of his class, he felt and thought the same as the feudal landlord rulers

fellow like Master Chen have taken to smoking opium?

What Old Tung Pao could never understand was why the fall of the House of Chen should affect his own family. They certainly hadn't kept any of the "Long Hairs'" gold. True, his father had related that when grandfather was escaping from the "Long Hairs'" camp he had run into a young "Long Hair" on patrol and had to kill him. What else could he have done? It was "fate"! Still from Tung Pao's earliest recollections, his family had prayed and offered sacrifices to appease the soul of the departed young "Long Hair" time and time again. That little wronged spirit should have left the nether world and been reborn long ago by now! Although Old Tung Pao couldn't recall what sort of man his grandfather was, he knew his father had been hard-working and honest — he had seen that with his own eyes. Old Tung Pao himself was a respectable person; both Ah Sze, his elder son, and his daughter-in-law were industrious and frugal. Only his younger son, Ah To, was inclined to be a little flighty. But youngsters were all like that. There was nothing really bad about the boy. . . .

Old Tung Pao raised his wrinkled face, scorched by years of hot sun to the colour of dark parchment. He gazed bitterly at the canal before him, at the boats on its waters, at the mulberry trees along its banks. All were approximately the same as they had been when he was twenty. But the world had changed. His family now often had to make their meals of pumpkin instead of rice. He was over three hundred silver dollars in debt. . . .

Toot! Toot-toot-toot. . . .

Far up the bend in the canal a boat whistle broke the silence. There was a silk filature over there too. He could see vaguely the neat lines of stones embedded as reinforcement in the canal bank. A small oil-burning river boat came puffing up pompously from beyond the silk filature, tugging three larger craft in its wake. Immediately the peaceful water was agitated with waves rolling towards the banks on both sides of the canal. A peasant, poling a tiny boat, hastened to shore and clutched a clump of reeds growing in the shallows. The waves tossed him and his little craft up and down like a see-saw. The peaceful green countryside was filled with the chugging of the boat engine and the stink of its exhaust.

Hatred burned in Old Tung Pao's eyes. He watched the river boat approach, he watched it sail past and glared after it until it went tooting around another bend and disappeared from sight. He had always abominated the foreign devils' contraptions. He himself had never met a foreign devil, but his father had given him a description of one Old Master Chen had seen — red eyebrows, green eyes and a stiff-legged walk! Old Master Chen had hated the foreign devils too. "The foreign devils have swindled our money away," he used to say. Old Tung Pao was only eight or nine the last time he saw Old Master Chen. All he remembered about him now were things he had heard from others. But whenever Old Tung Pao thought of that remark — "The foreign devils have swindled our money away" — he could almost picture Old Master Chen, stroking his beard and wagging his head.

How the foreign devils had accomplished this, Old Tung Pao wasn't too clear. He was sure, however, that Old Master Chen was right. Some things he himself had seen quite plainly. From the time foreign goods — cambric, cloth, oil — appeared in the market town, from the time the foreign river boats increased on the canal, what he produced brought a lower price in the market every day, while what he had to buy became more and more expensive. That was why the property his father left him had shrunk until it finally vanished completely; and now he was in debt. It was not without reason that Old Tung Pao hated the foreign devils!

In the village, his attitude towards foreigners was well known. Five years before, in 1927, someone had told him: The new Kuomintang government says it wants to "throw out" the foreign devils. Old Tung Pao didn't believe it. He heard those young propaganda speech makers the Kuomintang sent when he went into the market town. Though they cried "Throw out the foreign devils," they were dressed in Western style clothing. His guess was that they were secretly in league with the foreign devils, that they had been purposely sent to delude the countryfolk! Sure enough, the Kuomintang dropped the slogan not long after, and prices and taxes rose steadily. Old Tung Pao was firmly convinced that all this occurred as part of a government conspiracy with the foreign devils.

Last year something had happened that made him almost sick with fury: Only the cocoons spun by the foreign strain silkworms could be sold at a decent price. Buyers paid ten dollars more per load for them than they did for the local variety. Usually on good terms with his daughter-in-law, Old Tung Pao had quarrelled with her because of this. She had wanted to raise only foreign silkworms, and Old Tung Pao's younger son Ah To had agreed with her. Though Ah Sze didn't say much, in his heart he certainly had also favoured this course. Events had proved they were right, and they wouldn't let Old Tung Pao forget it. This year, he had to compromise. Of the five trays they would raise, only four would be silkworms of the local variety; one tray would contain foreign silkworms.

"The world's going from bad to worse! In another couple of years they'll even be wanting foreign mulberry trees! It's enough to take all the joy out of life!"

Old Tung Pao picked up his long pipe and rapped it angrily against a clod of dry earth. The sun was directly overhead now, foreshortening his shadow till it looked like a piece of charcoal. Still in his padded jacket, he was bathed in heat. He unfastened the jacket and swung its opened edges back and forth a few times to fan himself. Then he stood up and started for home.

Behind the row of mulberry trees were paddy fields. Most of them were as yet only neatly ploughed furrows of upturned earth clods, dried and cracked by the hot sun. Here and there, the early crops were coming up. In one field, the golden blossoms of rape-seed plants emitted a heady fragrance. And that group of houses way over there, that was the village where three generations of Old Tung Pao's family were living. Above the houses, white smoke from many kitchen stoves was curling lazily upwards into the sky.

After crossing through the mulberry grove, Old Tung Pao

walked along the raised path between the paddy fields, then turned and looked again at that row of trees bursting with tender green buds. A twelve-year-old boy came bounding along from the other end of the fields, calling as he ran:

"Grandpa! Ma's waiting for you to come home and eat!"

It was Little Pao, Old Tung Pao's grandson.

"Coming!" the old man responded, still gazing at the mulberries. Only twice in his life had he seen these finger-like buds appear on the branches so soon after Clear and Bright. His family would probably have a fine crop of silkworms this year. Five trays of eggs would hatch out a huge number of silkworms. If only they didn't have another bad market like last year, perhaps they could pay off part of their debt.

Little Pao stood beside his grandfather. The child too looked at the soft green on the gnarled fist branches. Jumping happily, he clapped his hands and chanted:

> *Green, tender leaves at Clear and Bright,*
> *The girls who tend silkworms*
> *Clap hands at the sight!*

The old man's wrinkled face broke into a smile. He thought it was a good omen for the little boy to respond like this on seeing the first buds of the year. He rubbed his hand affectionately over the child's shaven pate. In Old Tung Pao's heart, numbed wooden by a lifetime of poverty and hardship, suddenly hope began to stir again.

## II

The weather remained warm. The rays of the sun forced open the tender, finger-like, little buds. They had already grown to the size of a small hand. Around Old Tung Pao's village, the mulberry trees seemed to respond especially well. From a distance they gave the appearance of a low grey picket fence on top of which a long swath of green brocade had been spread. Bit by bit, day by day, hope grew in the hearts of the villagers. The unspoken mobilization order for the silkworm

campaign reached everywhere and everyone.  Silkworm rearing
equipment that had been laid away for a year was again brought
out to be scrubbed and mended.  Beside the little stream which
ran through the village, women and children, with much laughter
and calling back and forth, washed the implements.

None of these women or children looked really healthy.  Since
the coming of spring, they had been eating only half their fill;
their clothes were old and torn.  As a matter of fact, they weren't
much better off than beggars.  Yet all were in quite good spirits,
sustained by enormous patience and grand illusions.  Burdened
though they were by daily mounting debts, they had only one
thought in their heads — If we get a good crop of silkworms,
everything will be all right! . . .  They could already visualize
how, in a month, the shiny green leaves would be converted
into snow-white cocoons, the cocoons exchanged for clinking
silver dollars.  Although their stomachs were growling with
hunger, they couldn't refrain from smiling at this happy prospect.

Old Tung Pao's daughter-in-law was among the women by
the stream.  With the help of her twelve-year-old son, Little
Pao, she had already finished washing the family's large trays
of woven bamboo strips.  Seated on a stone beside the stream,
she wiped her perspiring face with the edge of her tunic.  A
twenty-year-old girl, working with other women on the opposite side of the stream, hailed her:

"Are you raising foreign silkworms this year too?"

It was Sixth Treasure, sister of young Fu-ching, the neighbour who lived across the stream.

The thick eyebrows of Old Tung Pao's daughter-in-law at
once contracted.  Her voice sounded as if she had just been
waiting for a chance to let off steam.

"Don't ask me; what the old man says, goes!" she
shouted.  "He's dead set against it, won't let us raise more
than one batch of foreign breed!  The old fool only has to
hear the word 'foreign' to send him up in the air!  He'll take
dollars made of foreign silver, though; those are the only
'foreign' things he likes!"

The women on the other side of the stream laughed.  From

the threshing ground behind them a strapping young man
approached. He reached the stream and crossed over on the
four logs that served as a bridge. Seeing him, his sister-in-law
dropped her tirade and called in a high voice:

"Ah To, will you help me carry these trays? They're as
heavy as dead dogs when they're wet!"

Without a word, Ah To lifted the six big trays and set them,
dripping, on his head. Balancing them in place, he walked
off, swinging his hands in a swimming motion. When in a
good mood, Ah To refused nobody. If any of the village
women asked him to carry something heavy or fish something
out of the stream, he was usually quite willing. But today he
probably was a little grumpy, and so he walked empty-handed
with only six trays on his head. The sight of him, looking as
if he were wearing six layers of wide straw hats, his waist
twisting at each step in imitation of the ladies of the town, sent
the women into peals of laughter. Lotus, wife of Old Tung
Pao's nearest neighbour, called with a giggle:

"Hey, Ah To, come back here. Carry a few trays for me
too!"

Ah To grinned. "Not unless you call me a sweet name!"
He continued walking. An instant later he had reached the
porch of his house and set down the trays out of the sun.

"Will 'kid brother' do?" demanded Lotus, laughing boisterously. She had a remarkably clean white complexion, but her
face was very flat. When she laughed, all that could be seen
was a big open mouth and two tiny slits of eyes. Originally
a slavey in a house in town, she had been married off to Old
Tung Pao's neighbour — a prematurely aged man who walked
around with a sour expression and never said a word all day.
That was less than six months ago, but her love affairs and
escapades already were the talk of the village.

"Shameless hussy!" came a contemptuous female voice from
across the stream.

Lotus' piggy eyes immediately widened. "Who said that?"
she demanded angrily. "If you've got the brass to call me

names, let's see you try it to my face! Come out into the open!"

"Think you can handle me? I'm talking about a shameless, man-crazy baggage! If the shoe fits, wear it!" retorted Sixth Treasure, for it was she who had spoken. She too was famous in the village, but as a mischievous, lively young woman.

The two began splashing water at each other from opposite banks of the stream. Girls who enjoyed a row took sides and joined the battle, while the children whooped with laughter. Old Tung Pao's daughter-in-law was more decorous. She picked up her remaining trays, called to Little Pao and returned home. Ah To watched from the porch, grinning. He knew why Sixth Treasure and Lotus were quarrelling. It did his heart good to hear that sharp-tongued Sixth Treasure get told off in public.

Old Tung Pao came out of the house with a wooden tray-stand on his shoulder. Some of the legs of the uprights had been eaten by termites, and he wanted to repair them. At the sight of Ah To standing there laughing at the women, Old Tung Pao's face lengthened. The boy hadn't much sense of propriety, he well knew. What disturbed him particularly was the way Ah To and Lotus were always talking and laughing together. "That bitch is an evil spirit. Fooling with her will bring ruin on our house," he had often warned his younger son.

"Ah To!" he now barked angrily. "Enjoying the scenery? Your brother's in the back mending equipment. Go and give him a hand!" His inflamed eyes bored into Ah To, never leaving the boy until he disappeared into the house.

Only then did Old Tung Pao start work on the tray-stand. After examining it carefully, he slowly began his repairs. Years ago, Old Tung Pao had worked for a time as a carpenter. But he was old now; his fingers had lost their strength. A few minutes' work and he was breathing hard. He raised his head and looked into the house. Five squares of cloth to which sticky silkworm eggs were adhered, hung from a horizontal bamboo pole.

His daughter-in-law, Ah Sze's wife, was at the other end

of the porch, pasting paper on big trays of woven bamboo strips. Last year, to economize a bit, they had bought and used old newspaper. Old Tung Pao still maintained that was why the eggs had hatched poorly — it was unlucky to use paper with writing on it for such a prosaic purpose. Writing meant scholarship, and scholarship had to be respected. This year the whole family had skipped a meal and with the money saved, purchased special "tray pasting paper." Ah Sze's wife pasted the tough, gosling-yellow sheets smooth and flat; on every tray she also affixed three little coloured paper pictures, bought at the same time. One was the "Platter of Plenty"; the other two showed a militant figure on horseback, pennant in hand. He, according to local belief, was the "Guardian of Silkworm Hatching."

"I was only able to buy twenty loads of mulberry leaves with that thirty silver dollars I borrowed on your father's guarantee," Old Tung Pao said to his daughter-in-law. He was still panting from his exertions with the tray-stand. "Our rice will be finished by the day after tomorrow. What are we going to do?"

Thanks to her father's influence with his boss and his willingness to guarantee repayment of the loan, Old Tung Pao was able to borrow the money at a low rate of interest — only twenty-five per cent a month! Both the principal and interest had to be repaid by the end of the silkworm season.

Ah Sze's wife finished pasting a tray and placed it in the sun. "You've spent it all on leaves," she said angrily. "We'll have a lot of leaves left over, just like last year!"

"Full of lucky words, aren't you?" demanded the old man, sarcastically. "I suppose every year'll be like last year? We can't get more than a dozen or so loads of leaves from our own trees. With five sets of grubs to feed, that won't be nearly enough."

"Oh, of course, you're never wrong!" she replied hotly. "All I know is with rice we can eat, without it we'll go hungry!" His stubborn refusal to raise any foreign silkworms last year had left them with only the unsalable local breed. As a result, she was often contrary with him.

The old man's face turned purple with rage. After this, neither would speak to the other.

But hatching time was drawing closer every day. The little village's two dozen families were thrown into a state of great tension, great determination, great struggle. With it all, they were possessed of a great hope, a hope that could almost make them forget their hungry bellies.

Old Tung Pao's family, borrowing a little here, getting a little credit there, somehow managed to get by. Nor did the other families eat any better; there wasn't one with a spare bag of rice! Although they had harvested a good crop the previous year, landlords, creditors, taxes, levies, one after another, had cleaned the peasants out long ago. Now all their hopes were pinned on the spring silkworms. The repayment date of every loan they made was set for the "end of the silkworm season."

With high hopes and considerable fear, like soldiers going into a hand-to-hand battle to the death, they prepared for their spring silkworm campaign!

"Grain Rain" day — bringing gentle drizzles — was not far off. Almost imperceptibly, the silkworm eggs of the two dozen village families began to show faint tinges of green. Women, when they met on the public threshing ground, would speak to one another agitatedly in tones that were anxious yet joyful.

"Over at Sixth Treasure's place, they're almost ready to incubate their eggs!"

"Lotus says her family is going to start incubating tomorrow. So soon!"

"Huang 'the Priest' has made a divination. He predicts that this spring mulberry leaves will go to four dollars a load!"

Old Tung Pao's daughter-in-law examined their five sets of eggs. They looked bad. The tiny seed-like eggs were still pitch black, without even a hint of green. Her husband, Ah Sze, took them into the light to peer at them carefully. Even so, he could find hardly any ripening eggs. She was very worried.

"You incubate them anyhow. Maybe this variety is a little slow," her husband forced himself to say consolingly.

Her lips pressed tight, she made no reply.

Old Tung Pao's wrinkled face sagged with dejection. Though he said nothing, he thought their prospects were dim.

The next day, Ah Sze's wife again examined the eggs. Ha! Quite a few were turning green, and a very shiny green at that! Immediately, she told her husband, told Old Tung Pao, Ah To . . . she even told her son Little Pao. Now the incubating process could begin! She held the five pieces of cloth to which the eggs were adhered against her bare bosom. As if cuddling a nursing infant, she sat absolutely quiet, not daring to stir. At night, she took the five sets to bed with her. Her husband was routed out, and had to share Ah To's bed. The tiny silkworm eggs were very scratchy against her flesh. She felt happy and a little frightened, like the first time she was pregnant and the baby moved inside her. Exactly the same sensation!

Uneasy but eager, the whole family waited for the eggs to hatch. Ah To was the only exception. We're sure to hatch a good crop, he said, but anyone who thinks we're going to get rich in this life, is out of his head. Though the old man swore Ah To's big mouth would ruin their luck, the boy stuck to his guns.

A clean dry shed for the growing grubs was all prepared. The second day of incubation, Old Tung Pao smeared a garlic with earth and placed it at the foot of the wall inside the shed. If, in a few days, the garlic put out many sprouts, it meant the eggs would hatch well. He did this every year, but this year he was more reverential than usual, and his hands trembled. Last year's divination had proved all too accurate. He didn't dare to think about that now.

Every family in the village was busy "incubating." For the time being there were few women's footprints on the threshing ground or the banks of the little stream. An unofficial "martial law" had been imposed. Even peasants normally on very good terms stopped visiting one another. For a guest to come and frighten away the spirits of the ripening eggs — that would be no laughing matter! At most, people exchanged a few words in low tones when they met, then quickly separated. This was the "sacred" season!

Old Tung Pao's family was on pins and needles. In the five sets of eggs a few grubs had begun wriggling. It was exactly one day before Grain Rain. Ah Sze's wife had calculated that most of the eggs wouldn't hatch until after that day. Before or after Grain Rain was all right, but for eggs to hatch on the day itself was considered highly unlucky. Incubation was no longer necessary, and the eggs were carefully placed in the special shed. Old Tung Pao stole a glance at his garlic at the foot of the wall. His heart dropped. There were still only the same two small green shoots the garlic had originally! He didn't dare to look any closer. He prayed silently that by noon the day after tomorrow the garlic would have many, many more shoots.

At last hatching day arrived. Ah Sze's wife set a pot of rice on to boil and nervously watched for the time when the steam from it would rise straight up. Old Tung Pao lit the incense and candles he had bought in anticipation of this event. Devoutly, he placed them before the idol of the Kitchen God. His two sons went into the fields to pick wild flowers. Little Pao chopped a lamp-wick into fine pieces and crushed the wild flowers the men brought back. Everything was ready. The sun was entering its zenith; steam from the rice pot puffed straight upwards. Ah Sze's wife immediately leaped to her feet, stuck a "sacred" paper flower and a pair of goose feathers into the knot of hair at the back of her head and went to the shed. Old Tung Pao carried a wooden scale-pole; Ah Sze followed with the chopped lamp-wick and the crushed wild flowers. Daughter-in-law uncovered the cloth pieces to which the grubs were adhered, and sprinkled them with the bits of wick and flowers Ah Sze was holding. Then she took the wooden scale-pole from Old Tung Pao and hung the cloth pieces over it. She next removed the pair of goose feathers from her hair. Moving them lightly across the cloth, she brushed the grubs, together with the crushed lamp-

wick and wild flowers, on to a large tray. One set, two sets . . .
the last set contained the foreign breed. The grubs from this
cloth were brushed on to a separate tray. Finally, she removed
the "sacred" paper flower from her hair and pinned it, with the
goose feathers, against the side of the tray.

A solemn ceremony! One that had been handed down through
the ages! Like warriors taking an oath before going into battle!
Old Tung Pao and family now had ahead of them a month of
fierce combat, with no rest day or night, against bad weather,
bad luck and anything else that might come along!

The grubs, wriggling in the trays, looked very healthy. They
were all the proper black colour. Old Tung Pao and his
daughter-in-law were able to relax a little. But when the old
man secretly took another look at his garlic, he turned pale! It
had grown only four measly shoots! Ah! Would this year be
like last year all over again?

### III

But the "fateful" garlic proved to be not so psychic after all.
The silkworms of Old Tung Pao's family grew and thrived!
Though it rained continuously during the grubs' First Sleep and
Second Sleep, and the weather was a bit colder than at Clear
and Bright, the "little darlings" were extremely robust.

The silkworms of the other families in the village were not
doing badly either. A tense kind of joy pervaded the countryside. Even the small stream seemed to be gurgling with bright
laughter. Lotus' family was the sole exception. They were
only raising one set of grubs, but by the Third Sleep their
silkworms weighed less than twenty catties. Just before the
Big Sleep, people saw Lotus' husband walk to the stream and
dump out his trays. That dour, old-looking man had bad luck
written all over him.

Because of this dreadful event, the village women put Lotus'
family strictly "off limits." They made wide detours so as not
to pass her door. If they saw her or her taciturn husband, no
matter how far away, they made haste to go in the opposite

direction. They feared that even one look at Lotus or her spouse, the briefest conversation, would contaminate them with the unfortunate couple's bad luck!

Old Tung Pao strictly forbade Ah To to talk to Lotus. "If I catch you gabbing with that baggage again, I'll disown you!" he threatened in a loud, angry voice, standing outside on the porch to make sure Lotus could hear him.

Little Pao was also warned not to play in front of Lotus' door, and not to speak to anyone in her family.

The old man harped at Ah To morning, noon and night, but the boy turned a deaf ear to his father's grumbling. In his heart, he laughed at it. Of the whole family, Ah To alone didn't place much stock in taboos and superstitions. He didn't talk with Lotus, however. He was much too busy for that.

By the Big Sleep, their silkworms weighed three hundred catties. Every member of Old Tung Pao's family, including twelve-year-old Little Pao, worked for two days and two nights without sleeping a wink. The silkworms were unusually sturdy. Only twice in his sixty years had Old Tung Pao ever seen the like. Once was the year he married; once when his first son was born.

The first day after the Big Sleep, the "little darlings" ate seven loads of leaves. They were now a bright green, thick and healthy. Old Tung Pao and his family, on the contrary, were much thinner, their eyes bloodshot from lack of sleep.

No one could guess how much the "little darlings" would eat before they spun their cocoons. Old Tung Pao discussed the question of buying more leaves with Ah Sze.

"Master Chen won't lend us any more. Shall we try your father-in-law's boss again?"

"We've still got ten loads coming. That's enough for one more day," replied Ah Sze. He could barely hold himself erect. His eyelids weighed a thousand catties. They kept wanting to close.

"One more day? You're dreaming!" snapped the old man impatiently. "Not counting tomorrow, they still have to eat three more days. We'll need another thirty loads! Thirty loads, I say!"

Loud voices were heard outside on the threshing ground. Ah To had arrived with men delivering five loads of mulberry branches. Everyone went out to strip the leaves. Ah Sze's wife hurried from the shed. Across the stream, Sixth Treasure and her family were raising only a small crop of silkworms; having spare time, she came over to help. Bright stars filled the sky. There was a slight wind. All up and down the village, gay shouts and laughter rang in the night.

"The price of leaves is rising fast!" a coarse voice cried. "This afternoon, they were getting four dollars a load in the market town!"

Old Tung Pao was very upset. At four dollars a load, thirty loads would come to a hundred and twenty dollars. Where could he raise so much money! But then he figured — he was sure to gather over five hundred catties of cocoons. Even at fifty dollars a hundred, they'd sell for two hundred and fifty dollars. Feeling a bit consoled, he heard a small voice from among the leaf-strippers.

"They say the folks east of here aren't doing so well with their silkworms. There won't be any reason for the price of leaves to go much higher."

Old Tung Pao recognized the speaker as Sixth Treasure, and he relaxed still further.

The girl and Ah To were standing beside a large basket, stripping leaves. In the dim starlight, they worked quite close to each other, partly hidden by the pile of mulberry branches before them. Suddenly, Sixth Treasure felt someone pinch her thigh. She knew well enough who it was, and she suppressed a giggle. But when, a moment later, a hand brushed against her breasts, she jumped; a little shriek escaped her.

"Aiya!"

"What's wrong?" demanded Ah Sze's wife, working on the other side of the basket.

Sixth Treasure's face flamed scarlet. She shot a glance at Ah To, then quickly lowered her head and resumed stripping leaves. "Nothing," she replied. "I think a caterpillar bit me!"

Ah To bit his lips to keep from laughing aloud. He had been half starved the past two weeks and had slept little. But in spite of having lost a lot of weight, he was in high spirits. While he never suffered from any of Old Tung Pao's gloom, neither did he believe that one good crop, whether of silkworms or of rice, would enable them to wipe off their debt and own their own land again. He knew they would never "get out from under" merely by relying on hard work, even if they broke their backs trying. Nevertheless, he worked with a will. He enjoyed work, just as he enjoyed fooling around with Sixth Treasure.

The next morning, Old Tung Pao went into town to borrow money for more leaves. Before leaving home, he had talked the matter over with daughter-in-law. They had decided to mortgage their grove of mulberries that produced fifteen loads of leaves a year as security for the loan. The grove was the last piece of property the family owned.

By the time the old man ordered another thirty loads, and the first ten were delivered, the sturdy "little darlings" had gone hungry for half an hour. Putting forth their pointed little mouths, they swayed from side to side, searching for food. Daughter-in-law's heart had ached to see them. When the leaves were finally spread in the trays, the silkworm shed at once resounded with a sibilant crunching, so noisy it drowned out conversation. In a very short while, the trays were again empty of leaves. Another thick layer was piled on. Just keeping the silkworms supplied with leaves, Old Tung Pao and his family were so busy they could barely catch their breath. But this was the final crisis. In two more days the "little darlings" would spin their cocoons. People were putting every bit of their remaining strength into this last desperate struggle.

Though he had gone without sleep for three whole days, Ah To didn't appear particularly tired. He agreed to watch the shed alone that night until dawn to permit the others to get some rest. There was a bright moon and the weather was a trifle cold. Ah To crouched beside a small fire he had built in the shed. At about eleven, he gave the silkworms their second feeding, then returned to squat by the fire. He could hear the loud rustle of the "little darlings" crunching through the leaves. His eyes closed. Suddenly, he heard the door squeak, and his eyelids flew open. He peered into the darkness for a moment, then shut his eyes again. His ears were still hissing with the rustle of the leaves. The next thing he knew, his head had struck against his knees. Waking with a start, he heard the door screen bang and thought he saw a moving shadow. Ah To leaped up and rushed outside. In the moonlight, he saw someone crossing the threshing ground towards the stream. He caught up in a flash, seized and flung the intruder to the ground. Ah To was sure he had nabbed a thief.

"Ah To, kill me if you want to, but don't give me away!"

The voice made Ah To's hair stand on end. He could see in the moonlight that queer flat white face and those round little piggy eyes fixed upon him. But of menace, the piggy eyes had none. Ah To snorted.

"What were you after?"

"A few of your family's 'little darlings'!"

"What did you do with them?"

"Threw them in the stream!"

Ah To's face darkened. He knew that in this way she was trying to put a curse on the lot. "You're pure poison! We never did anything to hurt you."

"Never did anything? Oh yes, you did! Yes, you did! Our silkworm eggs didn't hatch well, but we didn't harm anybody. You were all so smart! You shunned me like a leper. No matter how far away I was, if you saw me, you turned your heads. You acted as if I wasn't even human!"

She got to her feet, the agonized expression on her face terrible to see. Ah To stared at her. "I'm not going to beat you," he said finally. "Go on your way!"

Without giving her another glance, he trotted back to the shed. He was wide awake now. Lotus had only taken a handful and the remaining "little darlings" were all in good condition. It didn't occur to him either to hate or pity Lotus, but the last thing she had said remained in his mind. It seemed to him there was something eternally wrong in the scheme of human relations; but he couldn't put his finger on what it was exactly, nor did he know why it should be. In a little while, he forgot about this too. The lusty silkworms were eating and eating, yet, as if by some magic, never full!

Nothing more happened that night. Just before the sky began to brighten in the east, Old Tung Pao and his daughter-in-law came to relieve Ah To. They took the trays of "little darlings" and looked at them in the light. The silkworms were turning a whiter colour, their bodies gradually becoming shorter and thicker. They were delighted with the excellent way the silkworms were developing.

But when, at sunrise, Ah Sze's wife went to draw water at the stream, she met Sixth Treasure. The girl's expression was serious.

"I saw that slut leaving your place shortly before midnight," she whispered. "Ah To was right behind her. They stood here and talked for a long time! Your family ought to look after things better than that!"

The colour drained from the face of Ah Sze's wife. Without a word, she carried her water bucket back to the house. First she told her husband about it, then she told Old Tung Pao. It was a fine state of affairs when a baggage like that could sneak into people's silkworm sheds! Old Tung Pao stamped with rage. He immediately summoned Ah To. But the boy denied the whole story; he said Sixth Treasure was dreaming. The old man then went to question Sixth Treasure. She insisted she had seen everything with her own eyes. The old man didn't know what to believe. He returned home and looked at the "little darlings." They were as sturdy as ever, not a sickly one in the lot.

But the joy that Old Tung Pao and his family had been feeling was dampened. They knew Sixth Treasure's words couldn't be entirely without foundation. Their only hope was that Ah To and that hussy had played their little games on the porch rather than in the shed!

Old Tung Pao recalled gloomily that the garlic had only put forth three or four shoots. He thought the future looked dark. Hadn't there been times before when the silkworms ate great quantities of leaves and seemed to be growing well, yet dried up and died just when they were ready to spin their cocoons? Yes, often! But Old Tung Pao didn't dare let himself think of such a possibility. To entertain a thought like that, even in the most secret recesses of the mind, would only be inviting bad luck!

## IV

The "little darlings" began spinning their cocoons, but Old Tung Pao's family was still in a sweat. Both their money and their energy were completely spent. They still had nothing to show for it; there was no guarantee of their earning any return. Nevertheless, they continued working at top speed. Beneath the racks on which the cocoons were being spun fires had to be kept going to supply warmth. Old Tung Pao and Ah Sze, his elder son, their backs bent, slowly squatted first on this side then on that. Hearing the small rustlings of the spinning silkworms, they wanted to smile, and if the sounds stopped for a moment their hearts stopped too. Yet, worried as they were, they didn't dare to disturb the silkworms by looking inside. When the silkworms squirted fluid in their faces as they peered up from beneath the racks, they were happy in spite of the momentary discomfort. The bigger the shower, the better they liked it.*

Ah To had already peeked several times. Little Pao had caught him at it and demanded to know what was going on. Ah To made an ugly face at the child, but did not reply.

After three days of "spinning," the fires were extinguished. Ah Sze's wife could restrain herself no longer. She stole a

---

*The emission of the fluid means the silkworm is about to spin its cocoon

look, her heart beating fast. Inside, all was white as snow.
The brush that had been put in for the silkworms to spin on
was completely covered over with cocoons. Ah Sze's wife had
never seen so successful a "flowering"!

The whole family was wreathed in smiles. They were on
solid ground at last! The "little darlings" had proved they
had a conscience; they hadn't consumed those mulberry leaves,
at four dollars a load, in vain. The family could reap its
reward for a month of hunger and sleepless nights. The Old
Lord of the Sky had eyes!

Throughout the village, there were many similar scenes of
rejoicing. The Silkworm Goddess had been beneficent to the
tiny village this year. Most of the two dozen families garnered
good crops of cocoons from their silkworms. The harvest of
Old Tung Pao's family was well above average.

Again women and children crowded the threshing ground
and the banks of the little stream. All were much thinner than
the previous month, with eyes sunk in their sockets, throats
rasping and hoarse. But everyone was excited, happy. As they
chattered about the struggle of the past month, visions of piles
of bright silver dollars shimmered before their eyes. Cheerful
thoughts filled their minds — they would get their summer
clothes out of the pawnshop; at Dragon-Boat Festival perhaps
they could eat a fat golden fish. . . .

They talked, too, of the farce enacted by Lotus and Ah To
a few nights before. Sixth Treasure announced to everyone she
met, "That Lotus has no shame at all. She delivered herself
right to his door!" Men who heard her laughed coarsely.
Women muttered a prayer and called Lotus bad names. They
said Old Tung Pao's family could consider itself lucky that a
curse hadn't fallen on them. The gods were merciful!

Family after family was able to report a good harvest of
cocoons. People visited one another to view the shining white
gossamer. The father of Old Tung Pao's daughter-in-law came
from town with his little son. They brought gifts of sweets and
fruits and a salted fish. Little Pao was happy as a puppy
frolicking in the snow.

The elderly visitor sat with Old Tung Pao beneath a willow beside the stream. He had the reputation in town of a "man who knew how to enjoy life." From hours of listening to the professional story-tellers in front of the temple, he had learned by heart many of the classic tales of ancient times. He was a great one for idle chatter, and often would say anything that came into his head. Old Tung Pao therefore didn't take him very seriously when he leaned close and queried softly:

"Are you selling your cocoons, or will you spin the silk yourself at home?"

"Selling them, of course," Old Tung Pao replied casually.

The elderly visitor slapped his thigh and sighed, then rose abruptly and pointed at the silk filature rearing up behind the row of mulberries, now quite bald of leaves.

"Tung Pao," he said, "the cocoons are being gathered, but the doors of the silk filatures are shut as tight as ever! They're not buying this year! Ah, all the world is in turmoil! The silk houses are not going to open, I tell you!"

Old Tung Pao couldn't help smiling. He wouldn't believe it. How could he possibly believe it? There were dozens of silk filatures in this part of the country. Surely they couldn't all shut down? What's more, he had heard that they had made a deal with the Japanese; the Chinese soldiers who had been billeted in the silk houses had long since departed.

Changing the subject, the visitor related the latest town gossip, salting it freely with classical aphorisms and quotations from the ancient stories. Finally he got around to the thirty silver dollars borrowed through him as middleman. He said his boss was anxious to be repaid.

Old Tung Pao became uneasy after all. When his visitor had departed, he hurried from the village down the highway to look at the two nearest silk filatures. Their doors were indeed shut; not a soul was in sight. Business was in full swing this time last year, with whole rows of dark gleaming scales in operation.

He felt a little panicky as he returned home. But when he saw those snowy cocoons, thick and hard, pleasure made him smile. What beauties! No one wants them? — Impossible. He still had to hurry and finish gathering the cocoons; he hadn't thanked the gods properly yet. Gradually, he forgot about the silk houses.

But in the village, the atmosphere was changing day by day. People who had just begun to laugh were now all frowns. News was reaching them from town that none of the neighbouring silk filatures was opening its doors. It was the same with the houses along the highway. Last year at this time buyers of cocoons were streaming in and out of the village. This year there wasn't a sign of even half a one. In their place came dunning creditors and government tax collectors who promptly froze up if you asked them to take cocoons in payment.

Swearing, curses, disappointed sighs! With such a fine crop of cocoons the villagers had never dreamed that their lot would be even worse than usual! It was as if hailstones dropped out of a clear sky. People like Old Tung Pao, whose crop was especially good, took it hardest of all.

"What is the world coming to!" He beat his breast and stamped his feet in helpless frustration.

But the villagers had to think of something. The cocoons would spoil if kept too long. They either had to sell them or remove the silk themselves. Several families had already brought out and repaired silk reels they hadn't used for years. They would first remove the silk from the cocoons and then see about the next step. Old Tung Pao wanted to do the same.

"We won't sell our cocoons; we'll spin the silk ourselves!" said the old man. "Nobody ever heard of selling cocoons until the foreign devils' companies started the thing!"

Ah Sze's wife was the first to object. "We've got over five hundred catties of cocoons here," she retorted. "Where are you going to get enough reels?"

She was right. Five hundred catties was no small amount. They'd never get finished spinning the silk themselves. Hire outside help? That meant spending money. Ah Sze agreed with his wife. Ah To blamed his father for planning incorrectly.

"If you listened to me, we'd have raised only one tray of foreign breed and no locals. Then the fifteen loads of leaves from our own mulberry trees would have been enough, and we wouldn't have had to borrow!"

Old Tung Pao was so angry he couldn't speak.

At last a ray of hope appeared. Huang the Priest had heard somewhere that a silk house below the city of Wusih was doing business as usual. Actually an ordinary peasant, Huang was nicknamed "The Priest" because of the learned airs he affected and his interests in Taoist "magic." Old Tung Pao always got along with him fine. After learning the details from him, Old Tung Pao conferred with his elder son Ah Sze about going to Wusih.

"It's about 270 *li* by water, six days for the round trip," ranted the old man. "Son of a bitch! It's a goddam expedition! But what else can we do? We can't eat the cocoons, and our creditors are pressing hard!"

Ah Sze agreed. They borrowed a small boat and bought a few yards of matting to cover the cargo. It was decided that Ah To should go along. Taking advantage of the good weather, the cocoon selling "expeditionary force" set out.

Five days later, the men returned — but not with an empty hold. They still had one basket of cocoons. The silk filature, which they reached after a 270-*li* journey by water, offered extremely harsh terms — Only thirty-five dollars a load for foreign breed, twenty for local; thin cocoons not wanted at any price. Although their cocoons were all first class, the people at the silk house picked and chose, leaving them one basket of rejects. Old Tung Pao and his sons received a hundred and ten dollars for the sale, ten of which had to be spent as travel expenses. The hundred dollars remaining was not even enough to pay back what they had borrowed for that last thirty loads of mulberry leaves! On the return trip, Old Tung Pao became ill with rage. His sons carried him into the house.

Ah Sze's wife had no choice but to take the ninety odd catties they had brought back and reel the silk from the cocoons herself. She borrowed a few reels from Sixth Treasure's family and worked for six days. All their rice was gone now. Ah Sze took the silk into town, but no one would buy it. Even the pawnshop didn't want it. Only after much pleading was he able to persuade the pawnbroker to take it in exchange for a load of rice they had pawned before Clear and Bright.

That's the way it happened. Because they raised a crop of spring silkworms, the people in Old Tung Pao's village got deeper into debt. Old Tung Pao's family raised five trays and gathered a splendid harvest of cocoons. Yet they ended up owing another thirty silver dollars and losing their mortgaged mulberry trees — to say nothing of suffering a month of hunger and sleepless nights in vain!

*November 1, 1932*

# AUTUMN HARVEST

It wasn't until the end of the fifth lunar month that Old Tung Pao gradually began to recover. He had taken no medicine except that he ate some incense ash which his daughter-in-law had begged from the temple. His poverty-toughened body licked the demon of his illness single-handed.

But with the very first step he took from his bed, he felt that something was wrong. His legs seemed to be treading on heaped cotton; they were soft and weak. And try as he might, he couldn't straighten up.

"Lying around so long, my bones are rusty!" he said to himself, making an effort to assume an air of youthful vigour. But when he saw his reflection in the water of the wash-basin, he couldn't help sighing. Was that really his face? Gaunt cheekbones, thin sharp nose, large sunken eyes, hair all awry, greyish-brown whiskers framing his jaws, Adam's apple protruding like a small fist — he didn't look even half human! Old Tung Pao stared and stared. Uncontrollable tears dripped from his face into the wash-basin.

It was the first time in many years the rugged old man had wept. During his forty years of bitter struggle to win some security for his family there were only two things he had worshipped — the gods, and health. He was firmly convinced that without the protection of the gods, no matter how shrewd you were, you could never make your money or property "put on flesh." And without health, even if the gods protected you, you still couldn't earn a living.

The only god in which Old Tung Pao had any real faith was the God of Wealth. Twice a month — at the time of the new moon, and when the moon was full — he went to the dilapidated

shrine of the God of Wealth near the little bridge outside the
village. There he banged his head in fervent kowtows, always
the same way for more than forty years.

Now a severe illness had transformed him into something that
looked seven-tenths ghoul. This hurt him even worse than having had to sell his silkworm cocoons at a sacrifice. He felt that
he and his family were beyond all hope of recovery.

"I only spent a month or so in bed, but see what's become of
me!" he protested weakly to the wife of his elder son, Ah Sze.
She was puffing up the fire of the kitchen stove.

No answer. Ah Sze's wife, hair dishevelled, was blowing
with such intensity that she seemed in some danger of putting
her head right into the stove. White smoke filled the room and
poured out through the front and back doors. But the half-green
reeds refused to kindle. Little Pao, Old Tung Pao's twelve-year-
old grandson, came running in from the threshing ground and
was choked by the smoke. Between coughs, he complained that
he was hungry. The old man, also coughing, approached the
stove on trembling legs, intending to lend his daughter-in-law
a hand. Just then there was a flash in the door of the stove, and
the reeds began to blaze with a soft crackling sound. After
throwing in a few mulberry twigs, Ah Sze's wife finally raised
her head. Her face was stained with tears — whether from the
smoke or for some other reason we don't really know. In any
event, this woman who spoke little and worked hard, was
weeping.

The old man and his daughter-in-law, the eyes of both wet
with tears, examined each other in silence. The stove was burning brightly now, tongues of flame licking out through the open
stove door. Daughter-in-law's face was burnished by the fire-
light. Although the glow disguised her pallor, it could not conceal how thin her face had become. Little Pao too had been reduced to a mere bag of bones. The boy had been growing very
slowly anyhow, but now he looked like nothing more than a
wizened little monkey! In the dimness of his sickroom Old Tung
Pao had realized that the boy was much thinner when he had
held his hand. But he hadn't been able to see so clearly then.

Old Tung Pao was suddenly swept by a wave of grief. He almost cried aloud.

"What's happened to you, Little Pao? You look like one of those T.B. kids!" The old man spoke in gasps, his large sunken eyes fixed on his daughter-in-law.

Still no response. Ah Sze's wife wiped her eyes with the hem of her tattered blouse.

The pot on the stove began to emit puffs of fragrant white steam. Little Pao sidled close to the steam and sniffed. Then, pouting, he turned to his mother.

"Pumpkin again! *Niang,* why do you always make that old pumpkin? I wish we could eat some white rice for a change!"

The woman grabbed a mulberry branch as though to use it on her cheeky young son. But she only slapped it against the floor, breaking it into pieces which she tossed in the fire. She did not look around or reply.

"There'll be white rice when your father comes back," Old Tung Pao assured the boy. "Your *Tieh* has gone to see your other grandpa — to get him to borrow some money for us. When we get the money we'll buy rice and cook it up for you."

He stroked the little boy's shaven pate with a trembling withered hand. It was true enough. Early that morning Ah Sze had gone into the town to seek his father-in-law to ask him to be guarantor on a loan of five or ten dollars from Master Wu, who specialized in "rural credit."

Little Pao didn't believe his grandfather. He had been hearing his *Tieh* and *Niang* talking about "borrowing money to buy rice" for the past month and a half. But they still ate nothing but pumpkin and yams! He didn't mind the yams so much. Piping hot with a little salt they tasted fine. But that pumpkin — all mush. Without even any sugar to put on, how could you bear it day after day? Worst of all, for the past two weeks, two meals out of three were nothing but that dull old pumpkin! It made Little Pao sick just to think about it. His stomach rumbling emptily, with tears in his eyes, he looked at his grandfather. It seemed to him that his *Tieh,* his *Niang* and his grandfather, were all hard-hearted and bad. He only hoped his uncle Ah To would come home soon. Perhaps that wild young stallion of an uncle would bring a few sesame buns like last time and let him savour them again in secret.

Ah To had been away for three days and two nights. Little Pao missed him terribly!

In the pot, the pumpkin was done and was sending out hissing jets of steam. Old Tung Pao raised the lid. There was less than half a pot of pumpkin, dry, the bits against the sides of the pot crusted brown. The old man frowned. His daughter-in-law was too wasteful, he thought. Before they had become busy with the silkworm season, then too, for a while, his family had eaten pumpkin instead of rice. But they had cooked it with plenty of water, and all five of them, big and small, had been able to fill up by drinking several bowls of pumpkin soup each. Now, though he had been ill for only little more than a month, the young people were already well on the road to "extravagance." This would never do! Anger brought a bit of colour to his pallid cheeks. He walked shakily to the large vat and scooped out a dipperful of water to put in the pot. But his daughter-in-law quickly forestalled him by pouring the pumpkin stew into bowls and placing the bowls on the table.

"Don't add any water," she said in a hoarse voice. "There's only the three of us and we don't have to leave any over. The boy's father is sure to bring back a few pecks of rice tonight. . . . Little Pao, the stew isn't so thin this time, it'll taste better. Try and eat an extra bowl!"

Deftly, she scraped the bits of crust from the sides of the pot. Old Tung Pao was furious beyond words. On trembling legs he strode to the porch with his bowl and sat down on the high doorstep. Slowly sipping the pumpkin stew, he was gripped by an uneasiness he couldn't define.

The threshing ground in front of him was bathed in dazzling sunlight. Beyond, the little stream was a strip of flowing gold. But its water level had dropped considerably; the weeping willows along its banks had a parched look. Both sides of the stream were silent and deserted; not even a dog or chicken was in sight. Usually at this noon hour there were women and children washing clothes and dishes by the stream, while the men lolled in the shade of the trees along the threshing ground and smoked their after-dinner pipes. Or at least there would be people like Old Tung Pao sitting on the doorsteps of their porches, chatting with their neighbours while they ate. But now, though the village basked in the sun and the waters of the stream flowed quietly, the place was a barren wilderness! It was only a month and a half since Old Tung Pao had last come out on his porch, yet the village had changed almost beyond recognition — just as Little Pao had become thinner almost beyond recognition!

Old Tung Pao had long since finished the pumpkin stew, but he continued sipping mechanically, staring with large sunken eyes at the little stream and the lonely thatched hut a short distance beyond it. He made no attempt to guess why the villagers had all disappeared. He could only wonder at how much the world had changed since he had fallen ill! First himself, then the members of his family — his daughter-in-law and Little Pao — and now this village where he had lived so long and which he knew so well. Again he suddenly felt himself on the verge of tears — he who almost never wept. Instinctively, he put the bowl down beside him and supported his head with both hands, his thoughts a jumble.

He remembered the stories his father and grandfather used to spread about the "Long Hairs." They alleged that the "Long Hairs" "cleaned out" villages, "slaughtering" the entire population, "plundering" them of everything of value. Early this year, when the Japanese devils attacked Shanghai, "respectable" people said, "It's the 'Long Hairs' all over again!" But then, later, Old Tung Pao heard that there had been an armistice agreement. And while he was ill, nobody had mentioned anything about "Long Hairs." Yet the village resembled nothing more than his imagined picture of the aftermath of a "Long Hairs'" raid! He also recollected his grandfather saying that sometimes the "Long Hairs" didn't kill everyone but forced them to join the gang instead. Grandfather had claimed that the people had to pack up and move out, leaving behind an empty village. Was it possible that all his neighbours had gone off to become "Long Hairs"? He had heard of other districts where the "Long Hairs" had been active for many years. But the people in his village were "good" peasants. Surely they couldn't have joined the "Long Hairs" during the few days he had been unconscious? The more he thought of it, the more unlikely it seemed.

Suddenly, he heard footsteps approaching and he quickly raised his head. Directly in front of him a pair of piggy eyes gleamed from a wide flat face. The visitor was the notorious manchaser, Lotus, wife of Old Tung Pao's neighbour across the stream! Though she too was thinner, the slimming down had made her prettier. Her little eyes were more appealing than ever; they shone with sympathy and with shock at the old man's appearance. But Old Tung Pao immediately recalled the grudge his family held against her because of what she had tried to do to their silkworms. What's more, he felt it very unlucky that the first person he saw on his recovery — not counting his immediate family — was that "witch"! Vehemently, he spat on the ground, then dropped his head and turned his face away.

When he looked up again some time later, Lotus was gone and the sunlight had crept close to his feet. The boat from the town to the village must be setting sail now. Perhaps his elder son Ah Sze was on it, with the money; perhaps he had already bought some rice. Old Tung Pao mentally smacked his lips. He too was sick and tired of pumpkin stew. The thought of nice cooked rice made his mouth water.

"Little Pao! Little Pao! Come here to Grandpa!" he called. Thinking of the rice had brought to his mind his pitiful half-starved grandson. It was the first time since he left his bed that Old Tung Pao raised his voice in a healthy shout.

No answer. He glanced up at the sky, then shouted louder. To his surprise, Little Pao came running out of Lotus' house with a round flat object in his hand that looked like a sesame bun. The skinny monkey of a child bounded up to him and waved the thing in his face.

"Look, Grandpa," the child cried, "a sesame bun!" — and excitedly crammed it into his own mouth.

Old Tung Pao swallowed involuntarily, the merest flicker of an envious smile curling the corners of his lips. But immediately his face fell, and he asked in a low voice:

"Who gave it to you?"

"Lo — Lo —" was the best reply Little Pao could manage with his mouth full of bun.

Actually, the old man already knew. His expression grew sterner. His mind was troubled. Little Pao was eating a gift from an "enemy" — what a loss of face! And by what justice was Lotus' family able to afford sesame buns in the first place? Gritting his teeth, the old man was ready to fly into a rage. But he didn't have the heart to beat Little Pao. By then the child had already finished the bun and announced with much satisfaction:

"I got it from Lotus, Grandpa. Lotus is a good woman; she has sesame buns!"

"Stuff and nonsense!" His face brick-red, the old man raised his hand as if to strike.

But Little Pao wasn't afraid. "She has, too!" he insisted. "She brought 'em from town. She says tomorrow she's going for rice, white rice!"

The old man sprang to his feet, trembling all over. His belly hadn't known rice for a month and a half. Just hearing that another family had rice was enough to turn him green with envy. But, worst of all, it had to be Lotus' family — people he had always looked down on!

"What's so wonderful about that!" he exploded, dark as a thundercloud. "They probably stole the stuff! One of these days they'll be caught and beheaded! That's just what they deserve!"

But Old Tung Pao kept his voice down as he ranted. He was already wondering what to say if Lotus came out to "give battle." After all, to label people robbers without any proof was no joke. Strangely enough, there was no response from Lotus. But tactless Little Pao stirred his grandfather up again by prattling:

"Oh no, Grandpa, Lotus is good. She's got sesame buns and she's willing to give me some!"

The old man went pale. Without a sound he reached for a bamboo stick. Sensing the change in the atmosphere, Little Pao ran out as fast as his legs could carry him — and just for spite, right back to Lotus' house. Old Tung Pao was in hot pursuit when suddenly he saw stars and his legs turned to rubber. He had to sit down on the ground, the stick cast aside. It was then that a man appeared on the other side of the stream. He came across the little bridge and hailed Old Tung Pao:

"Congratulations! So you're out moving around today!"

Though a few black stars were still floating before his eyes, Old Tung Pao recognized the caller — Huang the Priest. He was glad to see him. They were old friends. When Old Tung Pao became ill, Huang the Priest was one of his most frequent visitors. The two were known in the village as a couple of "queers." Old Tung Pao earned his reputation by his stubborn hatred of any and all things "foreign." Huang the Priest was famous for being always ready to trot out the few cultured phrases he had picked up in the town. He was full of archaic ceremonial turns of speech. The way he kept muttering them under his breath sounded to the villagers like the incantations of a Taoist priest — thus, his nickname. Old Tung Pao was one of the few who understood Huang's elegant language. As he often said to his elder son, he considered it a great "waste of talent" that a man like Huang the Priest should spend his time tilling the fields.

Now, Old Tung Pao poured out to him all his irritations.

"Priest, it's enough to smother a man! I'm laid up for only a little over a month and the whole world goes to pot! The village looks as if the "Long Hairs" have been through it. And that bitch vixen, I don't know how, but somewhere she got hold of some sesame buns. Little Pao can't keep away from 'em, the shameless brat. What do you say, Priest, should I beat him or not?" Old Tung Pao picked up the bamboo stick and struck it against the ground.

Huang the Priest listened with the learned air he had copied from the fortune-teller in the town temple, who advertised his occult arts as having been "handed down through three generations." All during Old Tung Pao's speech, Huang kept nodding his head and sighing. Finally, Huang said softly:

"The world will be plunged into insurrection and turmoil! Elder Brother, do you know where our villagers have gone? To raid the rice bins of the grain merchants and the wealthy! The day before yesterday the peasants in Paichiping started it; today our village follows their example. Your honourable younger scion is among them. But, Elder Brother, you have just recovered from your illness. Pretend you know nothing of the activities of your younger son. Forgive me, I have said too much!"

At last Old Tung Pao understood. He jumped up, his eyes glaring. But at once, something seemed to bang him on the skull and he again collapsed weakly to the ground, his lips trembling. Raiding the rice bins of the wealthy? The news frightened and pleased him at the same time. He was pleased because he knew now that he had guessed right about Lotus' sesame buns. They had not been obtained by honourable means. He was frightened that because his son Ah To was involved, retribution might fall on his own head.

"Pardon, pardon!" cried Huang the Priest, squinting in alarm. "Your precious health is most important, most important! My words have agitated you! I beg your pardon! But compose yourself. We hear that the officials are not inclined to take harsh measures. Simply warn your honourable son and all will be well!"

"Ah, Priest, to tell you the truth, I've always known that young wretch had no sense of morality. For a long time I've feared that the spirit of the 'Long Hair' my grandfather killed would be born again in another body to torment us! And that's just what's happened! If he doesn't come home — all right. If he does — I'll bury the young fiend alive! Priest, thank you for bringing me the news. I've been living in the dark till now!"

Old Tung Pao's lips quivered with anger. Closing his eyes, he could almost see the spirit of the murdered "Long Hair." Huang the Priest hadn't suspected that his news would have such a violent effect on the old man, and he rather regretted having been so loquacious. He hastened to disown Old Tung Pao's thanks.

"Nothing at all, nothing at all! I have a small matter to attend to; I beg your leave. Preserve your honourable health!"

Huang the Priest fled, leaving the old man alone, dazedly trying to collect his thoughts. A powerful sun beat down on him, but Old Tung Pao was unaware of its heat. The wild stories his father and grandfather had told him about the "Long Hairs" raced confusedly through his mind. And he recalled the latter half of the seventies when the emperor Kuang Hsu had just come to the throne. The peasants had risen, all over the county. The Manchu rulers had retaliated swiftly and cruelly — with his own eyes he had seen bloody heads roll in the dust. His reasoning could lead to only one conclusion:

"If rebellion was any use, the 'Long Hairs' would have won the throne years ago!"

It seemed to him that no sooner had he become ill and gone to bed than the world turned upside-down. Although his family had seldom been more than barely self-sufficient and now was virtually bankrupt, he still harboured illusions about the sanctity of authority. Besides, the present unrest frightened him!

## II

At sunset, Old Tung Pao's elder son Ah Sze returned. He had not been able to borrow any money. Nevertheless, he brought back three pecks of rice.

"Master Wu said he had no money. He looked mad," said Ah Sze gloomily, pouring the rice into two large vats. "But then he got generous and gave me three pecks on credit. Those bins behind his rice shop are crammed full. No wonder the peasants haven't any rice! For these three pecks we have to give him five at harvest time — and he still claims he's doing us a favour. That's how the rich keep getting richer!" He went out to the pig pen in the back-yard where he talked in undertones with his wife.

Old Tung Pao gazed morosely at his son and daughter-in-law,

then at the two vats of rice. There was something wrong with his son's manner today. The story about how he got those three pecks wasn't quite clear, but Old Tung Pao was afraid to question him too closely. He had already quarrelled with his daughter-in-law over Ah To's "misbehaviour." She had called the old man a "muddle-head" and even dared to laugh at him.

"Go ahead, put in a complaint about Ah To," she had taunted. "You'll have him buried alive and the rich masters will reward you with a gold ingot!"

Although Old Tung Pao had retorted with a traditional axiom from the sages — "However poor, a man must remain righteous" — his words hadn't had the slightest effect. You can't eat "righteousness," his daughter-in-law had snapped. She maintained it wasn't even as good as pumpkin, which at least could serve as a substitute for rice!

The quarrel had added to Old Tung Pao's worries. He knew that while Ah Sze was a "loyal, respectable" citizen, he couldn't resist his wife's urgings. And now they were whispering beside the pig pen! Old Tung Pao ground his teeth, but there was nothing he could do about it. As he watched them, his thoughts switched to the pig pen itself. Five or six years ago, he had built it with his own hands. It was a handsome job; he had spent over ten dollars on wood alone. But last year they had stopped using it; this year they probably couldn't afford to buy little piglets either. When he hired that necromancer to choose a propitious site for the pig pen, he had just been wasting his money!

Nursing a bellyful of resentment against the pen, he walked unsteadily towards his son and daughter-in-law.

"I hear that Master Chen is looking for some old wood," he called to Ah Sze. "Tomorrow, take down that pig pen and sell it to him — it's unlucky. Since we can't afford to raise pigs, the damn thing isn't doing us any good just standing there!"

The two stopped whispering and turned towards the old man. The wife's face looked very excited in the twilight; her cheekbones were splotched with red.

"It's not worth the trouble," Ah Sze quickly replied. "Dirty old wood. Master Chen probably wouldn't take it."

"He will!" Old Tung Pao insisted angrily. "He'll take it for my sake. Our families have been connected for three generations. He couldn't refuse!"

The old man based his confidence on the "glorious past," when his grandfather and the grandfather of Master Chen had escaped together from the "Long Hairs' " camp. This had given his grandfather a high standing in the House of Chen. Old Tung Pao himself had received exceptionally good treatment. At times, Master Chen even addressed him as Elder Brother Tung Pao! Such kindness had strengthened Old Tung Pao's conviction that respect for one's betters was the only proper course.

He waited until his daughter-in-law, pouting, had walked away, then hotly questioned his elder son.

"What's Ah To up to anyway? Tell me! Don't you think I can guess? As long as I'm alive, you'll still be under my control!"

A crow, perched on the ridge of the roof, cawed raucously. Ah Sze threw a piece of broken tile at the bird and spat. He silently shook his head. How could he speak? What could he say? His father talked one way, his wife another, and his younger brother yet another. He was a simple honest fellow. To him, they all sounded reasonable. He could never form his own opinions.

"They'll lop off heads! Whole families will die! I've seen it happen plenty of times!"

"But . . . there are so many. Can they kill us all?" Ah Sze replied weakly. But seeing his father's staring eyes and the veins standing out on his forehead, Ah Sze added quickly, "There's nothing to worry about. Ah To only went along to see the excitement. They didn't go into town today —"

"You're crazy!" the old man cut in. "Huang the Priest told me so himself! Do you mean to say he's lying?" Old Tung Pao was sure now the brothers and his daughter-in-law were in league with each other.

"Really they didn't go to town. Huang the Priest has got it all wrong!" Upset by his father's persistence, Ah Sze spilled out the truth: "They just went to that village east of here — Yangchia Bridge. The old women and the girls took the lead;

the men are only helping them row the boats. Ah To is helping too. That's the whole story!"

Ah Sze was violating his wife's instructions by telling this much, but there were still two facts he was holding back: One was that "helpful" Ah To was actually the leader of the expedition. The other was that Ah Sze himself had already agreed with his wife that in the event he should be unable to borrow money and buy rice, tomorrow he too would "help with the rowing."

Old Tung Pao looked at Ah Sze sceptically, but remained silent.

It was nearly dark. White smoke rose from the kitchen chimney. Little Pao was singing in the front room. His wife called to Ah Sze, who was glad to have an excuse to get away from the old man. He started towards the house, then halted and said to his father with a sigh:

"The three pecks of rice will last eight or nine days. When Ah To comes home tonight just tell him not to help with the rowing any more."

"I still want the pen taken apart. It'll only get worse, standing out in the wind and rain. At least we can get a little money for the wood."

What Old Tung Pao seemed actually to be implying was — we aren't so poor yet that we have to fly in the face of the "Emperor's Laws"! He rapped the pig pen with his knuckles like an experienced carpenter appraising the value of the wood, then stalked off into the house.

Voices were heard on the threshing ground. The villagers were returning from their "excursion." Little Pao scurried out like a rabbit to find his uncle Ah To. The boy's mother crammed some wood into the stove, then rushed to the threshing ground too. She was anxious to learn the news. The pot on the stove puffed merrily, this time with the fragrance of fresh rice. It made Old Tung Pao's mouth water, and his stomach began to rumble. But his mind was on other matters. He was thinking how to control Ah To, his wild colt of a younger son, and how to prepare for the harvest season. The gathering of the crops was still more than a month off. Probably, at the moment, Old Tung Pao was the only one in the village worrying about it.

But Ah To had not come back with the others after all, nor had Lu Fu-ching, one of the neighbours across the stream. The two young men were said to be spending the night at Yangchia Bridge; tomorrow they intended to "help row" to Duck's Mouth Bar, where the peasants of three villages would join forces and march on the town. This news was transmitted to Ah Sze's wife by Sixth Treasure, Fu-ching's sister. The whole village was discussing the plan excitedly. But no one dared tell Old Tung Pao. Everyone knew his peculiar disposition.

"It's just as well he hasn't come home. The rascal! I'll disown him!" the old man growled at supper time, his eyes on his elder son. He seemed to know what was in the wind.

Ah Sze only clucked his tongue. His wife glanced sideways at her father-in-law and snorted incredulously.

That night, the old man slept badly. He began to dream the moment he closed his eyes. His dreams were quite short, but as each one ended he leaped into wakefulness as if someone had hit him with a stick. Though extremely tired, he was afraid to sleep. His eyelids seemed to weigh a thousand catties. In a hazy half-awake state, he could hear his son talking in the next room. He assumed that husband and wife were discussing household matters, and didn't listen. But suddenly Ah Sze raised his voice in words that caught the old man's attention:

"Ah To, *Tieh* wants to bury you alive! Of course you're right, but the old man doesn't understand the times. I'm worried about you; it's a serious crime. Suppose when it comes to a showdown the others run off and leave you to face the music alone? . . ."

He must be dreaming! But Old Tung Pao had heard everything very clearly. His hair stood on end; his eyes were wide open now. He raised himself on one elbow and shouted to his elder son.

No answer. Little Pao laughed in his sleep. Ah Sze's wife said something in a fretful indistinct voice. Then the bed creaked, and the snoring resumed.

Sleep out of the question, the old man stared into the empty darkness, his mind racing. He remembered the daily increasing good fortune of his family in the "Golden Age" thirty years before. All that remained of that happy period were some old account books. He had lost money again this year on his silkworms. . . . His mind drifted to a contemplation of his family's "righteousness" — upheld by every succeeding generation since his grandfather. When Old Master Chen was still alive, he had often praised them. From the time he was twenty, Old Tung Pao had resolutely modelled himself after the "gentlemen masters" in the town. Even though he only wielded a hoe, he too was "righteous." But now what had befallen him? The Old Lord of the Sky must be blind to let a good man like him have a son like Ah To! Could Ah To really be possessed by the spirit of the young "Long Hair" Old Tung Pao's grandfather had been forced to kill sixty years ago? The old man broke into a cold sweat — Ah To's actions were exactly those of the "Long Hairs"! About five years ago, when many people were crying "Down with the landlord gentry!" hadn't Ah To taken out and played with the big sword Old Tung Pao's grandfather brought home when he escaped from the "Long Hairs' " camp? The very sword which had cut down the young "Long Hair"! It must have been fated that one day Ah To should take up this sword!

He thought it all out, and the more he thought, the more frightened Old Tung Pao became. There was one little thing he hadn't thought of, something he couldn't have guessed in a million years. At the very moment he was gritting his teeth in rage at his younger son, thirty peasants from Yangchia Bridge were approaching through the dawn mist; and they were being led by his son Ah To and his neighbour Fu-ching! Moreover, the peasants in his own village, after excitedly dreaming of the band's arrival all night, had now arisen and were preparing to go out and give the visitors a hearty greeting!

Through a crack in the wall, the sky was a fish-belly grey. Sparrows chirped on the threshing ground. The only rooster left

in the village — the precious possession of Huang the Priest —
began to crow. From afar, it sounded like a woman crying.

Old Tung Pao fell into an uneasy doze. In a kind of dream
he could see the "Long Hairs'" sword gleaming brightly before
him. The hand of a muscular arm grasped its hilt. Then he saw
a face with large round eyes beneath bushy brows. Ah To! Uttering a cry of anger tempered with fear, Old Tung Pao jumped
to the floor. It was broad daylight. Ah Sze's wife was cooking gruel; flames danced in the opening of the stove. Taking a
grip on himself, the old man returned to bed.

Suddenly, a great storm of voices surged in from the threshing
ground, followed by the crash of a violently beaten gong.

"Whose house is on fire?" yelled the old man, rushing out to
see.

When he reached the threshing ground, he finally understood.
The scene that met his eye was exactly the same as the one he
saw when the peasants "revolted" against the emperor Kuang
Hsu in the early days of his reign! The peasants from Yangchia
Bridge — men and women, young and old — were moving in a
dense black crowd across the threshing ground. "Come out!
Let's all go together!" they were shouting. Ah To was among
them. In fact he was the one beating the gong! Ah To strode
to the fore and bounded right up to his father. Old Tung Pao's
face flamed; his eyes shot sparks.

"Fool! They'll cut your head off!"

"That's one way of dying," Ah To laughed. "But unless we
get rice we'll be just as dead when we starve to death! We're
going! Where's brother? And sister-in-law? We'll all go!"

Deafened by fury, the old man raised his fist to strike. Ah
Sze darted out and rushed between them.

"Ah To," he pleaded, "listen to me! Don't go. Yesterday, I
borrowed three pecks of rice. Our family can eat!"

Ah To's thick brows jumped and his expression changed. But
before he could reply, a man stepped out from behind him. It
was their neighbour, Fu-ching. Laughing, Fu-ching pushed Ah
Sze aside and shouted:

"So you've got three pecks of rice? That's fine! The Yangchia Bridge people haven't had their morning gruel yet. Everybody come this way!"

What! Eat his family's rice? Ah Sze couldn't believe his ears. But the Yangchia Bridge peasants surged into his house, cheering. Old Tung Pao howled as if his heart were being hacked by a knife, then his eyes went black and his legs turned to cotton. He had to sit down. Raging insanely, Ah Sze flung himself on Fu-ching and tried to throttle him.

"Are you crazy?" said Fu-ching, holding him off. "What are you doing? Listen to me, Brother Ah Sze! Ah To, what's wrong with him?"

Ah Sze abruptly released Fu-ching and whirled on Ah To. He seized his young brother and began to punch him, yelling tearfully:

"Even a snake doesn't foul its own nest, but you bring people to eat up your family's rice! You let them eat us out of house and home!"

He had one arm locked tight around Ah To's head, smothering him. Fu-ching couldn't pry them apart. The old man, sitting on the floor swearing a blue streak, showed no inclination to intervene. Luckily Fu-ching's younger sister Sixth Treasure came in just then, and with her help Fu-ching managed to separate the two brothers.

"You've got a way out, you borrowed rice," Ah To panted. "But the others have no way out. What are they going to do? You've got a little rice, so you don't want to go. But if we can't pull this thing off because we're short of men, then what? — And you'll get the rice back. Come with us to the town. You'll get your share!"

But Ah Sze was squatting on his heels, his face wooden. Fu-ching patted him on the shoulder with one hand while rubbing his own bruised neck with the other.

"We all agreed we'd eat whatever rice we could find here, then take the owners of the rice along with us to the town. Don't hold it against me, Ah Sze. Everybody agreed!"

"Even the 'Long Hairs' weren't so rude, so blasted savage!"

muttered Old Tung Pao, but he kept his eyes down. He didn't have the courage to upbraid the men to their faces.

He knew what was going on now. Good, he thought, go ahead, go to the town! You'll get what's coming to you there! The Old Lord of the Sky has eyes! Then you'll know that you should have listened to this old man. He's no flea living blindly on some dog's back. He's learned a thing or two in all these years!

At that moment, the Yangchia Bridge peasants swept noisily out of the house, carrying with them the two large rice vats. Ah Sze's wife, her hair streaming wildly, weeping and yelling, trailed in their wake.

"They belong to us! They're ours! How can you steal our food? Thieves! Murderers!"

No one paid any attention to her. The peasants set the vats in the middle of the threshing ground and someone began beating the gong again. It took all of Sixth Treasure's strength to pull Ah Sze's wife back.

"Whoever has rice has to share it with everybody! Can't you understand?" the girl shouted at her. "Who told you to kowtow and humble yourself? Who told you to borrow rice on credit? That may work for you, but others have no place to borrow! Others are starving; are they supposed to stand by and watch your family stuffing itself? Hush now! Crying and carrying on like you'd just lost your grandfather! We're eating your rice, it's true, but we'll help you get it back soon enough! What are you crying about?"

The woodenly squatting Ah Sze rose to his feet with a sigh and walked over to his wife.

"It was all your idea. Now we've ended up with nothing," he berated her. Then he urged, "Let's go along with them. What else can we do? We're all in the same boat now. If the sky falls, everyone will get crushed!"

Two large cauldrons made their appearance on the threshing ground, and soon the local villagers and the Yangchia Bridge peasants were busy cooking gruel. The early mist had vanished. Golden sunlight, slanting down on the threshing ground, added a touch of colour to the pasty faces of the eaters. At the eastern end of the stream, where it flowed fairly wide and deep, people were singing happily as they pushed half a dozen boats into the water. These boats would take the peasants to the town!

Old Tung Pao squatted in silence, glaring venomously. He watched the crowd boisterously finish the gruel; he watched them noisily board the boats. It was all like a dream. He saw Ah To vigorously plying a sculling oar. Ah Sze, looking tragic, his wife, and Sixth Treasure, sat together. The two women were chatting quite amiably now. Little Pao stood in the stern, imitating the motions of his uncle Ah To.

Then, as if awakening, Old Tung Pao jumped up and ran at top speed along the stream, all the way to its western end. Why, he didn't know. A weight seemed to be pressing down on his heart. He simply had to find someone to talk to. But the whole village was silent and deserted. Not even a child remained.

Finally, however, when he came back to the eastern end of the stream, he saw someone far on the opposite side, rushing madly in his direction. Old Tung Pao couldn't distinguish the man's features at first; the only thing he could see clearly was a white turban. But when the fellow came running across the little bridge, Old Tung Pao identified him as Huang the Priest. Much relieved, the old man called out:

"Even the 'Long Hairs' weren't so rude! I haven't spent all my years living like a flea on some dog's back! I've seen a thing or two! Mark my words! They'll catch it when they get to town! The murdering thieves!"

Huang the Priest stopped and looked at him without recognition. Only after carefully scrutinizing the old man for half a minute did Huang the Priest speak, and then in an indignant wail:

"Utterly unprincipled! Utterly unprincipled! They ate my rooster I tell you! Utterly unprincipled!"

"Murderers! Your rooster, eh? That's nothing. They'll be killing men next! The assassins!" Old Tung Pao stumped off home.

That night all the villagers returned safely. Much to the old man's astonishment, each was carrying five pints of rice. It seemed to him that the "gentlemen masters" of the town weren't like the "gentlemen masters" of the old days. A hundred or so peasants from three small villages march on the town and the gentry become so frightened that they immediately talk terms and give each peasant half a peck of rice. These modern "gentlemen masters" have no backbone; all his years might just as well have been spent as a flea on a dog's back for the way the town gentry fall down on his predictions! The world has changed beyond all understanding. Ah To and his kind are riding high!

### III

The storm of raids on the rice bins spread. Within a radius of seventy-five miles, almost every day hungry peasants "breached the public peace" in more than a dozen small towns. To the gentry in these towns, this conduct seemed entirely too impolite. They dropped their mask of benevolent concern and took steps to "preserve order." The county and district governments, even the towns' merchant guilds, issued impressive proclamations which were circulated throughout the countryside: Attacks on the bins of the rice merchants and the wealthy must cease; all problems can be peaceably negotiated. . . . At the same time, "fair-minded" gentry came forward to request the rice merchants and the pawnshops to "take a loss" and "give special facilities" to help the "poor suffering peasants" get through this time of stress.

But the hungry bellies of the peasants couldn't wait for the gentry and merchants to define what exactly they meant by "special facilities." The proclamations were in vain; the urgings of the village heads (usually former leaders of the local gentry's armed "protection corps") proved equally useless. Raids continued and increased. Peasants' bands were no longer one hundred in number but five hundred, a thousand! And now they were ranging far beyond neighbouring towns. They were forming "expeditionary armies" which marched on the cities!

In a small prosperous city about twenty miles from Old Tung Pao's village, hungry peasants clashed with the police. The police fired in the air as a warning, then arrested a few dozen demonstrators. The next day, thousands of angry peasants surrounded the city and cut it off completely from all contact with the outside world.

This left the city with no choice but to offer "special facilities" immediately. There were three: The peasants could borrow rice on credit from the grain merchants, to be returned at harvest time on a bushel for bushel basis. Pawnshops would give interest-free loans. The city's merchant guild would donate 425 bushels of rice to the peasants' village, which the village head would distribute. . . . Realizing the danger in the situation, the merchants and gentry did everything they could to minimize it. As to the loss they would take on the gift of 425 bushels, they could make that up with a levy on the people of the city.

In the meanwhile, the provincial government was stationing troops at key arteries in the countryside. This, added to the "special facilities," resulted in a gradual subsiding of the storm of raids on the rice bins. It was nearly the end of the sixth lunar month by then; the peasants' busy season was fast approaching.

Thanks to the storm, Old Tung Pao's family was able to eat one meal with rice and two with gruel every day. Nor was their indebtedness in any way increased by this rice, except for the unfortunate three pecks which Ah Sze had previously borrowed. However, they would have to start planting their rice paddy fields soon, and both Ah Sze and his wife feared that the family's pile of debts would rise still higher.

As a result, they worked without enthusiasm, and this added to Old Tung Pao's irascibility. His prestige had suffered a serious blow in the past month, but now it was rice-planting not rice-bin-raiding time! He fancied himself a kind of elder statesman in agriculture, an old war horse who could find his way under any conditions. He talked ceaselessly to his daughter-in-law and Ah Sze about how the planting should be done. He

told them how diligent he had been as a youth, how his grandfather had never lost heart but worked and worked until he had
won security for the family.

One day, as Old Tung Pao returned from the fields, he
shouted at Ah Sze:

"We'll transplant our rice sprouts tomorrow or the day after
at the latest. Why haven't you figured out yet how much we'll
have to spend for fertilizer? Have you lost your wits?"

"We still have a sack left from last year," his son replied
listlessly.

The old man glared, furious. "That chemical stuff! Poison!
Poison made by the foreign devils to kill people! I only know
the bean-cake fertilizer our ancestors used. Fine, strong! That
chemical powder ruins the land. Tomorrow, we'll buy bean
cake!"

"Where will we get the money? People say that chemical fertilizer loses strength if you keep it too long; you have to add
half as much new powder for it to be any good. But in our state,
there's no use even thinking of that!"

"Poppycock and piffle!" roared the old man, shaking his
finger under his son's nose. "According to you, we shouldn't
plant at all! What are you going to eat if we don't plant? How
will we pay off our debts?"

An Sze sighed. He knew the old man was right; it was only
from the fields that they could earn their food and clothing,
get money to return what they had borrowed. But his experience
in recent years had also taught him that borrowing in order to
plant simply made you the creditor's draught ox in your own
fields — no, not even that, for draught oxen at least could eat
their fill, something his family seldom did. Why plant rice? —
his wife had often asked him. They both felt that what Ah To
said was right — "The peasant who borrows is finished!" But
since working in the fields was the only way they could live,
husband and wife had come to a decision. Under no circumstances would they seek any more loans to invest in the land.

When his son remained silent, the old man sulked, said he
was "fed up with them." The same afternoon, he went to town

and complained to Ah Sze's father-in-law and to Master Chen about how his son was "ruining the family." Both men urged Old Tung Pao not to take things too seriously — sons had their own lives to live too. The old man spent the night in town. Early the next morning he barged in on Master Chen and asked him for a loan. It wasn't a large sum — only enough to buy a cake of pressed bean fertilizer. Master Chen had just finished his morning opium pipe and was dying to sleep. But when he saw that he couldn't put the old man off, he got up, went with him to the bean-pressing shop and vouched for his credit.

Old Tung Pao returned home with the bean cake, smiling all the way. After placing it on the porch, he turned to his daughter-in-law and Ah Sze and told them grimly:

"Until I've turned up my toes, you'll listen to me! Don't ask where I got the money. Just do your work!"

Now that the tender rice was sprouting in the fields, the illusions he had cherished during the silkworm season again flourished in his stubborn old brain. Bathed in golden sunlight, caressed by soft breezes, the rice grew extremely fast, almost as if someone were pulling it upwards. But the village stream rapidly shrank, and treadmills had to be placed on the embankment to push the water into the paddy fields. Ah Sze couldn't manage their mill alone indefinitely, and Old Tung Pao tried to relieve him. But after a few minutes on the treadmill, the old man was panting hard, his back stiff, his legs aching. He had to come down and let his daughter-in-law take his place.

The rice grew like mad, and it consumed water like mad. Yet every day, like a fiery dragon, the sun drank of the little stream, steadily lowering its level. Everywhere in the village the cry was raised — "We need help!" Everywhere people were begged to take a turn at the treadmill. Lotus and her silent dour husband had only planted a few small cereal crops and they were relatively free. People forgot that she was a "witch." She and her husband were in great demand wherever there was a treadmill. Young neighbour Fu-ching had returned his leased land that year and, with his sister, he frequently called at Old Tung

Pao's and lent a hand. Ah To seldom came to the village; when he did, he helped other families, since the old man refused to see him.

Each morning the clear blue of the sky made the peasants frown. A few white clouds at dusk would send the whole village into transports of delight. Old ladies would peer up near-sightedly, chanting thankful prayers. But always their joy proved premature. In almost a month they didn't have a single drop of rain!

Old Tung Pao's paddy field, being on high ground, was particularly difficult to manage. Muddy water had to be pushed up painfully from the drying stream through a ditch seventy feet long; the parched soil consumed half the water before it even reached the field. The rice shoots, originally so lusty, seemed stricken with anemia. They grew more brown and withered by the day. It hurt Old Tung Pao to see them; he stamped in helpless frustration. His son Ah Sze looked tragic but said nothing. His daughter-in-law said a great deal — all cold and biting. She predicted that this year's harvest would be a miserable failure, a waste of effort; she bemoaned the new debt incurred for the bean cake!

"If we only had water, we'd have a fine crop," the old man retorted weakly. He couldn't bear listening to her any longer.

"Water! Water!" snapped Ah Sze's wife. "It's more precious to you than our blood! Fu-ching and his sister help part-time; they can count as only one. Altogether that makes just three of us on the treadmill. How much blood can you get out of three people? This month the mill has worked us dry! Ah To is young and strong, but you won't let him come! . . ."

"Why not send for Ah To?" agreed Ah Sze. "He's like an ox!"

Old Tung Pao spat without replying.

The next day Ah To, all smiles, came to help at the treadmill. But it was already too late. Only a trickle of water still flowed in the centre of the stream bed. The men attached three lengths of trough to extend their ditch to the shrunken stream. But a few hours later the water level had dropped so low that even

Ah To, with his ox-like strength, couldn't pump any water into their paddy field. About twenty yards to the west, the stream ran deeper — it was up to Ah To's waist. But at that point there was no embankment on which to mount the treadmill. Unless it rained that night, Old Tung Pao's rice would be finished.

Nor was his the only family in trouble. Every paddy field in the village was drying and cracking like an old tortoise-shell. People climbed high trees to peer at the distant horizons. There was not a speck of cloud in the wide blue sky.

The last remaining chance was to hire a "foreign pump" from town. Old Tung Pao was displeased when he heard the word "foreign"; he didn't believe the gadget could do much good anyhow. During last year's flood, peasants in a neighbouring village had hired the pump to free their inundated fields. Though he himself had not seen the pump in operation, Huang the Priest, who loved to poke his nose into other people's business, had praised it highly. But then it was only siphoning water out. Would it prove so effective when it had to pump water in — and over a distance of several hundred yards? Before he had a chance to express his doubts, however, his daughter-in-law spoke up grumpily:

"The foreign pump is good, but what about the hiring fee? We haven't any money! They say it costs over a dollar to fill one section of paddy field!"

Old Tung Pao couldn't make up his mind. He hurried to the dilapidated shrine of the God of Wealth near the little bridge outside the village, and banged his head against the ground in resounding kowtows. "Display your power," he begged. "Give us some rain today!" He promised to offer a substantial sacrifice if his prayer should be answered.

That night, because there was no water left for the treadmill to pump, the family was able to sleep right through until morning. But Old Tung Pao never closed his eyes. He heard a hissing sound of some sort and mistook it for rain. Bounding out of bed, he rushed to the porch for a look. It wasn't raining, but the sky was grey and overcast. Though disappointed, he clutched at this straw of hope and dropped on his knees and prayed. The

third time he got out of bed to examine the sky, it was already
light in the east. He hurried to the field to look at his precious
crop. There had been some dew during the night; the rice seemed a little stronger than when he had last seen it — in the light
of the pitiless sun. But the field was badly parched. Even when
he put his fingers deep into the cracks he could feel no softness
in the soil. Old Tung Pao's heart thumped. He knew that in
a short while the sun would come out and his rice would die.
That would mean the end of him and his family.

He returned to the threshing ground in front of his door. A
blood-red sun was just showing its head in the east. Weeds
choked the trickle that remained of the stream. Some villagers
had planted maize in the exposed stream bed; it was already as
tall as a man. Half a dozen people were standing beside the
maize, arguing in loud voices. Old Tung Pao listlessly drifted
over to them. They were discussing whether to pool their funds
and hire the "foreign" pump. The man known as Li the Tiger
was insisting:

"If we're going to hire it, we'd better be quick about it. That
pump is kept busy every day. Last night, though, I heard that
no one had hired it yet for today. We'll lose it if we don't
hurry. Then we'll be in a fix. Will you come in for a share,
Old Tung Pao?"

The old man stared straight ahead, as if he hadn't understood.
Two things prevented him from replying — he was afraid the
"foreign" pump wouldn't help, and he had no money. He figured it would be better to let others try the pump first. If it
really worked, he could use it too. As to the money, perhaps he
could manage a loan for a couple of days.

That morning, he and his family wandered through the paddy
field as if keeping vigil at the bedside of a dying patient. The
rice shoots went from bad to worse, drooping their heads at
first, then finally bending in the middle. The soil emitted
parched cracked sighs. Now the entire village was idle. Treadmills stood motionless; the stream was too low for them to be
of any use. A few peasants stood on the small bridge outside

the village, anxiously awaiting the arrival of the "foreign" pump — the doctor who could save their sick crops!

Towards noon, when the wretched sun was blazing like fire, the people on the bridge set up a cry: It's coming! . . . A small boat came sailing down the canal. On it was mounted an engine — the "foreign" pump! It didn't look particularly impressive, but people said it could pump water faster than eight robust young men. The whole village turned out, including Old Tung Pao and his sons. The boat did not land but remained floating in the canal. Several dozen yards of shiny rubber hose thick as a man's arm were unreeled. Then, one end was hauled ashore and hung over the embankment of a paddy field.

"The water will come out here and irrigate the field!" the operator from town announced dramatically.

Soon, the engine on the boat began to pant like an old asthma victim and water spewed in jerks out of the rubber hose, then settled down to a steady flow. The peasants shouted and laughed for joy, forgetting that this water would cost money.

Standing off to one side, Old Tung Pao watched bug-eyed. He was sure some demon must be concealed in the noisy pump engine and the long snaky hose. Maybe it was the mud-fish spirit that inhabited the slimy pool in front of the village's Temple of Earth. The water probably was the saliva of the mud-fish spirit; tonight the spirit might decide to suck it all back. Then tomorrow the man could come from town again and swindle some more money!

But none of these suspicions could withstand the spreading expanse of green water. By the time the pump finished irrigating the second section of paddy field, Old Tung Pao decided to beg the assistance of this mechanized mud-fish spirit. He would take his hoe and guard his field all night just to make sure it didn't come sneaking through the darkness to steal back its saliva.

Without consulting either his son Ah Sze or his daughter-in-law, he got Li the Tiger and Huang the Priest to be his guarantors, and promised the pump operator to pay eight dollars after harvest plus twenty per cent monthly interest. The hose was then placed in his field.

An inch of oily green water covered Old Tung Pao's paddy land before sunset. Light breezes stirred ripples like the wrinkles on an old lady's face. Very happy, Old Tung Pao ignored his daughter-in-law's nagging protests — "Now we owe another eight dollars!" Of course eight dollars was no small sum, but wouldn't they be getting at least ten dollars a load for their rice at harvest? Why, last year, even second-rate rice sold for ten and a half! Old Tung Pao's illusions had again taken full possession of him.

But Ah Sze still stared at the field mournfully. The rice continued to droop in spite of the water. It was too late. The sun had sapped the life out of the delicate shoots.

"Put a little chemical fertilizer on the rice tonight and tomorrow it'll be all right," said Ah To.

The unexpected sound of Ah To's voice in his ear made Ah Sze jump. That's right, they still had a sack of fertilizer! If they were ever going to use it, this was certainly the time. Spoil the land? So what! Use it!

But Old Tung Pao overheard Ah To's remark and rushed at him like a maddened tiger.

"That stuff is poison, you 'Long Hair' spawn! Murderer! Do you want to spread poison?"

It took several people to hold off the old man and calm him down. There was no further talk about using the fertilizer.

"You'll see, by tomorrow morning the rice will be fine," Old Tung Pao said to Ah Sze, though not entirely pacified. "Chemical fertilizer! Poison!"

The old man vowed to himself he would guard his field that night if it killed him. Now he had not only the mud-fish spirit to fear, but also his sons. They might come and secretly sprinkle the powder while he slept. But the mud-fish spirit was what worried him most. He had no intention of revealing his "occult knowledge" however, and merely announced he would protect the paddy field from any plot that Ah To might persuade Ah Sze to join. The old man was notoriously stubborn!

But the night passed peacefully. Neither the mud-fish spirit nor the unruly, fertilizer-advocating brothers made any appearance. The rice still bent listlessly however, in fact a few stalks were in worse condition than the day before. Though the rice in other fields that had been irrigated was again green and strong, Old Tung Pao began to suspect the effectiveness of the mud-fish spirit's saliva. His daughter-in-law raged, "The old muddle-head is sending us all to the grave!" Worried frantic, he turned the colour of pig's liver. Young neighbour Fu-ching urged him at least to try the chemical fertilizer and see whether it did any good, but he continued to sit silent and wooden. Meanwhile, his sons had gone to work spreading the fertilizer. The old man kept his eyes averted from their direction. He didn't want to see.

Fortunately, the next two days a curtain of clouds protected the fields from the blistering sun. About half an inch of water still remained on the paddy ground. The rice became green once again. While the old man would not give any credit to the chemical fertilizer, he no longer said it was poison. After the cloudy weather, a fine rain fell, followed by bland sunny days. The rice flourished and the peasants sighed with relief. Their lives were saved. The Old Lord of the Sky had taken pity on them!

The cool fresh breezes of autumn began to blow, ending like a bad dream the more than forty days of scorching weather. The villagers were happy. They could tell from experience that this year's crop would not be bad. Old Tung Pao, now positive that he had not spent all his years in vain like a flea on a dog's back, was predicting a harvest for his family of four loads to the *mou* — a bumper crop! At times, as he carefully fondled the heavy rice heads, he dreamed they might even reap five loads. And every grain was so full and solid!

And he calculated: Even at only four and a half loads to the *mou*, that would still be a total of forty loads. After paying almost seven loads for rent, at ten dollars a load his family would earn more than three hundred dollars. With such a sum, he could pay off half his debts. Besides, they'd probably get more than ten dollars a load. That was the very minimum!

With one good harvest, the peasants could get on their feet

again. The Old Lord of the Sky had eyes after all. He saw where His mercy was needed!

But the merchants in town had eyes too, and they saw only where the profits lay. The price of rice in town fell before the harvest even began. When the peasants gathered the fruits of their months of back-breaking toil and packed the full solid grains into bags, the price dropped to six dollars. While the peasants were virtually going blind at the difficult job of milling, rice in town was falling to four dollars for second grade. By the time they painstakingly sorted out the rough grain and brought it to town, it was difficult to find buyers even at three! The rice merchants looked coldly at the stricken peasants and said indifferently:

"That's today's price. Tomorrow it may go lower!"

Creditors descended on the village like a swarm of locusts, fierce and angry. Take rice in payment? All right — two dollars and ninety cents for second grade, three-sixty for white rice!

Old Tung Pao's illusions burst like a soap bubble. The villagers wept and cursed.

Ah Sze's wife raged to everyone she met. "What's the good of tilling the land? We nearly killed ourselves with work and we're still in debt!"

His bitter experience with the silkworms had laid Old Tung Pao low. His bitter experience with the rice harvest sent him to his grave. As he was breathing his last, though he had already lost the power of speech, his eyes were clear. He gazed at Ah To as if to say:

"So you were right all along! Amazing! Who could have believed it!"

*January 1933*

# WINTER RUIN

Strong winds blowing from the northwest for several successive days stripped the remaining leaves from the branches of the trees. Dying grass beside the little stream faded from bright gold to greyish brown. In a few places, where mischievous children had tried to simulate a prairie fire, the grass was black and scorched.

When the weather was clear, you might find a skinny dog sunning himself on the threshing ground, and maybe a villager or two, still wearing light autumn clothing, squatting in the sunlight picking lice. On the dark days when the northwest wind made the branches creak and clouds scudded across the sky like wild horses, the threshing ground was devoid of any signs of life. Then the entire village seemed dead. Everything was a mortuary ashen colour.

The only sign of green was just north of the village in the Chang family cemetery. This was the ancestral burial ground of Chang the landlord, who lived in town, and it had many tall fir trees.

The cemetery was one of the banes of the villagers' existence. Whenever a fir tree was cut down and stolen, Chang insisted that the village compensate him for its loss — even though the thieves were usually people from outside.

One morning, in spite of the fact that the sunlight was only a dull yellow and bare branches groaned in the northwest wind, people gathered on the open threshing ground. Lotus, reviled by many as a witch, was addressing the assembled crowd, gesticulating vigorously.

"I just went by there. Sure enough, another one's gone! Chips lying all around, still smelling fragrant and sweet — the thieves must have stolen it this morning. And a whopping big one it was too! Like this!" she said, showing the width of the tree with her hands.

Her listeners frowned and sighed. "Let's get word to Chang quickly —" one of them started to say.

"What for?" another man cut in. "You don't think if we tell him that old skinflint will let us off, do you? Huh! Not him!"

Lotus' dour husband nodded. "Every day we put it off is a day less trouble. Let's take our chances on what happens when he finds out."

Surprisingly enough, Lotus was the first to disagree. "What do you mean — take our chances? Do you think we'll have money to pay him then? And even if we do — I don't think we ought to give him a penny! We don't eat his food or use his money. What do the trees in his family cemetery have to do with us?"

"You can't reason with him," Ah Sze interrupted. "Last year, Li the Tiger swore at him, and he had Li arrested and put in jail!"

"Those damn tree-snatchers are ruining us!" Ah Sze's wife cried tearfully. In her heart she agreed with Lotus' husband.

The others joined in warmly cursing the thieves. They were sure the culprits were the poor peasants who lived in a settlement of thatched shacks not far from the village. They had suffered at the hands of the avaricious Chang and had probably stolen his tree for revenge. But the result was they were getting others into trouble! Someone proposed going to the settlement and recovering the "purloined object."

Ah To, who until now hadn't spoken, could restrain himself no longer.

"Take the tree back? That's a fine idea! You're not Skinflint Chang's stinking son! Why sweat over this for him?"

"You don't have to get tough about it!" the man retorted. "You didn't steal the tree. Why are you getting all worked up?"

Lotus' husband pulled Ah To back. "We're only talking," he said soothingly. "Nobody's really going for the tree. Keep your shirt on."

"That's not the point! Those people who took the tree weren't trying to hurt us. If Skinflint Chang tries to make us pay for it, that'll be because he's a dirty son of a bitch! Why should we help him find his damn tree? He's nothing to us. . . ."

Ah Sze, Ah To's elder brother, dragged him off into the house.

Muttering imprecations against the hateful Chang, the gathering broke up. Only Lotus and Ah Sze's wife remained, staring absently in the direction of the green cemetery ground. Suddenly, as if a curtain had been lifted, the view cleared and the dull yellow sunlight brightened into gold. The wind stopped too. The two women raised their faces to the sky and took a deep breath. Of one accord, they squatted on their heels to enjoy the warmth of the sun.

Lotus had been a slavey to a rich family in town and knew all the gossip. To Ah Sze's wife she said in a whisper:

"Skinflint Chang is a crook himself! He's got a hand in plenty of shady deals!"

"Oho!"

"Salt smugglers, opium pedlars — he works with 'em all! Last year wasn't there a gang that specialized in stealing draught oxen from the thatched shack settlement? And they robbed the flour shops in town too. Well, Skinflint Chang was their fence!"

"But surely the authorities must know about it?"

"Hah! Authorities! The chief of police is in on the rackets himself!"

Lotus pursed her mouth scornfully, her eyes screwed almost shut. She had become much thinner lately and her white skin had taken on a bluish tinge. Her mouth looked larger than ever, further accentuating the tininess of her piggy eyes.

Ah Sze's wife wagged her head and sighed. Then she rose to her feet and said angrily:

"No wonder Ah To says that the meek and humble haven't a chance!"

"He's right. The world's going to turn head over heels!"

"My father-in-law used to say the 'Long Hairs' will be coming again. I hear there are women 'Long Hairs' too. You know,

we've got a big 'Long Hair' sword in our house. . . . But my
father says the True Emperor* hasn't been born yet."

"Bah, how does he know? Do you think Heaven would tell
him first? Last month there was a red star in the western sky —
big as a wine cup, and with eight points! That was the star of
the True Emperor! Eight points means he was born eight years
ago. Hasn't been born yet, has he?"

"A rebel! My father says that kind of person is a rebel
usurper! What do you know anyhow! Damn witch!"

"What!" Lotus leaped up, her piggy eyes squinting balefully.

The two women stood glaring at each other; it hadn't taken
much to revive the old animosity between them. Ah Sze's wife
had always been contemptuous of Lotus, considering her "a
slavey, a bit of fluff, a tart!" Lotus, no milksop and full of resentment, had tried to steal the other's silkworm eggs and dump
them into the stream. That was six months ago, and since then
the two cut each other dead whenever they chanced to meet.
Only recently, after Old Tung Pao died, did they begin to act
like neighbours. Now, an inconsequential point had set them to
wrangling again, each convinced of her own righteousness.

Ah Sze's wife spat on the ground with a lordly air, deciding
to make light of this small matter. But as she turned to go, Lotus, who preferred a drubbing any day to silent "cultured" scorn,
jumped forward and cried in a strained voice:

"Anyone who curses and runs away is made of pretty poor
stuff!"

"Better than cheap stuff like you! Witch!" Ah Sze's wife continued on her way. But she did not go home. Instead she went
to the other side of the little stream.

Not having been able to provoke her, Lotus felt very lonely.
She loved "excitement" — even if it were the excitement of a
quarrel, even if she came out the loser. At times she got severely pounded, but she never regretted it. To her anything was

---

* Old popular superstition had it that emperors were ordained by Heaven,
and when a dynasty became helplessly corrupt, Heaven sent a new "true"
emperor to be born in a mortal body. It was his task to overthrow the old
regime and the people were morally bound to support him.

better than being ignored. She hated not being considered "human." When she had been a slavey, the master treated her like a soulless being, an inanimate object, lower than even a cat or a dog. But Lotus knew that she had a soul, and this treatment was one of the reasons she hated her former master.

When she was able to stop being a slavey and became a wife, Lotus was overjoyed. She was sure she could start being a person. Unfortunately, half a month after her marriage, her husband fell seriously ill; then their poultry and livestock were stricken by disease. Her reputation was ruined — she was a witch! In the village she was not considered "human" either! But since it was only a little country village after all, Lotus found ways to hit back. She quarrelled with the village women whenever she had the chance, and she played around with the unmarried young men. For it was only when engaged in a hot wrangle or while dallying in amorous pursuits that she was able to feel, at least to some extent — "I'm a human being too."

When, after the debacle of the spring silkworms, starving peasants took to raiding the rice bins of the grain merchants and the wealthy, Lotus' stock as a "human being" rose considerably. For a long time no one called her by the epithet she so abhorred — "witch." She behaved better too. But now Ah Sze's wife had prodded her old scar. What's more, she did it with a lofty air — as if Lotus were not even worth a quarrel!

Lotus gritted her teeth. She was suffering a pain much worse than any beating could have caused. The northwest wind suddenly rose again. Its swishing sound seemed to mock her — "Witch, witch, witch!"

At the bank of the stream, Ah Sze's wife stopped abruptly. She turned around to glance at Lotus, then quickly averted her face and spat. That was adding fuel to the flames! With a cry, Lotus rushed after her tormentor. But before she had gone two steps, she slipped and sat down so heavily that she saw stars.

"Ha, ha, ha! Witch!" Ah Sze's wife taunted from the distance. At the same time another woman came running across the threshing ground, clapping her hands and laughing. It was Sixth Treasure, also one of Lotus' foes.

"Just wait for me, if you've got any guts!" Lotus panted angrily, turning her flat face in the direction of the newcomer. Though Lotus had come down hard and her backside was smarting, her fury made her forget the pain. She had to give vent to her wrath. But there were two of them against her now. A swearing bout? Sixth Treasure was famed in the village for her sharp tongue. A fight? How could she cope with two? Getting to her feet, she hesitated. Just then a man came walking in her direction from the east. When Lotus saw who he was, she changed her plans.

## II

The new arrival was Huang the Priest. With the death of Old Tung Pao, he had lost another of the few persons with whom he could chat. The younger villagers didn't pay much attention to him. Most people had begun to forget the very existence of this queer old fogy. Originally, he had been a peasant too. But one year he was dragged off to carry ammunition for the army. The rice was just sprouting when he left. When he returned, it was already winter. He consoled himself with the thought that anyhow he could enjoy the New Year meal at home. Then his wife died. He was left alone; they had no children. He sold his small paddy field, retaining only a tiny plot on which he raised vegetables to sell in the town. That was how he lived from year to year. Sometimes the villagers wouldn't see him for four or five days at a stretch. People who went to market in the town said Huang spent the money he received for his vegetables on wine; he sat all day with flushed face discussing the "news" with the professional fortune-teller outside the temple; at night he slept beneath the sacrificial altar.

This manner of living turned Huang "queer." He picked up the highflown phrases of some of the townspeople — a cross between chanted scriptures and involved literary aphorisms. None of the villagers could understand him, nor were they particularly interested in what he had to say.

Recently, because he couldn't even earn enough for food from the sale of his vegetables, Huang gave up drinking. On the rare occasions when he went to town, he returned in half a day at the latest. Then he would squat on his heels beneath a tree beside the little stream and stare vacantly into space. If anyone who crossed his line of vision happened to glance at him, he would jump up and seize the person by the arm and shout:

"The world is going to be plunged into turmoil! In the northeast — in the northeast the True Emperor has appeared!" He would go on ranting until his listener would spit in disgust and flee.

But ever since the northwest wind had begun to blow, the village had seen very little of him, under the trees or anywhere else. He stayed in his small shack, pottering around mysteriously. Someone who had peeked through a split in Huang's door said "the crackpot" seemed to be praying in all directions; he had set up a shrine with three small effigies made of straw.

The younger villagers said Huang the Priest had gone crazy, but the old women and children kept after him to learn what spirits the three straw figures represented. The young women were also determined to get to the bottom of the matter. Huang the Priest answered them all evasively, and pasted paper over the cracks in his door.

But although Huang was not inclined to talk about his three effigies, he was quite willing to babble of other things. The "pointed star" which Lotus had spoken of was something she had acquired from the store of learning of Huang the Priest. And so, when she now saw him approaching, his eyes staring widely, she hastened to greet him. She wanted to enlist his aid in her feud with Sixth Treasure and Ah Sze's wife.

"Hey, Priest," she called. "Can you imagine? That woman says the red star means a rebel usurper! What a fool!" Lotus faced her two enemies with a wild laugh. Suddenly, she became aware of her aching backside. A look of grief wiped the laugh from her face, and her hands went behind her.

The eyes of Huang the Priest grew larger. He stared at the two women, then he looked at Lotus and shook his head.

"The True Emperor has come into the world," he intoned.

"He is as far away as the horizon, yet he may be right before your eyes! At the foot of a mountain outside Nanking is an old man in a little beancurd shop. Every morning he gets up before dawn to mill his beancurd. Rap, rap, rap! Every morning, someone knocks on the shop door and asks, 'Is it light yet? Is it light yet?' Ha-ha, of course it isn't light yet, so the old man answers, 'No!' He doesn't know that the questioner is the True Emperor!"

"And suppose he answers, 'The sky is light'? Then what?" Sixth Treasure drew near to ask, her eyes fixed on the face of Huang the Priest.

"If he said, 'The sky is light'? In that case, in that case. . . ." Huang the Priest squinted up at the sky, then shook his head in a profoundly mysterious manner.

"In that case we poor people'll be able to rise!" Lotus burst out impatiently at Sixth Treasure, her painful buttocks again forgotten.

"Right, right!" breathed Huang the Priest. He felt quite grateful to Lotus. "We're sure to get some good from it. Like a three-year rent holiday, for example."

But Sixth Treasure was nothing if not thorough. Ignoring Lotus, she continued to press Huang the Priest for an answer.

"Won't it be wonderful if the old man decides to say 'The sky is light' real soon!" Ah Sze's wife muttered dully.

"Oh, no! That would never do! He couldn't breach the heavenly edict! It isn't time yet! Why, why when he says 'The sky is light,' the heavenly hosts and generals must come down and help the True Emperor win the throne!" Huang the Priest turned to the younger woman. "Sixth Treasure, you know it would never do to call them all down before the time is ripe!"

"Oh," said Sixth Treasure, somewhat dissatisfied. She pressed her lips together and shook her head.

Lotus burst into laughter. Seeing Sixth Treasure's tight-lipped expression, Lotus thought she ought to find her a good nickname.

"And is the old man an immortal too?" Ah Sze's wife asked in a hushed voice. "Tell me, Priest, how do you know that the one who knocks at the door and asks, 'Is it light yet?' is the True Emperor? What does he look like?"

Huang the Priest laughed coldly. "How do I know? Of course I know. That old man in the beancurd shop has his proof. Rap, rap, rap — every morning the same knock on his door. You understand? A knock on his door, not on anyone else's! 'Is it light yet? Is it light yet?' Every morning the same question! The old man only hears the voice, he doesn't see the speaker. Would he dare to steal a look? Certainly not! That would be breaking heaven's edict — he'd be struck by lightning! Anyhow it is the True Emperor, no doubt about it!"

With this concluding sentence, the face of Huang the Priest grew solemn and his eyes distended in an awesome majesty. The women went goose-pimply all over. They could almost hear the knocking at the door.

Buffeted by the northwest wind, the four of them shivered with cold. Sixth Treasure wiped her streaming eyes.

"What about your three straw men?" she asked.

"There is reason for them, there is reason!" Huang the Priest replied theatrically, showing the whites of his eyes. He raised his left hand and pointed at the northern sky with his middle finger. His face became even more grave than before.

The three women looked in the direction he was pointing. It seemed to Ah Sze's wife that the skinny black finger of Huang the Priest was stabbing something in the heavens. Her heart beat faster.

"From there comes the True Emperor, there is the Gory Glow! You understand? The Gory Glow!" Huang the Priest said in a piercing voice, his large eyes staring at the three women.

They all started with fright. Though none of them was very clear what was meant exactly by "Gory Glow," because of the solemnity of Huang the Priest's manner, they felt they really did understand. The wife of Ah Sze especially was suddenly blessed with clear vision. She knew that "Gory Glow" meant many people would die, many people definitely had to die. The place that produced the True Emperor had to be paid its price.

Again Huang the Priest raised his hand and stabbed his finger three times into the northern sky. Each time the heart of Ah Sze's wife leaped. Then he brought his hand down and pointed at the ground on which they stood.

"Here too there will be a Gory Glow," he intoned in a muffled voice. "In six months, a year, you all will fall beneath the blade! This village shall be scourged from the face of the earth!" He let his head droop, his lips moving either with trembling or inaudible incantations.

The three women sighed. Lotus looked at Sixth Treasure as if to say, "Let's see who'll be the first to die — you or me!" But Sixth Treasure was eyeing Huang the Priest a bit sceptically. After a pause, Ah Sze's wife suddenly blurted:

"Then there's no salvation? Does that —"

"Who says so!" Huang the Priest interrupted aggressively, fairly hopping with excitement. "I'm ordering my three straw figures to serve as substitute victims! Seven sevens make forty-nine days — a few days still remain. Bring me your written horoscope, plus fifty coppers, and a straw man will meet the disaster in your place. You understand? There are only a few days left."

"But the True Emperor — when is he coming?" asked Lotus. The base of her spine still ached a little.

Huang the Priest stared straight ahead as if he hadn't heard the question. The cutting northwest wind was making everyone's eyes stream. The fir trees in the Chang family cemetery were groaning in the gale. Huang the Priest wiped his eyes with his middle finger and looked grave.

"When is he coming? When all the fir trees in the Chang family cemetery are dead and gone — then he will come!"

"Ah, the fir trees!" chorused the three women. Their eyes shone with both fear and hope. They would be punished by Skinflint Chang each time a tree disappeared; of this they were afraid. Yet hope lurked behind their fear. And so, in spite of themselves, they couldn't help having a certain amount of confidence in Huang the Priest's rambling blether.

## III

Ah Sze's wife had been fretting over a problem for several days. Her father had advised her to take a job as a servant in town — she would get her food and could earn a little money besides. She thought her father's advice was good. But her husband wanted to continue tilling his rented land, as it was much harder for a man to find work in town than a woman. If he still were to tend his fields, he would need her help.

Ah To disagreed with his elder brother. "Till rented land?" he scoffed. "You break your back over it but starve just the same! In a good year we can get fifteen loads of rice from our fields. After paying six and a half for rent we ought to have enough left to eat. But there's the interest on our debt . . . and fertilizer costs money too. By the time you get through paying this and paying that, you find you've been working for nothing. We don't even have enough for thin gruel!"

Ah Sze said nothing, his face bitter. He knew they couldn't live off rented land. His wife could earn some money as a servant and, as for himself, he could get by doing odd jobs. But something seemed to stick in his chest. He felt to take such a step would mean the end. He looked at his wife, waiting for her to speak.

"What's the use of putting it off?" demanded Ah To. "We've had to sell all our land. We're up to our ears in debt. Even this broken-down house doesn't belong to us any more. What are we hanging around here for? The way I see it, you two ought to go into town and get jobs where you can eat. As to the debts the old man piled up, I say the hell with 'em!"

"Little Pao could stay with my father," mused the wife, then caught herself. Her father had no home of his own. He too was living at his place of employment. One grandson was staying with him already and his boss grumbled about it at times. It was hardly likely he could get away with bringing in another grandson. It might even result in his losing his job. No one in town liked to hire people who brought children with them. . . .

When she thought of this, the idea of eating an employer's food didn't seem quite so attractive.

"I've been thinking too," said Ah Sze. He was almost in tears as he watched her face. "The trouble is we have no place to send the kid."

"I've never seen anybody shilly-shally like you!" cried Ah To. "I'll take Little Pao and I guarantee he'll have enough to eat and enough to wear! He's twelve years old already. You can't always coddle him like a suckling babe!"

Ah Sze unhappily shook his head and his wife retorted:

"No, no, I'd worry too much! Ai! What would our family come to — scattering to the four winds! It's no good for a family to split up like that!"

"Hah! With the world all going to hell, people starving by the thousands — what does it matter if we do split up!" Ah To exploded. "In these times a man can die like a dog and no one will care. What's so terrible about splitting up!" He glared at his brother and sister-in-law as if he wanted to swallow down the irresolute pair in one gulp.

Because he was angry, they did not reply. But his blistering wrath did its work. The thing that had been weighing on Ah Sze's chest — making him want to continue tilling the fields in the same old way even though it was rented land, making him reluctant to work for others, making him feel perpetually depressed and unable to come to any decisions — that thing now seemed, with one kick of Ah To's foot, to have been smashed wide open. And what was revealed inside was merely a fear of splitting the family!

They had always been a closely knit family in the past, and once owned their own land. Later, they had been willing to till rented land because they thought in that way they would hold the family together. To drift off in various directions now — wouldn't that be letting down their ancestors, and wouldn't it be letting down Little Pao, their son? The "family" had long been the only thing in which they had any faith. Ruined though they were, how could they abandon a faith that had been so many years in the building?

Yet Ah To's words had hewn that faith asunder, like a knife hacking through their hearts. "With all the world going to hell . . . what does it matter if we do split up! In these times a man can die like a dog and no one will care!"

The more the wife thought of it, the worse she felt. She began to cry. When is the True Emperor coming? she wondered tearfully. Can the three straw men of Huang the Priest do any good?

In spite of her sorrowful state of mind, she thought she saw a ray of hope.

## IV

The weather became colder every day. It snowed. Many vegetables were spoiled by frost. The villagers had nothing left to exchange in town for rice. Often there was no traffic between town and village for several days. In a neighbouring hamlet the people were starving.

Someone discovered that the roots of the mulberry tree were edible — they tasted rather like yams. Everyone began digging up mulberry roots.

The wife of Ah Sze viewed the roots with enmity now, though she had formerly cherished the mulberry trees as her very life. They were a painful reminder of the blow her family had suffered when they last raised silkworms — fed on the leaves of the mulberry — and of the fact that their own grove of trees had already been pledged with the local money lender.

A few young men disappeared from the village. Sixth Treasure's brother Fu-ching, Li the Tiger whom Skinflint Chang had persecuted, and Ah To, one day suddenly were gone. But none of the villagers cared. What they were most concerned about was the fir trees in the Chang family cemetery. Even though it was snowing, some of them went to see how many trees remained. The prediction of Huang the Priest had quickly become known to everyone in the village and many people believed it.

More and more slips of paper were pinned on the three straw men in Huang the Priest's ramshackle hut. These were the horoscopes of various villagers — Little Pao's among them. Ah Sze's wife was trying to raise another fifty coppers so as to be able to add her husband's horoscope to the others.

Of all the women, Sixth Treasure was the only one who placed no credence in Huang the Priest's raving. But she was not in the village either. Some said she had gone to work in a factory in Shanghai; others claimed she had moved to town.

Shortly before the winter solstice a rumour flew through the village that the True Emperor had made his appearance in the neighbouring hamlet of Chichia Creek. Chao, one of the villagers, was holding forth about this miracle to a group on the threshing ground as if he had seen the Emperor with his own eyes:

"He's only twelve. A snot-nose kid, just like Little Pao. . . ."

Several listeners burst into laughter and Chao's face turned red. "If you don't believe me, go and see for yourselves!" he shouted. "Ha, talk about 'The immortals among us do not reveal themselves' — this case really proves it. Don't rush me now, let me think. Ah, that's right — last summer, the kid — the True Emperor — was very ill, unconscious for three days and three nights. When he came to, he had the Golden Mouth! Nobody knew it at first. Then, on Mid-Autumn Festival Day, he went out with the others, picking yams. There was a big rock blocking the path and he hollered at it — 'Roll away!' And what do you know — that big rock just picked itself up and rolled right out of the path! He's got the Golden Mouth!"

Chao's audience stared at him wide-eyed. A few people turned to look at the painfully thin Little Pao, standing behind his mother.

"The True Emperor should have come into the world long ago," someone said softly, almost sighing.

Ah Sze wasn't satisfied. "What else did the Golden Mouth say? Tell us, Brother Chao!"

But Chao could only gaze at him vacantly, mouth agape. A simple fellow who told exactly what he knew, and no more, Chao was incapable of embroidering a tale. After a pause, he again burst out agitatedly:

"All the villages are talking about it! *He* has come! About twelve years old — the same as Little Pao!"

"Ai! Only twelve! By the time he mounts the throne our bones will be turning soft!" Ah Sze's wife interrupted, her shoulders hunched as if against the cold.

Lotus saw a chance to pick a quarrel and immediately sprang to arms. "Who says so?" she demanded. "Actually it might happen very soon! The stars will be helping him! Emperors whose luck was strong mounted the throne before at eleven or twelve! If we have to wait till your bones turn soft, we'll all be dead and buried!"

"So now you've got the Golden Mouth too!" retorted Ah Sze's wife. "Shameless hussy!" In her heart she thought Lotus was probably right, but she was unwilling to admit it in the presence of so many people.

The two were getting ready to start another row. Huang the Priest intervened.

"We mustn't quarrel among ourselves," he insisted. Then he asked Chao, "How far is Chichia Creek from here? Not even three miles, is it? That puts our village right in the Gory Glow! A few days ago the idol in the little shrine near the bridge shed tears and the waters of the stream shone red. Oh, woe! Soon! Half a year, one year! Remember what I am saying!"

His last few words were like the shriek of an owl. His listeners shivered, fear creeping into their hope. They could visualize his straw men, festooned with slips of paper. Those who had already paid their fifty coppers sighed with relief and gazed respectfully at the face of Huang the Priest.

"In the past few days, three more fir trees have been cut down!" Lotus mumbled, looking north towards the patch of green that was the Chang family cemetery.

Everyone nodded. A few sighed softly.

Chao hadn't expected that his story about the True Emperor would lead to such serious consequences, and he became alarmed. He had not yet pinned his horoscope to a straw man in spite of his wife's prodding. They had quarrelled about it, but now he felt he had better spend the money after all. Although fifty coppers was a large sum, he thought he probably could manage it. He already owed last month's levy for the village "Protection Corps" — a kind of militia maintained by the wealthy. Why not miss another month's payment and be done with it? Wouldn't that give him the money he needed?

Chao was not the only one thinking along these lines. Quite a number of people had already transferred their assessment for the "Protection Corps" to the keeping of Huang the Priest's straw men. They had reasoned it out quite clearly — the Protection Corps levy had to be paid every month, but Huang the Priest only required one payment; what's more, they didn't believe that the Protection Corps' "Combined Armoured Company," stationed in the Temple of Earth a mile outside the village, could be of much use in an emergency. The combined armour of the company was exactly three rifles, manned by the company's full complement — a captain, a sergeant and a private. It seemed to the villagers that as protectors these three warriors would be far inferior to the three straw men of Huang the Priest.

Nor did they believe it was ever the intention of the Combined Armoured Company to protect anything of theirs. The three riflemen had arrived at the end of summer, when the peasants had nothing to eat and were raiding rice bins. What property worthy of protection could starving people have?

Nevertheless, the Combined Armoured Company concerned itself with many things, and in a highly efficient manner. Although because of the cold the members of the Company spent all day in the Temple of Earth, they knew about the True Emperor in Chichia Creek and they knew about the three straw men of Huang the Priest. Even the words which Chao and the others had spoken on the threshing ground that day had reached their ears.

In addition, the fact that many of the villagers were using their Protection Corps assessment money to buy the privilege of pinning horoscopes on the straw men was also known to the Combined Armoured Company!

Four days after Chao made his startling announcement, the

Combined Armoured Company made an expedition to Chichia
Creek and arrested the child with the Golden Mouth and conducted him to the Temple of Earth "for investigation." This was
on a grey afternoon. There was a fine drizzle that threatened to
turn to snow.

The interior of the temple was very dark. The entire company
— that is to say the captain, the sergeant and the private — was
exhausted from its long expedition. The captain issued an order
to tie the child to the baked mud leg of the temple's idol, appoint-
ed the sergeant Officer of the Day and directed the private to
stand sentry at the door. On the morrow, he said, they would
report the capture to their superiors and request instructions.

The True Emperor squatted at the feet of the clay idol, weeping softly.

Extracting a wrinkled cigarette from the pocket of his tunic,
the captain carefully pinched it straight. He lit up, inhaled
deeply, then expelled the smoke and said to his Officer of the
Day:

"We've broken this case. How much of a reward do you think
we'll get?"

"There's no use talking about rewards," the Officer of the Day
replied coldly. "I hear our battalion hasn't even issued our
winter uniforms yet."

The captain frowned and took another drag on his cigarette.

It was much darker now. The Officer of the Day lit an oil
lamp. He was about to relieve the sentry so that the latter could
come in and make their supper, when the captain abruptly clapped his hands together and stood up. Taking the oil lamp, the
captain shone it on the True Emperor's face, peering at the boy
intently.

"So you want to be emperor?" he intoned threateningly. "You
can lose your head for a crime like this. Lose your head, understand?"

The child said nothing. He was too frightened even to cry.

"Who else is in your gang? Speak up!" shouted the Officer
of the Day. He had come to stand beside the captain.

The only reply was a shake of the head.

Furious, the captain set down the lamp, grabbed the child by the hair and pulled his head back. Glaring cruelly at the up-turned dirty thin face, the captain yelled:

"Are you deaf? Who's in your gang? Speak up and you won't be beaten!"

"I don't know! All I know is gathering fuel and picking herbs. I can't help what people call me. That's all I know."

"You're lying, you little bastard!"

The captain banged the boy's head against the leg of the idol, repeatedly. The child bleated like a lamb at the slaughter, clay dust raining down on his head from the idol's leg.

Hands behind his back, the Officer of the Day gazed at the decayed remainder of the white beard of the idol. He knew what the captain had in mind, but he could also see that the child was unspeakably stupid. He waited until the captain had spent his anger, then tugged him by the tunic and whispered something in his ear. The two walked off to one side and conferred in low tones.

The boy's head was swelling out in lumps. Frightened beyond tears, he stared with large terrified eyes.

"Tomorrow we'll arrest Huang the Priest and bring him here. Then we'll get something done," were the concluding words of the Officer of the Day.

Smiling, the captain nodded. Again he approached the child, not the least fierce now, in fact very amiable.

"We've wronged you, little boy. Tomorrow, we'll send you home. But first you must tell me — which families in your village have money? If you don't speak, I'll hit you again!" Here, the captain's face suddenly grew savage, and he stamped his foot.

Trembling all over, the child raised his face. He shivered violently for a moment, but finally only shook his head and wept.

"Dirty dog!" roared the captain. "Unless you're beaten, you won't talk, eh!"

The Officer of the Day took up a stick and stood waiting for the captain's order.

Suddenly there were wild yells outside the temple. The two men wheeled around to see their sentry, shielding his head with his arms, coming flying in the doorway, closely pursued by the dark figures of several men. The Officer of the Day dropped his stick and fled through the little door beside the throne of the idol. No coward, the captain dashed for his rifle hanging at the side of the room. But by the time he got his hands on the gun, he was seized around the waist. A crushing blow from the handle of a hoe felled him dead to the ground.

Fu-ching had grabbed the sentry and relieved him of his cartridge belt.

"One got away!" shouted Ah To mopping his face. He was spattered with the captain's blood.

"But we got the three rifles and all their cartridges. Let's grant a pardon to the one who ran," said Li the Tiger.

The three peasants laughed.

Ah To broke open the cords that bound the True Emperor, then raised the lamp to examine the boy's face. The child was dazed with terror, his eyes large, his teeth chattering. Fu-ching and Li the Tiger raised the child from the floor and kneaded his chest. After a moment, he came to his senses. He burst into tears.

Putting down the lamp, Ah To smiled. "So this is the True Emperor! Go on, run along home!"

Outside the temple door, the wind rose, driving before it a storm of whirling snowflakes.

*July 1, 1933*

# EPITOME

The girl's name was Ling, or maybe it was Lin. Who knows? That kind of person never has any definite family name. People call them whatever they like.

The day she arrived, she first walked softly into the room of the *Lao Taitai** to pay her respects. The old lady was munching some water chestnuts her granddaughter's husband had sent, and didn't hear her enter. When she suddenly became aware of the girl kowtowing in front of her, *Lao Taitai* started with surprise. She considered being shocked like this, at first meeting, a bad omen. It made her feel ill. What's more, the girl's modern hair-do, with its mass of curls, hurt the old lady's eyes. And so, although her son's wife had died some years ago and there was no proper mistress of the house, she refused to recognize this girl as a "wife." Still chewing her water chestnuts, *Lao Taitai* addressed her contemptuously as "Miss" Ling.

So it was "Miss" Ling! The family matriarch had used the term herself. From then on, this teen-aged girl, Ling, or Lin — or whatever her name was — was permanently relegated to the status of concubine.

Miss Ling had a mother. The Master, her present husband, while in Shanghai on business, had told her mother, "In the future, we shall treat each other as relatives." This was after sleeping with Miss Ling, whom he had met in one of the big department stores. Miss Ling had no brothers; her mother relied on her entirely for support in her old age. All this was made plain to the Master before Miss Ling left Shanghai with him.

But now everything had changed. The *Lao Taitai* naturally

---

*Courteous title for an older woman who is the mistress of the house.

wouldn't recognize such "relatives." The Master forgot his promises completely. Whenever there was an opportune moment, Miss Ling would remark to him that her mother back in Shanghai must be having a hard time. But usually, these hints found him deaf and dumb. At other times he would glare and snort impatiently:

"What expenses does an old woman have! It's only been a few months; she couldn't have spent the whole three hundred dollars I gave her!"

The *Lao Taitai* was very displeased about this gift. She berated the Master severely, right in front of a woman servant who had been with the family for years.

"You give three hundred dollars for a smelly piece of trash you pick up off the streets of Shanghai? You spend money like water! When your own daughter got married you spent less than three hundred dollars. The wardrobe trunk you bought her was imitation leather; its lid dropped off the same day. Her in-laws still sneer at us about it. Anyhow, it was a very unlucky thing to happen. Three times she's given birth, but not one baby has lived more than a hundred days! But you, you scrape together a little cash, running 'black' goods,* and you throw it around any old way! *Omitofu!* Carrying on with a slut like that! Heaven might strike you dead!"

The *Lao Taitai* was famous for her nasty disposition, and the Master was a little afraid of her. Besides, now that he thought of it, Miss Ling hardly seemed worth three hundred dollars. She actually wasn't much better than that certain lady he knew right here in town. Regretting the money and smarting from the *Lao Taitai*'s sharp tongue, the Master took it out on Miss Ling. This was the first lesson she received from his fists and feet. . . . She had been "Miss" Ling for just two months then.

Of course she didn't look the same as when she first came. There was no hairdressing shop in the town, and there certainly was no place to get a permanent wave. Miss Ling's modern

---

*Opium.

curly mop had long since been pressed straight by her pillow.
Her hair was now tied together at the back in a bun like a
duck's rump. She didn't look any different from any of the
town's other girls. Her lipstick was finished, her eyebrow
tweezers were broken. You couldn't buy these things in the
town, and the Master wouldn't buy them in Shanghai, though
he often made trips there. Miss Ling grew less attractive every
day, at least she was no longer particularly alluring.

Then the Master discovered something about Miss Ling that
made him even more dissatisfied. Two days after the Master
beat Miss Ling for the first time, he drank heavily. Although the
sun was shining brightly outside, he dallied with her endlessly
in their bedroom. Suddenly he noticed faint silvery lines on her
abdomen — a tell-tale sign that a woman has borne a child. The
Master was just coming out of a drunken haze. Seeing this
sobered him almost completely. Suddenly, he leaped up, flung
Miss Ling to the floor and slapped her face twice, hard.

"Stinking whore!" he grated through clenched teeth. "And
I thought I was getting the original package! You put on a
great show that first night in Shanghai!"

Miss Ling was afraid to utter a word. She wept, muffling her
sobs.

When news of this afternoon amorousness reached the *Lao
Taitai*'s religious ears, the lot of Miss Ling grew harder still.
To revile Miss Ling directly or indirectly became *Lao Taitai*'s
daily task. At times, quite forgetting her Buddhist principles
of simple placid living, the old lady would work herself into
a fine rage, pounding the table and kicking over the chairs,
cursing Miss Ling till the girl barely dared to breathe. When
a weasel stole one of the hens, *Lao Taitai* blamed that on
Miss Ling too. Poking her finger at the girl's face, she swore
shrilly.

"Slut! Vixen! Doing those things in broad daylight is a sin!
No wonder the weasel got away with our hen! You'll die a
horrible death, sinning against the Sun Buddha like that!
Shameless hussy!"

## II

The Master's business took him to Shanghai at least once a month. Each trip required three days to a week; there was no telling. On those occasions Miss Ling was happier than a condemned man with a last minute reprieve from the axe. Although the *Lao Taitai*'s steady stream of abuse was worse than when the Master was at home, at least Miss Ling was freed from those episodes she had grown to fear more and more every day.

The Young Master, about her own age, was as lecherous as his father. Apricot, the little slavey, shivered at the sight of the Young Master like a mouse when it sees a cat. If there was no one else around, the Young Master went after Miss Ling too. He would scratch his finger against the palm of her hand, or pat her face, or feel her breasts. Miss Ling didn't have the courage to make a row. All she could do was flee, her face crimson. The Young Master would gaze after her, but made no attempt to pursue.

More difficult to cope with was the Master's son-in-law — husband of that daughter the *Lao Taitai* so often mentioned. Just looking at him, the young concubine could tell he was the same kind of rake as the Master. He too addressed her as "Miss" Ling. Even in the presence of an old shrew like the *Lao Taitai*, he had the temerity to pinch the girl's thigh under the table. Miss Ling avoided him in much the same manner as Apricot tried to steer clear of the Young Master.

Son-in-law had a post of some sort in the local police department. When the Master was away, son-in-law would become especially diligent about paying his respects to his wife's family. He would call often, with a pistol holster strapped round his waist. Miss Ling knew that the holster contained a gun, and her heart beat fearfully. At times like this she felt that things were better when the Master was at home, and even looked forward to his return.

The town had a "Protection Corps" which the local gentry and landlords had organized, allegedly for protection against "marauding bandits." The Master was the "Director" of this

Corps. Each time he returned with "merchandise" from Shanghai, his "Captains" came to report. There were two of them, and two pairs of shifty evil eyes would glide over Miss Ling's contours at every opportunity.

Back from his latest trip, the Master was conferring with these worthies in his parlour. Off to one side were two large packages, wrapped in matting — fruits of the visit to Shanghai. The Captains had been conferring with him for some time when, abruptly, the Master became incensed.

"He gets twenty per cent for sitting around doing nothing, and he's still not satisfied!" he shouted. "So he wants to make trouble, does he? What kind of fight can his men put up — those scabby-headed rats! If he wants to get tough we can get tough too! Tomorrow, a hundred catties of the stuff is coming on the river steamer. You fellows be down there and stand guard. We'll give them a battle if that's what they're after; they're the ones who are starting this thing! . . . Tomorrow morning, five o'clock! Get up early. This is our public duty. We shouldn't be afraid of a little trouble!"

"Our men —" one of the Captains began hesitantly.

"After we've won," the Master interrupted, "there'll be two ounces of opium apiece for each and every one!" His tone was still very angry.

Miss Ling, all ears outside the door, was taken completely unawares when someone came up and pinched her arm. She nearly cried out, but caught herself in time. The one who had pinched her was son-in-law! Lust gleamed in his eyes. He looked as if he wanted to swallow her in one gulp. And the Master was just on the other side of the door! Miss Ling's heart pounded.

Controlling himself with a visible effort, son-in-law turned and went into the next room. He conferred in low tones with the Master for several minutes.

"That son of a bitch!" Miss Ling heard the Master explode hoarsely. "We'll take care of him, then! Tomorrow morning, I'll be there too!"

Son-in-law hooted his weird-sounding laugh. It grated on Miss Ling's ears like the cry of an owl.

Until dusk that day, the Master's face was dark iron. He spoke very little. He took his pistol apart, inspected it carefully, put it together again and loaded it. Several times he practised aiming. Miss Ling's legs trembled whenever she had to pass near him. Then, without waiting for dinner, the Master took his gun and went out. There seemed to be a stone pressing in Miss Ling's bosom, and she was growing very frightened.

The *Lao Taitai* sat before a small Buddhist shrine, counting her beads with remarkable rapidity while muttering her prayers. Burning sandalwood in a little bronze urn glowed in front of the shrine.

About eleven that night, the Master finally returned, his face pale and splotchy. His bloodshot eyes looked smaller than usual. His head was steaming with sweat and he reeked of drink. He took out his pistol and thumped it down on the table. With palsied fingers, Miss Ling helped him remove his clothing. Suddenly, laughing boisterously, he grabbed her, lifted her up and tossed her on to the bed. This had often happened before, but this time it was unexpected. Miss Ling couldn't tell what kind of a mood he was in; she lay motionless, not daring to stir. The Master strode up to her and angrily yanked open her garments, the black gleaming pistol clutched in his right hand. Miss Ling went weak with terror. She stared at him, her eyes large and distended. He stripped her, and placed the icy muzzle of the pistol against her breast. Miss Ling was shivering so violently, the whole bed creaked.

"I'll practise on you first," she heard the Master say. "Let's see how good my gun is."

There was a roaring in Miss Ling's ears. Tears coursed down her cheeks.

"Afraid to die, slut? Hah! Don't worry, I still want to play around with you for a while yet!"

Laughing cruelly, the Master flopped into bed, and instantly began to snore, deep in slumber.

Miss Ling huddled to one side of the bed. She was afraid to

sleep; she was unable to sleep. If he had only pulled the trigger, she thought, my misery would have been ended, quick and clean. Stealthily she took the pistol, looked at it, then closed her eyes, her heart beating fast. But finally, she put it down again. Life was bitter, but death was too frightening.

Some time after three in the morning, people began beating on the compound gate. The Master raised his head and listened a moment. Picking up his pistol, he ran to the window and pushed it open.

"What are you making such a blasted racket about!" he yelled.

"The men are all here!" a voice replied.

The Master put on the fleece-lined gown, tightened a silk sash around his waist, shoved the pistol into the sash, and hurried out. Miss Ling heard him talking with the crowd outside the gate. He swore savagely, then they all departed.

Miss Ling gazed at the sky. A few scattered stars, one or two frozen grey clouds. She shivered and returned to bed, her mind a blur. I'd better not sleep, she thought as she slipped beneath the covers. But before long she began to doze; her head slid from the backboard down to her shoulder. She dreamed that the Master had shot her. She saw her mother, too. Her mother held her in her arms and cried, her mother cried distractedly. . . . Miss Ling woke with a start. Her mother wasn't there, but someone else was embracing her, murmuring passionately. Her eyes flew open. In the light of the oil lamp burning beside the bed, she saw his face. She blanched.

"Young Master, you —!"

She tried to fight him off. "If you don't go, I'll scream!"

"Go ahead! The old man's gone out to fight the police for opium and the *Lao Taitai* wouldn't care!" He grappled with her. Although only seventeen, he was much stronger than she.

"You're ruining me. . . ." Miss Ling wept. But finally she let him have his way.

The oil lamp on the table gradually burned out. The sky was turning a fish-belly white. A cock in the courtyard crowed once, twice. Next door, the neighbour's cock took up the cry.

Soon, cocks were crowing for miles around. . . .

Down the street a loud hubbub of men's voices could be heard coming closer. A moment later, and thunderous blows began to rain on the compound gate. Miss Ling, terrified, jumped up and ran to lock the bedroom door. The Young Master dashed past her.

"Have you lost your mind?" he demanded. "Wait till I get out of here!" He sped from the room.

Miss Ling hastily put something on, hopped back into bed and pulled the covers over her head. Trembling, she curled herself into a tight ball. There was a tremendous racket going on downstairs. The noise mounted till it was outside the door of the bedroom. She leaped up, took a grip on herself, and opened the door. Five or six men were waiting there, including the Master and son-in-law.

Two men were carrying the Master. His gown was opened at the chest. The white fleece lining was stained with blood. After putting him on the bed, the others went away, leaving only son-in-law and one of the Captains. The Master was bellowing like an injured bull. The Captain looked at his wound, then said to son-in-law:

"I don't think that wound can be treated here in town. It's queer, him getting shot like that. They were all in front of us, but he was hit from the side. Very strange. And that was no stray bullet. Whoever shot him was aiming for him! Anyhow, we did a fine job on that dog of a police chief!"

From the edge of the bed, Miss Ling saw son-in-law standing behind the Captain. He was concealing a grin.

Downstairs, the *Lao Taitai* could be heard throwing things around and cursing.

"It's retribution! Offending against the Sun Buddha! All because of that stinking baggage! I knew she was bad luck the day she came in the door! He doesn't need any doctor; just kill that dirty bitch and he'll get well! Kill her!"

## III

Before mid-morning the townspeople were animatedly discussing the ferocity of the robbers. The President of the Chamber of Commerce reported the affair by long-distance telephone to the county authorities. He stated that the chief of police had been killed while "apprehending the criminals" and that the Director of the Defence Corps, in the course of "assisting with the arrest," had been severely wounded. Relaying the report to the provincial government, the county converted the robbers into bandits, "between two and three hundred, all heavily armed, who came without warning and quickly disappeared after commission of the offence." On the basis of this information, the provincial authorities sent a company of troops to "eradicate" the bandits.

The day the troops arrived, they marched down the main street. Miss Ling saw them. She didn't know whether they had come to help the Master or to help son-in-law. For somehow she was positive that it was son-in-law who had shot the Master. But she kept this conviction to herself, not even mentioning it to the Young Master.

The Master's wound gradually healed. A tiny piece of bullet was still imbedded in his flesh, but the wound had closed. Miss Ling feared that he would soon be completely well and force himself on her again. All too familiar with his lecherous appetite, she was truly afraid.

She privately begged the Young Master to think of a way to rescue her. He said there wasn't anything he could do, and only laughed at her.

A few days later, and the Master was able to get up and walk around. Miss Ling was so worried, she couldn't eat.

But the Master seemed to have something on his mind. He didn't bother much with Miss Ling. One of the Captains came frequently to confer. They talked in low tones, the Master frowning continuously. Once, when Miss Ling was serving the Master some bird's-nest soup, she heard the Captain say:

"Every day the Chamber of Commerce has to provide banquet dinners for two hundred people. This has been going on for more than half a month now. It's cost the Chamber over two thousand silver dollars. The President of the Chamber wants them to leave right away, but the commander of the troops says he was sent here to wipe out the bandits; unless he has a battle with them, he can't go back and report 'mission completed.' "

"The hell with his 'mission completed'!" fumed the Master, but his frown deepened.

After a pause, the Captain whispered something in his ear. The Master bounded to his feet.

"What!" he yelled. "We gave them thirty ounces of opium yesterday and today they want more? The crooks!"

"That's not the worst of it — they're hijacking us! When our men go out to make deliveries to our big customers, they hold us up on the road and steal our stuff. They've only been here half a month, but they know all the ropes!"

"It's an outrage!" The Master pounded his fist on the table. Veins stood out on his forehead like little fingers.

Miss Ling was as terrified as if the Master again wanted to take his gun and shoot her.

"If they stay another half month, we'll be out of business! You've got to think of something, fast!"

The Captain heaved a sigh. The Master sighed too. Then they whispered together for a long time. Miss Ling could see a somewhat happier expression on the Master's face. He kept nodding his head.

"Don't worry about a thing, Your Worship. We'll disguise ourselves well," the Captain assured the Master as he was leaving. "There won't be any slip-ups! That village northwest of here will be best. The peasants there have still got a little grain and things left. We might as well 'subsidize' the trip while we're at it."

"Tell our scouts to look sharp. The moment they report that the troops have set out from town, you all get out of there. We don't want a real clash with the troops. We'll be the joke of the town if we're exposed!"

After the Captain had departed, the Master sat wrapped in thought, looking very serious. Then he dispatched a servant to bring his son-in-law. When she heard the word "son-in-law," Miss Ling felt very uneasy. She was dying to tell her suspicions to the Master, but in the end she said nothing and concentrated on staying out of the way.

Son-in-law talked with the Master for a while, rose and left quickly. He bumped into Miss Ling at the door and smirked at her, revealing big teeth in a wolfish grin. Her hair stood on end. She recoiled from him as from a poisonous snake.

In the evening at dinner, the Master began drinking. Miss Ling's heart became more troubled with each cup she poured him. She had a feeling that tonight was going to be bad. But oddly enough, besides drinking, the Master displayed no other inclinations. He drank from a small cup, sipping slowly and genteelly, putting it down from time to time and listening. At about nine, there was the sound of running feet in the street outside; someone was shouting commands. Obviously very concerned, the Master stopped drinking and lay down on the bed. He directed Miss Ling to knead his legs.

After another interval, rifles began popping in the distance. The Master jumped up and ran to the window. A patch of fire was gleaming to the northwest. The Master watched for a few minutes, then filled himself a big bowl of wine and drank it down. Wagging his head with satisfaction, he stretched forward his two arms. Miss Ling knew this was his signal to be undressed, and she trembled inwardly.

To her surprise, after having her knead his legs a little longer, the Master went to sleep.

The next morning in the kitchen, Miss Ling heard the water vendor say that bandits had attacked the village to the northwest the previous night. The troops had fought the raiders for hours and captured many peasants who were in league with them, as well as one wounded bandit. He was now locked up in the police station.

In the front room, the *Lao Taitai* was throwing another tantrum.

"That's what he gets for losing his head over a witch! Now he quarrels with his son-in-law! Anybody who sins against the Sun Buddha. . . ."

Carrying a bowl of lotus-seed broth upstairs, Miss Ling could hear the angry voices of the Master and his son-in-law. Just as she reached the door of the room, she heard the Master snarl:

"You're crazy! You dare to talk to me like that!"

"Didn't you get enough that last time you were shot?" hissed the son-in-law. He laughed coldly in a way that sent shivers up Miss Ling's spine.

Though her heart was thumping, she entered the room. There was a gleaming black pistol in son-in-law's hand and it was pointing at the Master. Miss Ling's legs turned to water. Her blood seemed to congeal in her veins.

"Kill me? Hah!" snorted the Master. "Just try, and —"

Bang!

At the sound, Miss Ling collapsed beside the door, her eyes staring. She saw the distorted evil face of son-in-law as he stepped across her body and went out. Everything faded into darkness after that.

## IV

It was the Master who had been shot, not Miss Ling. But she became ill, delirious. For two days she ran a high temperature. Her face was brick-red as if she had been drinking heavily, her eyes glassy. She ate nothing. At times she raved unintelligible gibberish. On the third day she was somewhat better, but quite weak. She felt dizzy, and slept most of the afternoon. Near dark, she awoke with a start, very thirsty. She saw Apricot, the little slavey, leaning over the window sill, looking out. Miss Ling couldn't understand why she was lying in bed; of the recent incident, she remembered nothing. She tried to sit up, but she didn't have the strength.

"Apricot," she said weakly, "what are you looking at? If the Master catches you there, he'll beat you!" She was feeling rather hungry.

The little slavey turned around and grinned at her.

"The Master's dead!" Apricot said with a ghoulish laugh. "See — he was lying right there, blood all over the place!"

Miss Ling shivered. She remembered now. Again her heart

beat fast, again her eyes blurred, again she drifted into a vague
dream world.  She saw the Master poking her breast with the
pistol muzzle, she saw son-in-law take murderous aim at the
Master.  Last of all, she saw a face — a face with cruelly twisting brows — looking at her avidly.  It was son-in-law!  She
thought she screamed, but the sound she heard seemed to be
coming from the other side of a thick wall.  A heavy weight was
crushing her bosom.  Again she sank into unconsciousness. . . .

When she awoke this time, Miss Ling was sure she was dead.
The lamp had already been lit and a man's shadow fell across
the bed.  Miss Ling recognized the Young Master, standing at
her bedside, his back to the lamp.  He was leaning very close.

"Am I dead?" she moaned.

"It isn't that easy to die!"

"I ache all over.  I think . . . son-in-law. . . ."

"He just left. . I used a trick to get him out."

"You're a smart little imp!"  She let the Young Master kiss
her cheek.  A smile played at the corners of her mouth.  She was
quite hungry.

The Young Master said that son-in-law had taken over the
post of Director of the Defence Corps.  He was running everything at home too.  Miss Ling was stunned.  She asked
hesitantly:

"Do you know how the Master died?"

"The old man was careless and shot himself while cleaning
his pistol."

"Who says so?"

"Son-in-law says so, and so does the *Lao Taitai*.  She says
the old man sinned against the Sun Buddha, so the spirits made
his mind wander and he shot himself.  She says you sinned
against the Sun Buddha too, and after he died, the old man
called you before the King of the Underworld to testify.  That's
why you've been dead for the past couple of days."

Abstractedly, Miss Ling considered this for several minutes,
then she shook her head.  She put her mouth close to the Young
Master's ear.

"It's not like that!  The Master didn't kill himself!  Now don't tell this to anybody. I saw it with my own eyes — son-in-law shot him dead!"

The Young Master gazed at her, only half convinced. "Who cares how he died," he said indifferently. "He's dead, and that's the end of it!"

"Ah, I know son-in-law, sooner or later, is going to kill you too! And my turn will also come."

The Young Master said nothing. With a slight frown, he gazed at her searchingly.

"Some day he'll kill us both. If he ever finds out that you and I. . . ." Miss Ling sighed.

Unable to think of any reply, the Young Master hung his head. She gave him a little shove.

"Don't hang around here. He'll be coming back soon!"

"That's what you think! He took office today. Tonight they're giving him a big feed at the house of that fancy lady in town. A fat chance of him coming back!"

"Bite your tongue — smarty!" Miss Ling giggled. She didn't urge the Young Master to leave again.

But, actually, he was a little afraid. After fooling around for a short time, he got up and went away. Miss Ling fell into a deep slumber. She had no idea how long she had been sleeping when someone shook her awake. Voices clamoured on the street; close by, rifles were popping like firecrackers on New Year's Eve. The Young Master, very frightened, was pulling Miss Ling out of bed.

"Real bandits have come!" he cried hysterically. "You hear? They're shooting! They're fighting at the west gate!"

Miss Ling was too terrified to speak. Through the window she could see the slanting rays of the setting sun shining golden in a corner of the courtyard. While the Young Master was hastening her into her clothes, he reported breathlessly:

"That day the old man sent his men to the village to the northwest, they robbed and set houses on fire. Then the troops grabbed a lot of the villagers and said they were bandits. Well, now real bandits have come, and the villagers who were falsely

accused have joined them! They want to kill our whole family
—"

Fierce yells from the street drowned out the rest of his words.
Shops which had not yet boarded up their windows for the night
were being broken into. The Young Master left Miss Ling and
ran downstairs. Her legs shaking, she stood by the window that
looked on to the street. The troops were running in disorder,
looting the unboarded shops as they retreated. Bang! Bang!
They fired crazily against the boards of the closed shops. Miss
Ling's legs collapsed under her. She sat down weakly on the
floor. Just then, the Young Master came running back and
pulled her to her feet.

"Bandits . . . fought their way into the town!" he panted.
"Son-in-law . . . killed!"

They hurried down the stairs. The *Lao Taitai* was on her
knees, kowtowing before the small shrine. Ignoring her completely, the Young Master dragged Miss Ling through the back
door as fast as she could travel. Where are we going? Miss
Ling kept wondering. She thought of her mother in Shanghai,
and tears ran down her ashen cheeks.

Suddenly, there were many short whistling sounds. The
Young Master was hit by a stray bullet; he fell like a log, pulling
Miss Ling down with him. As she sat up and held him in her
arms, another wild shot went through her chest. Her face
twitched, then, without a sound, she sprawled on her back and
moved no more. The corners of her lips seemed to curl with
laughter — and with hatred.

Black smoke rose from the house they had just left. There
was a burst of flame. Sparks flew in all directions.

*February 29, 1932*

# THE SHOP OF THE LIN FAMILY

Miss Lin's small mouth was pouting when she returned home from school that day. She flung down her books, and instead of combing her hair and powdering her nose before the mirror as usual, she stretched out on the bed. Her eyes staring at the top of the bed canopy, Miss Lin lay lost in thought. Her little cat leaped up beside her, snuggled against her waist and miaowed twice. Automatically, she patted his head, then rolled over and buried her face in the pillow.

"Ma!" called Miss Lin.

No answer. Ma, whose room was right next door, ordinarily doted on this only daughter of hers. On hearing her return, Ma would come swaying in to ask whether she was hungry. Ma would be keeping something good for her. Or she might send the maid out to buy a bowl of hot soup with meat dumplings from a street vendor. . . . But today was odd. There obviously were people talking in Ma's room — Miss Lin could hear Ma hiccuping too — yet Ma didn't even reply.

Again Miss Lin rolled over on the bed, and raised her head. She would eavesdrop on this conversation. Whom could Ma be talking to, that voices had to be kept so low?

But she couldn't make out what they were saying. Only Ma's continuous hiccups wafted intermittently to Miss Lin's ears. Suddenly, Ma's voice rose, as if she were angry, and a few words came through quite clearly:

"— These are Japanese goods, those are Japanese goods, hic! . . ."

Miss Lin started. She prickled all over, like when she was having a hair-cut and the tiny shorn hairs stuck to her neck. She had come home annoyed just because they had laughed at her and scolded her at school over Japanese goods. She swept aside the little cat nestled against her, jumped up and stripped off her new azure rayon dress lined with camel's wool. She shook it out a couple of times, and sighed. Miss Lin had heard that this charming frock was made of Japanese material. She tossed it aside and pulled that cute cowhide case out from under the bed. Almost spitefully, she flipped the cover open, and turning the case upside down, dumped its contents on the bed. A rainbow of brightly coloured dresses and knick-knacks rolled and spread. The little cat leaped to the floor, whirled and jumped up on a chair, where he crouched and looked at his mistress in astonishment.

Miss Lin sorted through the pile of clothes, then stood, abstracted, beside the bed. The more she examined her belongings, the more she adored them — and the more they looked like Japanese goods! Couldn't she wear any of them? She hated to part with them — besides, her father wouldn't necessarily be willing to have new ones made for her! Miss Lin's eyes began to smart. She loved these Japanese things, while she hated the Japanese aggressors who invaded the Northeast provinces. If not for that, she could wear Japanese merchandise and no one would say a word.

"Hic —"

The sound came through the door, followed by the thin swaying body of Mrs. Lin. The sight of the heap of clothing on the bed, and her daughter, bemused, standing in only her brief woollen underwear, was more than a little shock. As her excitement increased, the tempo of Mrs. Lin's hiccups grew in proportion. For the moment, she was unable to speak. Miss Lin, grief written all over her face, flew to her mother. "Ma! They're all Japanese goods. What am I going to wear tomorrow?"

Hiccuping, Mrs. Lin shook her head. With one hand she supported herself on her daughter's shoulder, with the other she kneaded her own chest. After a while, she managed to force out a few sentences.

"Child — hic — why have you taken off — hic — all your clothes? The weather's cold — hic — This trouble of mine —

hic — began the year you were born. Hic — lately it's getting worse! Hic —"

"Ma, tell me what am I going to wear tomorrow? I'll just hide in the house and not go out! They'll laugh at me, swear at me!"

Mrs. Lin didn't answer. Hiccuping steadily, she walked over to the bed, picked the new azure dress out of the pile, and draped it over her daughter. Then she patted the bed in invitation for Miss Lin to sit down. The little cat returned to beside the girl's legs. Cocking his head, with narrowed eyes he looked first at Mrs. Lin, then at her daughter. Lazily, he rolled over and rubbed his belly against the soles of the girl's shoes. Miss Lin kicked him away and reclined sideways on the bed, with her head hidden behind her mother's back.

Neither of them spoke for a while. Mrs. Lin was busy hiccuping; her daughter was busy calculating "how to go out tomorrow." The problem of Japanese goods not only affected everything Miss Lin wore — it influenced everything she used. Even the powder compact which her fellow students so admired and her automatic pencil were probably made in Japan. And she was crazy about those little gadgets!

"Child — hic — are you hungry?"

After sitting quietly for some time, Mrs. Lin gradually controlled her hiccups, and began her usual doting routine.

"No. Ma, why do you always ask me if I'm hungry? The most important thing is that I have no clothes. How can I go to school tomorrow?" the girl demanded petulantly. She was still curled up on the bed, her face still buried behind her mother.

From the start, Mrs. Lin hadn't understood why her daughter kept complaining that she had no clothes to wear. This was the third time and she couldn't ignore the remark any longer, but those damned hiccups most irritatingly started up again. Just then, Mr. Lin came in. He was holding a sheet of paper in his hand; his face was ashen. He saw his wife struggling with continuous agitated hiccups, his daughter lying on the clothing-strewn bed, and he could guess pretty well what was wrong. His brows drew together in a frown.

"Do you have an Anti-Japanese-Invasion Society in your school, Hsiu?" he asked. "This letter just came. It says that if you wear clothes made of Japanese material again tomorrow, they're going to burn them! Of all the wild lawless things to say!"

"Hic — hic!"

"What nonsense! Everyone has something made in Japan on him. But they have to pick on our family to make trouble! There isn't a shop carrying foreign goods that isn't full of Japanese stuff. But they have to make our shop the culprit. They insist on locking up our stocks! Huh!"

"Hic — hic — Goddess Kuanyin protect and preserve us! Hic —"

"Papa, I've got an old style padded jacket. It's probably not made of Japanese material, but if I wear it they'll all laugh at me, it's so out of date," said Miss Lin, sitting up on the bed. She had been thinking of going a step farther and asking Mr. Lin to have a dress made for her out of non-Japanese cloth, but his expression decided her against such a rash move. Still, picturing the jeers her old padded jacket would evoke, she couldn't restrain her tears.

"Hic — hic — child! — hic — don't cry — no one will laugh at you — hic — child. . . ."

"Hsiu, you don't have to go to school tomorrow! We soon won't have anything to eat; how can we spend money on schools!" Mr. Lin was exasperated. He ripped up the letter and strode, sighing, from the room. Before long, he came hurrying back.

"Where's the key to the cabinet? Give it to me!" he demanded of his wife.

Mrs. Lin turned pale and stared at him. Her eternal hiccups were momentarily stilled.

"There's no help for it. We'll have to make an offering to those straying demons —" Mr. Lin paused to heave a sigh. "It'll cost me four hundred at most. If the Kuomintang local branch thinks it's not enough, I'll quit doing business. Let them lock up the stocks! That shop opposite has more Japanese goods than I.

They've made an investment of over ten thousand dollars. They paid out only five hundred, and they're going along without a bit of trouble. Five hundred dollars! Just mark it off as a couple of bad debts! — The key! That gold necklace ought to bring about three hundred. . . ."

"Hic — hic — really, like a gang of robbers!" Mrs. Lin produced the key with a trembling hand. Tears streamed down her face. Miss Lin, however, did not cry. She was looking into space with misty eyes, recalling that Kuomintang committeeman who had made a speech at her school, a hateful swarthy pockmarked fellow who stared at her like a hungry dog. She could picture him grasping the gold necklace and jumping for joy, his big mouth open in a laugh. Then she visualized the ugly bandit quarrelling with her father, hitting him. . . .

"Aiya!" Miss Lin gave a frightened scream and threw herself on her mother's bosom. Mrs. Lin was so startled she had no time for hiccups.

"Child, hic — don't cry," Mrs. Lin made a desperate effort to speak. "After New Year your Papa will have money. We'll make a new dress for you, hic — Those black-hearted crooks! They all insist we have money. Hic — we lose more every year. Your Papa was in the fertilizer business, and he lost money, hic — Every penny invested in the shop belongs to other people. Child, hic, hic — this sickness of mine; it makes life hell — hic — In another two years when you're nineteen, we'll find you a good husband. Hic — then I can die in peace! Save us from our adversity, Goddess Kuanyin! Hic —"

## II

The following day, Mr. Lin's shop underwent a transformation. All the Japanese goods he hadn't dared to show for the past week, now were the most prominently displayed. In imitation of the big Shanghai stores, Mr. Lin inscribed many slips of coloured paper with the words "Big Sale 10% Discount!" and pasted them on his windows. Just seven days before New Year, this was the "rush season" of the shops selling imported goods

in the towns and villages. Not only was there hope of earning
back Mr. Lin's special expenditure of four hundred dollars;
Miss Lin's new dress depended on the amount of business done
in the next few days.

A little past ten in the morning, groups of peasants who had
come into town to sell their produce in the market began drifting
along the street. Carrying baskets on their arms, leading small
children, they chatted loud and vigorously as they strolled. They
stopped to look at the red and green blurbs pasted on Mr. Lin's
windows and called attention to them, women shouting to their
husbands, children yelling to their parents, clucking their tongues
in admiration over the goods on display in the shop windows.
It would soon be New Year. Children were wishing for a pair
of new socks. Women remembered that the family wash-basin
had been broken for some time. The single wash-cloth used by
the entire family had been bought half a year ago, and now
was an old rag. They had run out of soap more than a month
before. They ought to take advantage of this "Sale" and buy
a few things.

Mr. Lin sat in the cashier's cage, marshalling all his energies,
a broad smile plastered on his face. He watched the peasants,
while keeping an eye on his two salesmen and two apprentices.
With all his heart he hoped to see his merchandise start moving
out and the silver dollars begin rolling in.

But these peasants, after looking a while, after pointing and
gesticulating appreciatively a while, ambled over to the store
across the street to stand and look some more. Craning his neck,
Mr. Lin glared at the backs of the group of peasants, and sparks
shot from his eyes. He wanted to go over and drag them back!

"Hic — hic —"

Behind the cashier's cage were swinging doors which separated
the shop itself from the "inner sanctum." Beside these doors sat
Mrs. Lin releasing hiccups that she had long been suppressing
with difficulty. Miss Lin was seated beside her. Entranced,
the girl watched the street silently, her heart pounding. At least
half of her new dress had just walked away.

Mr. Lin strode quickly to the front of the counter. He

glared jealously at the shop opposite. Its five salesmen were waiting expectantly behind the counter. But not one peasant entered the store. They looked for a while, then continued on their way. Mr. Lin relaxed; he couldn't help grinning at the salesmen across the street. Another group of seven or eight peasants stopped before Mr. Lin's shop. A youngster among them actually came a step forward. With his head cocked to one side, he examined the imported umbrellas. Mr. Lin whirled around, his face breaking into a happy smile. He went to work personally on this prospective customer.

"Would you like a foreign umbrella, Brother? They're cheap. You only pay ninety cents on the dollar. Come and take a look."

A salesman had already taken down two or three imported umbrellas. He promptly opened one and shoved it earnestly into the young peasant's hand. Summoning all his zeal, the salesman launched into a high powered patter:

"Just look at this, young master! Foreign satin cloth, solid ribs. It's durable and handsome for rainy days or clear. Ninety cents each. They don't come any cheaper. . . . Across the street, they're a dollar apiece, but they're not as good as these. You can compare them and see why."

The young peasant held the umbrella and stood undecided, with his mouth open. He turned towards a man in his fifties and weighed the umbrella in his hand as if to ask "Shall I buy it?" The older man became very upset and began to shout at him.

"You're crazy! Buying an umbrella! We only got three dollars for the whole boatload of firewood, and your mother's waiting at home for us to bring back some rice. How can you spend money on an umbrella!"

"It's cheap, but we can't afford it!" sighed the peasants standing around watching. They walked slowly away. The young peasant, his face brick red, shook his head. He put down the umbrella and started to leave. Mr. Lin was frantic. He quickly gave ground.

"How much do you say, Brother? Take another look. It's fine merchandise!"

"It is cheap. But we don't have enough money," the older peasant replied, pulling his son. They practically ran away.

Bitterly, Mr. Lin returned to the cashier's cage, feeling weak all over. He knew it wasn't that he was an inept businessman. The peasants simply were too poor. They couldn't even spend ninety cents on an umbrella. He stole a glance at the shop across the way. There too people were looking, but no one was going in. In front of the neighbouring grocery store and the cookie shop, no one was even looking. Group after group of the country folk walked by carrying baskets. But the baskets all were empty. Occasionally, someone appeared with a homespun flowered blue cloth sack, filled with rice, from the look of it. The late rice which the peasants had harvested more than a month before had long since been squeezed out as rent for the landlords and interest for the usurers. Now in order to have rice to eat, the peasants were forced to buy a measure or two at a time, at steep prices.

All this Mr. Lin knew. He felt that at least part of his business was being indirectly eaten away by the usurers and landlords.

The hour gradually neared noon. There were very few peasants on the street now. Mr. Lin's shop had done a little over one dollar's worth of business, just enough to cover the cost of the "Big Sale 10% Discount" strips of red and green paper. Despondently, Mr. Lin entered the "inner sanctum." He barely had the courage to face his wife and daughter. Miss Lin's eyes were filled with tears. She sat in the corner with her head down. Mrs. Lin was in the middle of a string of hiccups. Struggling for control, she addressed her husband.

"We laid out four hundred dollars — and spent all night getting things ready in the shop — hic! We got permission to sell the Japanese goods, but business is dead — hic — my blessed ancestors! . . . The maid wants her wages —"

"It's only half a day. Don't worry." Mr. Lin forced a comforting note into his voice, but he felt worse than if a knife were cutting through his heart. Gloomily, he paced back and forth. He thought of all the business promotion tricks he knew, but none of them seemed any good. Business was bad. It had been bad in all lines for some time; his shop wasn't the only one having difficulty. People were poor, and there wasn't anything that could be done about it. Still, he hoped business would be better in the afternoon. The local townspeople usually did their buying then. Surely they would buy things for New Year! If only they wanted to buy, Mr. Lin's shop was certain of trade. After all, his merchandise was cheaper than other shops!

It was this hope that enabled Mr. Lin to bolster his sagging spirits as he sat in the cashier's cage awaiting the customers he pictured coming in the afternoon.

And the afternoon proved to be different indeed from the morning. There weren't many people on the street, but Mr. Lin knew nearly every one of them. He knew their names, or the names of their fathers or grandfathers. These were local townspeople, and as they chatted and walked slowly past his shop, Mr. Lin's eyes, glowing with cordiality, welcomed them, and sent them on their way. At times, with a broad smile he greeted an old customer.

"Ah, Brother, going out to the tea-house? Our little shop has slashed its prices. Favour us with a small purchase!"

Sometimes, the man would actually stop and come into the shop. Then Mr. Lin and his assistants would plunge into a frenzy of activity. With acute sensitiveness, they would watch the eyes of the unpredictable customer. The moment his eyes rested on a piece of merchandise, the salesmen would swiftly produce one just like it and invite the customer to examine it. Miss Lin watched from beside the swinging doors, and her father frequently called her out to respectfully greet the unpredictable customer as "Uncle." An apprentice would serve him a glass of tea and offer him a good cigarette.

On the question of price, Mr. Lin was exceptionally flexible. When a customer was firm about knocking off a few odd cents from the round figure of his purchase price, Mr. Lin would take the abacus from the hands of his salesman and calculate

personally.   Then, with the air of a man who has been driven to
the wall, he would deduct the few odd cents from the total bill.

"We'll take a loss on this sale," he would say with a wry
smile.   "But you're an old customer.   We have to please you.
Come and buy some more things soon!"

The entire afternoon was spent in this manner.   Including
cash and credit, big purchases and small, the shop made a total
of over ten sales.   Mr. Lin was drenched with perspiration, and
although he was worn out, he was very happy.   He had been
sneaking looks at the shop across the street.   They didn't seem
to be nearly so busy.   There was a pleased expression on the
face of Miss Lin, who had been constantly watching from beside
the swinging doors.   Mrs. Lin even jerked out a few less hiccups.

Shortly before dark, Mr. Lin finished adding up his accounts
for the day.   The morning amounted to zero; in the afternoon
they had sold sixteen dollars and eighty-five cents worth of
merchandise, eight dollars of it being on credit.   Mr. Lin smiled
slightly, then he frowned.   He had been selling all his goods at
their original cost.   He hadn't even covered his expenses for the
day, to say nothing of making any profit.   His mind was blank
for a moment.   Then he took out his account books and calculated
in them for a long time.   On the "credit" side there was a total
of over thirteen hundred dollars of uncollected debts — more
than six hundred in town and over seven hundred in the
countryside.   But the "debit" ledger showed a figure of eight
hundred dollars owed to the big Shanghai wholesale house
alone.   He owed a total of not less than two thousand dollars!

Mr. Lin sighed softly.   If business continued to be so bad, it
was going to be a little difficult for him to get through New
Year. He looked at the red and green paper slips on the window
announcing "Big Sale 10% Discount."   If we really cut prices
like we did today, business ought to pick up, he thought to
himself.   We're not making any profit, but if we don't do any
business I still have to pay expenses anyway.   The main thing is
to get the customers to come in, then I can gradually raise my
prices. . . .   If we can do some wholesale business in the countryside, that will be even better! . . .

Suddenly, someone broke in on Mr. Lin's sweet dream. A shaky old lady entered the shop carrying a little bundle wrapped in blue cloth. Mr. Lin yanked up his head to find her confronting him. He wanted to escape, but there was no time. He could only go forward and greet her.

"Ah, Mrs. Chu, out buying things for the New Year? Please come into the back room and sit down. — Hsiu, give Mrs. Chu your arm."

But Miss Lin didn't hear. She had left the swinging doors some time ago. Mrs. Chu waved her hand in refusal and sat down on a chair in the store. Solemnly, she unwrapped the blue cloth and brought out a small account book. With two trembling hands she presented the book under Mr. Lin's nose. Twisting her withered lips, she was about to speak, but Mr. Lin had already taken the book and was hastening to say:

"I understand. I'll send it to your house tomorrow."

"Mm, mm, the tenth month, the eleventh month, the twelfth month; altogether three months. Three threes are nine; that's nine dollars, isn't it? — you'll send the money tomorrow? Mm, mm, you don't have to send it. I'll take it back with me! Eh!"

The words seemed to come with difficulty from Mrs. Chu's withered mouth. She had three hundred dollars loaned to Mr. Lin's shop, and was entitled to three dollars interest every month. Mr. Lin had delayed payment for three months, promising to pay in full at the end of the year. Now, she needed some money to buy gifts for tomorrow's Kitchen God Festival, and so she had come seeking Mr. Lin. From the forcefulness with which she moved her puckered mouth, Mr. Lin could tell that she was determined not to leave without the money.

Mr. Lin scratched his head in silence. He hadn't been deliberately refusing to pay the interest. It was just that for the past three months business had been poor. Their daily sales had been barely enough to cover their food and taxes. He had delayed paying her unconsciously. But if he didn't pay her today, the old lady might raise a row in the shop. That would be too shameful and would seriously influence the shop's future.

"All right, all right. Take it back with you!" Mr. Lin finally said in exasperation. His voice shook a little. He rushed to the cashier's cage and gathered together all the cash that had been taken in that morning and afternoon. To that he added twenty cents from his own pocket, and presented the whole collection of dollars, pennies and dimes to the old lady. She carefully counted the lot over and over again, then with trembling hands wrapped the money in the blue cloth. Mr. Lin couldn't repress a sigh. He had a wild desire to snatch back a part of the cash.

"That blue handkerchief is too worn, Mrs. Chu," he said with a forced laugh. "Why not buy a good white linen one? We've also got top quality wash-cloths and soap. Take some to use over the New Year. Prices are reasonable!"

"No. I don't want any. An old lady like me doesn't need that kind of thing." She waved her hand in refusal. She put her account book in her pocket and departed, firmly grasping the blue cloth bundle.

Looking sour, Mr. Lin walked into the "inner sanctum." Mrs. Chu's visit reminded him that he had two other creditors. Old Chen and Widow Chang had put up two hundred and one hundred and fifty dollars respectively. He would have to pay them a total of ten dollars interest. He couldn't very well delay their money; in fact, he would have to pay them ahead of time. He counted on his fingers — twenty-fourth, twenty-fifth, twenty-sixth. By the twenty-sixth, he ought to be able to collect all the outstanding debts in the countryside. His clerk Shou-sheng had gone off on a collection trip the day before yesterday. He should be back by the twenty-sixth at the latest. The unpaid bills in town couldn't be collected till the twenty-eighth or twenty-ninth. But the collector from the Shanghai wholesale house to which Mr. Lin owed money would probably come tomorrow or the day after. Lin's only alternative was to borrow more from the local bank. And how would business be tomorrow? . . .

His head down, Mr. Lin paced back and forth, thinking. The voice of his daughter spoke into his ear:

"Papa, what do you think of this piece of silk? Four dollars and twenty cents for seven feet. That's not expensive, is it?"

Mr. Lin's heart gave a leap. He stood stock-still and glared, speechless. Miss Lin held the piece of silk in her hand and giggled. Four dollars and twenty cents! It wasn't a big sum, but the shop only did sixteen dollars worth of business all day, and really at cost price! Mr. Lin stood frozen, then asked weakly:

"Where did you get the money?"

"I put it on the books."

Another debit. Mr. Lin scowled. But he had spoiled his daughter himself, and Mrs. Lin would take the girl's side no matter what the case might be. He smiled a helpless bitter smile. Then he sighed.

"You're always in such a rush," he said, slightly reproving. "Why couldn't you wait till after New Year!"

### III

Another two days went by. Business was indeed very brisk in Mr. Lin's shop, with its "Big Sale." They did over thirty dollars in sales every day. The hiccups of Mrs. Lin diminished considerably; she hiccuped on the average of only once every five minutes. Miss Lin skipped up and back between the shop and the "inner sanctum," her face flushed and smiling. At times she even helped with the selling. Only after her mother called her repeatedly, did she return to the back room. Mopping her brow, she protested excitedly.

"Ma, why have you called me back again? It's not hard work! Ma, Papa's so tired he's soaking wet; his voice is gone! — A customer just made a five-dollar purchase! Ma, you don't have to be afraid it's too tiring for me! Don't worry! Papa told me to rest a while, then come out again!"

Mrs. Lin only nodded her head and hiccuped, followed by a murmur that "Buddha is merciful and kind." A porcelain image of the Goddess Kuanyin was enshrined in the "inner sanctum," with a stick of incense burning before it. Mrs. Lin swayed over to the shrine and kowtowed. She thanked the Goddess for Her Protection and prayed for Her Blessing on a number of matters — that Mr. Lin's business should always be good, that Miss Lin should grow nicely, that next year the girl should get a good husband.

But out in the shop, although Mr. Lin was devoting his whole being to business, though a smile never left his face, he felt as if his heart were bound with strings. Watching the satisfied customer going out with a package under his arm, Mr. Lin suffered a pang with every dollar he took in, as the abacus in his mind clicked a five per cent loss off the cost price he had raised through sweat and blood. Several times he tried to estimate the loss as being three per cent, but no matter how he figured it, he still was losing five cents on the dollar. Although business was good, the more he sold the worse he felt. As he waited on the customers, the conflict raging within his breast at times made him nearly faint. When he stole glances at the shop across the street, he had the impression that the owner and salesmen were sneering at him from behind their counters. Look at that fool Lin! they seemed to be saying. He really *is* selling below cost! Wait and see! The more business he does, the more he loses! The sooner he'll have to close down!

Mr. Lin gnawed his lips. He vowed he would raise his prices the next day. He would charge first-grade prices for second-rate merchandise.

The head of the Merchants Guild came by. It was he who had interceded with the Kuomintang chieftains for Mr. Lin on the question of selling Japanese goods. Now he smiled and congratulated Mr. Lin, and clapped him on the shoulder.

"How goes it? That four hundred dollars was well spent!" he said softly. "But you'd better give a small token to Kuomintang Party Commissioner Pu too. Otherwise, he may become annoyed and try to squeeze you. When business is good, plenty of people are jealous. Even if Commissioner Pu doesn't have any 'ideas,' they'll try to stir him up!"

Mr. Lin thanked the head of the Merchants Guild for his

concern. Inwardly, he was very alarmed. He almost lost his zest for doing business.

What made him most uneasy was that his assistant Shou-sheng still hadn't returned from the bill collecting trip. He needed the money to pay off his account with the big Shanghai wholesale house. The collector had arrived from Shanghai two days before, and was pressing Mr. Lin hard. If Shou-sheng didn't come soon, Mr. Lin would have to borrow from the local bank. This would mean an additional burden of fifty or sixty dollars in interest payments. To Mr. Lin, losing money every day, this prospect was more painful than being flayed alive.

At about four p.m., Mr. Lin suddenly heard a noisy uproar on the street. People looked very frightened, as though some serious calamity had happened. Mr. Lin, who could think only of whether Shou-sheng would safely return, was sure that the river boat on which Shou-sheng would come back had been set upon by pirates. His heart pounding, he hailed a passer-by and asked worriedly:

"What's wrong? Did pirates get the boat from Lishih?"

"Oh! So it's pirates again? Travelling is really too dangerous! Robbing is nothing. Men are even kidnapped right off the boat!" babbled the passer-by, a well-known loafer named Lu. He eyed the brightly coloured goods in the shop.

Mr. Lin could make no sense out of this at all. His worry increased and he dropped Lu to accost Wang, the next person who came along.

"Is it true that the boat from Lishih was robbed?"

"It must be Ah Shu's gang that did it. Ah Shu has been shot, but his gang is still a tough bunch!" Wang replied without slackening his pace.

Cold sweat bedewed Mr. Lin's forehead. He was frantic. He was sure that Shou-sheng was coming back today, and from Lishih. That was the last place on the account book list. Now it was already four o'clock, but there was no sign of Shou-sheng. After what Wang had said, how could Mr. Lin have any doubts? He forgot that he himself had invented the story of

the boat being robbed. His whole face beaded with perspiration, he rushed into the "inner sanctum." Going through the
swinging doors, he tripped over the threshold and nearly fell.

"Papa, they're fighting in Shanghai! The Japanese bombed
the Chapei section!" cried Miss Lin, running up to him.

Mr. Lin stopped short. What was all this about fighting in
Shanghai? His first reaction was that it had nothing to do with
him. But since it involved the "Japanese," he thought he had
better inquire a little further. Looking at his daughter's agitated
face, he asked:

"The Japanese bombed it? Who told you that?"

"Everyone on the street is talking about it. The Japanese
soldiers fired heavy artillery and they bombed. Chapei is
burned to the ground!"

"Oh, well, did anyone say that the boat from Lishih was
robbed?"

Miss Lin shook her head, then fluttered from the room like
a moth. Mr. Lin hesitated beside the swinging doors, scratching
his head. Mrs. Lin was hiccuping and mumbling prayers.

"Buddha protect us! Don't let any bombs fall on our heads!"

Mr. Lin turned and went out to the shop. He saw his
daughter engaged in excited conversation with the two
salesmen. The owner of the shop across the street had come
out from behind his counter and was talking, gesticulating
wildly. There was fighting in Shanghai; Japanese planes had
bombed Chapei and burned it; the merchants in Shanghai had
closed down — it all was true. What about the pirates robbing
the boat? No one had heard anything about that! And the
boat from Lishih? It had come in safely. The shopowner across
the street had just seen stevedores from the boat going by with
two big crates. Mr. Lin was relieved. Shou-sheng hadn't come
back today, but he hadn't been robbed by pirates either!

Now the whole town was talking about the catastrophe in
Shanghai. Young clerks were cursing the Japanese aggressors.
People were even shouting, "Anyone who buys Japanese goods
is a son of a bitch!" These words brought a scarlet blush to
Miss Lin's cheeks, but Mr. Lin showed no change of expression.

All the shops were selling Japanese merchandise. Moreover, after spending a few hundred dollars, the merchants had received special authorizations from the Kuomintang chieftains, saying, "The goods may be sold after removing the Japanese markings." All the merchandise in Mr. Lin's shop had been transformed into "native goods." His customers, too, would call them "native goods," then take up their packages and leave.

Because of the war in Shanghai, the whole town had lost all interest in business, but Mr. Lin was busy pondering his affairs. Unwilling to borrow from the local bank at exorbitant interest, he sought out the collector from the Shanghai wholesale house, to plead with him as a friend for a delay of another day or two. Shou-sheng would be back tomorrow before dark at the latest, said Mr. Lin. Then he would pay in full.

"My dear Mr. Lin, you're an intelligent man. How can you talk like that? They're fighting in Shanghai. Train service may be cut off tomorrow or the day after. I only wish I could start back tonight! How can I wait a day or two? Please, settle your account today so that I can leave the first thing tomorrow morning. I'm not my own boss. Please have some consideration for me!"

The Shanghai collector was uncompromisingly firm in his refusal. Mr. Lin saw that it was hopeless; he had no choice but to bear the pain and seek a loan from the local banker. He was worried that "Old Miser" knew of his sore need and would take advantage of the situation to boost the interest rate. From the minute he started speaking to the bank manager, Mr. Lin could feel that the atmosphere was all wrong. The tubercular old man said nothing when Mr. Lin finished his plea, but continued puffing on his antique water-pipe. After the whole packet of tobacco was consumed, the manager finally spoke.

"I can't do it," he said slowly. "The Japanese have begun fighting, business in Shanghai is at a standstill, the banks have all closed down — who knows when things will be set right again! Cut off from Shanghai, my bank is like a crab without legs. With exchange of remittances stopped, I couldn't do business even with a better client than you. I'm sorry. I'd love to help you but my hands are tied!"

Mr. Lin lingered. He thought the tubercular manager was putting on an act in preparation for demanding higher interest. Just as Mr. Lin was about to play along by renewing his pleas, he was surprised to hear the manager press him a step farther.

"Our employer has given us instructions. He has heard that the situation will probably get worse. He wants us to tighten up. Your shop originally owed us five hundred; on the twenty-second, you borrowed another hundred — altogether six hundred, due to be settled before New Year. We've been doing business together a long time, so I'm tipping you off. We want to avoid a lot of talk and embarrassment at the last minute."

"Oh — but our little shop is having a hard time," blurted the dumbfounded Mr. Lin. "I'll have to see how we do with our collections."

"Ho! Why be so modest! The last few days your business hasn't been like the others! What's so difficult about paying a mere six hundred dollars? I'm letting you know today, old brother. I'm looking forward to your settling your debt so that I can clear myself with my employer."

The tubercular manager spoke coldly. He stood up. Chilled, Mr. Lin could see that the situation was beyond repair. All he could do was to take a grip on himself and walk out of the bank. At last he understood that the fighting in distant Shanghai would influence his little shop too. It certainly was going to be hard to get through this New Year: The Shanghai collector was pressing him for money; the bank wouldn't wait until after the New Year; Shou-sheng still hadn't come back and there was no telling how he was getting on. So far as Mr. Lin's outstanding accounts in town were concerned, last year he had only collected eighty per cent. From the looks of things, this year there was no guarantee of even that much. Only one road seemed open to Mr. Lin: "Business Temporarily Closed — Balancing Books!" And this was equivalent to bankruptcy. There hadn't been any of his own money invested in the shop for a long time. The day the books were balanced and the creditors paid off, what would be left for him probably wouldn't be enough to stand between his family and nakedness!

The more he thought, the worse Mr. Lin felt. Crossing the bridge, he looked at the turbid water below. He was almost tempted to jump and end it all. Then a man hailed him from behind.

"Mr. Lin, is it true there's a war on in Shanghai? I hear that a bunch of soldiers just set up outside the town's east gate and asked the Merchants Guild for a 'loan.' They wanted twenty thousand right off the bat. The Merchants Guild is holding a meeting about it now!"

Mr. Lin hurriedly turned around. The speaker was Old Chen who had two hundred dollars loaned to the shop — another of Mr. Lin's creditors.

"Oh —" retorted Mr. Lin with a shiver. Quickly he crossed the bridge and ran home.

## IV

For dinner that evening, beside the usual one meat dish and two vegetable dishes, Mrs. Lin had bought a favourite of Mr. Lin's — a platter of stewed pork. In addition, there was a pint of yellow wine. A smile never left Miss Lin's face, for business in the shop was good, her new silk dress was finished, and because they were fighting back against the Japanese in Shanghai. Mrs. Lin's hiccups were especially sparse — about one every ten minutes.

Only Mr. Lin was sunk in gloom. Moodily drinking his wine, he looked at his daughter, and looked at his wife. Several times he considered dropping the bad news in their midst like a bombshell, but he didn't have that kind of courage. Moreover, he still hadn't given up hope, he still wanted to struggle; at least he wanted to conceal his failure to make ends meet.

And so when the Merchants Guild passed a resolution to pay the soldiers five thousand dollars and asked Mr. Lin to contribute twenty, he consented without a moment's hesitation.

He decided not to tell his wife and daughter the true state of
affairs until the last possible minute. The way he calculated it
was this: He would collect eight per cent of the debts due him,
he would pay eighty per cent of the money he owed. Anyhow,
he had the excuse that there was fighting in Shanghai, that remittances couldn't be sent. The difficulty was that there was
a difference of about six hundred dollars between what people
owed him and what he had to pay to others. He would have
to take drastic measures and cut prices heavily. The idea was
to scrape together some money to meet the present problem, then he would see. Who could think of the future in
times like these? If he could get by now, that would be enough.

That was how he made his plans. With the added potency
of the pint of yellow wine, Mr. Lin slept soundly all night,
without even the suggestion of a bad dream.

It was already six thirty when Mr. Lin awoke the next morning. The sky was overcast and he was rather dizzy. He gulp-
ed down two bowls of rice gruel and hurried to the shop. The
first thing to greet his eye was the Shanghai collector, sitting
with a stern face, waiting for his "answer." But what shocked
Mr. Lin particularly was the shop across the street. They too
had pasted red and green strips all over their windows; they
too were having a "Big Sale 10% Discount"! Mr. Lin's perfect
plan of the night before was completely snowed under by those
red and green streamers of his competitor.

"What kind of a joke is this, Mr. Lin? Last night you didn't
give a reply. That boat leaves here at eight o'clock and I have
to make connections with the train. I simply must catch that
eight o'clock boat! Please hurry —" said the Shanghai collector
impatiently. He brought his clenched fist down on the table.

Mr. Lin apologized and begged his forgiveness. Truly, it was
all because of the fighting in Shanghai and not being able to
send remittances. After all, they had been doing business for
many years. Mr. Lin pleaded for a little special consideration.

"Then am I to go back empty-handed?"

"Why, why, certainly not. When Shou-sheng returns, I'll give
you as much as he brings. I'm not a man if I keep so much as

half a dollar!" Mr. Lin's voice trembled. With an effort he held back the tears that brimmed to his eyes.

There was no more to be said; the Shanghai collector stopped his grumbling. But he remained firmly seated where he was. Mr. Lin was nearly out of his wits with anxiety. His heart thumped erratically. Although he had been having a hard time the past few years, he had been able to keep up a front. Now there was a collector sitting in his shop for all the world to see. If word of this thing spread, Mr. Lin's credit would be ruined. He had plenty of creditors. Suppose they all decided to follow suit? His shop might just as well close down immediately. In desperation, several times he invited the Shanghai gentleman to wait in the back room where it was more comfortable, but the latter refused.

An icy rain began to fall. The street was cold and deserted. Never had it appeared so mournful at New Year's time. Signboards creaked and clattered in the grip of a north wind. The icy rain seemed like to turn into snow. In the shops that lined the street, salesmen leaning on the counters looked up blankly.

Occasionally, Mr. Lin and the collector from Shanghai exchanged a few desultory words. Miss Lin suddenly emerged through the swinging doors and stood at the front window watching the cold hissing rain. From the back room, the sound of Mrs. Lin's hiccups steadily gathered intensity. While trying to be pleasant to their visitor, Mr. Lin looked at his daughter and listened to his wife's hiccups, and a wave of depression rose in his breast. He thought how all his life he had never known any prosperity, nor could he imagine who was responsible for his being reduced to such dire straits today.

The Shanghai collector seemed to have calmed down somewhat. "Mr. Lin," he said abruptly, in a sincere tone, "you're a good man. You don't go in for loose living, you're obliging and honest in your business practices. Twenty years ago, you would have gotten rich. But things are different today. Taxes are high, expenses are heavy, business is slow — it's an accomplishment just to get along."

Mr. Lin sighed and smiled in wry modesty.

After a pause, the Shanghai collector continued, "This year the market in this town was a little worse than last, wasn't it? Places in the interior like this depend on the people from the countryside for business, but the peasants are too poor. There's really no solution. . . . Oh, it's nine o'clock! Why hasn't your collection clerk come back yet? Is he reliable?"

Mr. Lin's heart gave a leap. For the moment, he couldn't answer. Although Shou-sheng had been his salesman for seven or eight years and had never made a slip, still, there was no absolute guarantee! And besides he was overdue. The Shanghai collector laughed to see Mr. Lin's doubtful expression, but his laugh had an odd ring to it.

At the window, Miss Lin whirled and cried urgently, "Papa, Shou-sheng is back! He's covered with mud!"

Her voice had a peculiar sound too. Mr. Lin jumped up, both alarmed and happy. He wanted to run out and look, but he was so excited that his legs were weak. By then Shou-sheng had already entered, truly covered with mud. The clerk sat down, panting for breath, unable to say a word. The situation looked bad. Frightened out of his wits, Mr. Lin was speechless too. The Shanghai collector frowned. After a while, Shou-sheng managed to gasp:

"Very dangerous! They nearly got me!"

"Then the boat was robbed?" the agitated Mr. Lin took a grip on himself and blurted.

"There wasn't any robbing. They were grabbing coolies for the army. I couldn't make the boat yesterday afternoon; I got a sampan this morning. After we sailed, we heard they were waiting at this end to grab the boat, so we came to port further down the river. When we got ashore, before we had come half a *li*, we bumped into an army pressgang. They grabbed the clerk from the clothing shop, but I ran fast and came back by a short cut. Damn it! It was a close call!"

Shou-sheng lifted his jacket as he talked and pulled from his money belt a cloth-bound packet which he handed to Mr. Lin.

"It's all here," he said. "That Huang Shop in Lishih is rotten. We have to be careful of customers like that next year.

. . . I'll come back after I have a wash and change my clothes."

Mr. Lin's face lit up as he squeezed the packet. He carried it over to the cashier's cage and unbound the cloth wrapping. First he added up the money due on the list of debtors, then he counted what had been collected. There were eleven silver dollars, two hundred dimes, four hundred and twenty dollars in banknotes, and two bank demand drafts — for the equivalent of fifty and sixty-five taels of silver respectively, at the official rate. If he turned the whole lot over to the Shanghai collector, it would still be more than a hundred dollars short of what he owed the wholesale house.

Deep in contemplation, Mr. Lin glanced several times out of the corner of his eye at the Shanghai collector who was silently smoking a cigarette. At last he sighed, and as though cutting off a piece of his living flesh, placed the two bank drafts and four hundred dollars in cash before the man from Shanghai. Then Mr. Lin spoke for a long time until he managed to extract a nod from the latter and the words "all right."

But when the collector looked twice at the bank drafts, he said with a smile, "Sorry to trouble you, Mr. Lin. Please get them cashed for me first."

"Certainly, certainly," Mr. Lin hastened to reply. He quickly affixed his shop's seal to the back of the drafts and dispatched one of his salesmen to cash them at the local bank. In a little while, the salesman came back empty-handed. The bank had accepted the drafts but refused to pay for them, saying they would be credited against Mr. Lin's debt. Though it was snowing heavily now, Mr. Lin rushed over to the bank without an umbrella to plead in person. But his efforts were in vain.

"Well, what about it?" demanded the Shanghai collector impatiently as Mr. Lin returned to the shop, his face anguished.

Mr. Lin seemed ready to weep. There was nothing he could say; he could only sigh. Except to beg the collector for more leniency, what else could he do? Shou-sheng came out and added his pleas to Mr. Lin's. He vowed that they would send the remaining two hundred dollars to Shanghai by the tenth of the new year. Mr. Lin was an old customer who had always paid his debts promptly without a word, said Shou-sheng. This thing today was really unexpected. But that was the situation; they couldn't help themselves. It wasn't that they were stalling.

The Shanghai collector was adamant. Painfully, Mr. Lin brought out the fifty dollars he had taken in during the past few days and handed it over to make up a total payment of four hundred and fifty dollars. Only then did that headache of a Shanghai collector depart.

By that time, it was eleven in the morning. Snowflakes were still drifting down from the sky. Not even half a customer was in sight. Mr. Lin brooded a while, then discussed with Shou-sheng means to be used in collecting outstanding bills in town. Both men were frowning; neither of them had any particular confidence that much of the six hundred dollars due from town customers could be collected. Shou-sheng bent close to Mr. Lin's ear and whispered:

"I hear that the big shop at the south gate and the one at the west gate are both shaky. Both of them owe us money — about three hundred dollars altogether. We better take precautions with these two accounts. If they fold up before we can collect, it won't be so funny!"

Mr. Lin paled; his lips trembled a little. Then, Shou-sheng pitched his voice lower still, and mumbled a bit of even more shocking news.

"There's another nasty rumour — about us. They're sure to have heard it at the bank. That's why they're pressing us so hard. The Shanghai collector probably got wind of it too. Who can be trying to make trouble for us? The shop across the street?"

Shou-sheng pointed with his pursed lips in the direction of the suspect, and Mr. Lin's eyes swung to follow the indicator. His heart skipping unevenly, his face mournful, Mr. Lin was unable to speak for some time. He had the numb and aching feeling that this time he was definitely finished! If he weren't ruined it would be a miracle: The Kuomintang chieftains were putting the squeeze on him; the bank was pressing him; his fellow shopkeepers were stabbing him in the back; a couple of his biggest debtors were going to default. Nobody could stand up under this kind of buffeting. But why was he fated to get such a dirty deal? Ever since he inherited the little shop from his father, he had never dared to be wasteful. He had been so obliging; he never hurt a soul, never schemed against anyone. His father and grandfather had been the same, yet all he was reaping was bitterness!

"Never mind. Let them spread their rumours. You don't have to worry," Shou-sheng tried to comfort Mr. Lin, though he couldn't help sighing himself. "There are always rumours in lean years. They say in this town nine out of ten shops won't be able to pay up their debts before the year is out. Times are bad, the market is dead as a doornail. Usually strong shops are hard up this year. We're not the only one having rough going! When the sky tumbles everyone gets crushed. The Merchants Guild has to think of a way out. All the shops can't be collapsing; that would make the market even less like a market."

The snowfall was becoming heavier; it was sticking to the ground now. Occasionally, a dog would slink by, shivering, its tail between its legs. It might stop and shake itself violently to dislodge the snow thickly matting its fur. Then, with tail drooping again, the dog would go on its way. Never in its history had this street witnessed so frigid and desolate a New Year season! And just at this time, in distant Shanghai, Japanese heavy artillery was savagely pounding that prosperous metropolis of trade.

## V

It was a gloomy New Year, but finally it was passed. In town, twenty-eight big and little shops folded up, including a "credit A-1" silk shop. The two stores that owed Mr. Lin three hundred dollars closed down too. The last day of the year, Shou-sheng had gone to them and plagued them for hours, but all he could extract was a total of twenty dollars. He heard that afterwards no other collector got so much as a penny out of them; the owners of the two shops hid themselves and couldn't be found. Thanks to the intervention of the head of the Merchants Guild, it wasn't necessary for Mr. Lin to hide. But he had to guarantee to wipe off his debt of four hundred dollars to the bank before the fifteenth of the first month, and he had to consent to very harsh terms: The bank would send a representative to "guard" all cash taken in starting from resumption of business on the fifth; eighty per cent of all money collected would go to the bank until Mr. Lin's debt to them was paid.

During the New Year holidays, Mr. Lin's house was like an ice box. Mr. Lin heaved sigh after sigh. Mrs. Lin's hiccups were like a string of firecrackers. Miss Lin, although she neither hiccuped nor sighed, moped around in the dazed condition of one who has suffered from years of jaundice. Her new silk dress had already gone to the only pawnshop in town to raise money for the maid's wages. An apprentice had taken it there at seven in the morning; it was after nine when he finally squeezed his way out of the crowd with two dollars in his hand. Afterwards, the pawnshop refused to do any more business that day. Two dollars! That was the highest price they would give for any article, no matter how much you had paid for it originally! This was called "two dollar ceiling." When a peasant, steeling himself against the cold, would peel off a cotton-padded jacket and hand it across the counter, the pawnshop clerk would raise it up, give it a shake, then fling it back with an angry "We don't want it!"

Since New Year's Day, the weather had been beautiful and clear. The big temple courtyard, as was the custom, was crowded with the stalls of itinerant pedlars and the paraphernalia of acrobats and jugglers. People lingered before the stalls, patted their empty money belts, and reluctantly walked on. Children dragged at their mothers' clothing, refusing to leave the stall where fireworks were on sale, until Mama was forced to give the little offender a hard slap. The pedlars, who had come specially to cash in on the usual New Year's bazaar trade, didn't even make enough to pay for their food. They couldn't pay their rent at the local inn and quarrelled with the innkeeper every day.

Only the acrobatic troupe earned the large sum of eight dollars. It had been hired by the Kuomintang chieftains to add to the atmosphere of "peace and normalcy."

On the evening of the fourth, Mr. Lin, who had with some difficulty managed to raise three dollars, gave the usual spread for his employees at which they all discussed the strategy for the morrow's re-opening of business. The prospects were already terribly clear to Mr. Lin: If they re-opened, they were sure to operate at a loss; if they didn't re-open, he and his family would be entirely without resources. Moreover, people still owed him four hundred dollars, the collection of which would be even more difficult, if he closed down. The only way out was to cut expenses. But taxes and levies for the soldiers were inescapable; there was even less chance of his avoiding being "squeezed." Fire a couple of salesmen? He only had three. Shou-sheng was his righthand man; the other two were poor devils; besides he really needed them to wait on the customers. He couldn't save any more at home. They had already let the maid go. He felt the only thing to do was to plunge on. Perhaps, when the peasants, with Buddha's blessing, earned money from their spring raw silk sales, he still might make up his loss.

But the greatest problem in resuming business was that he was short of merchandise. Without money to remit to Shanghai, he couldn't replenish his stock. The fighting in Shanghai was getting worse. There was no use in hoping for getting anything on credit. Sell his reserve? The shop was long since actually cleaned out. The underwear boxes on the shelves were empty; they were used only for show. All that was left were things like wash-basins and towels. But he had plenty of those.

Gloomily, the feasters sipped their wine. For all their perplexed reflection, no one could offer any solution to the problem. They talked of generalities for a while. Then suddenly Ashi, one of the salesmen, said:

"The world is going to hell. People live worse than dogs! They say Chapei was completely burned out. A couple of hundred thousand people had to flee, leaving all their belongings behind. There wasn't any fire in the Hongkew section, but everybody ran away. The Japanese are very cruel. They wouldn't let them take any of their things with them. House rent in safe quarters in Shanghai has skyrocketed. All the refugees are running to the countryside. A bunch came to our town yesterday. They all look like decent people, and now they're homeless!"

Mr. Lin shook his head and sighed, but Shou-sheng, on hearing these words, was suddenly struck with a bright idea. He put down his chopsticks, then raised his wine cup and drained it in one swallow. He turned to Mr. Lin with a grin.

"Did you hear what Ashi just said? That means our wash-basins, wash-cloths, soap, socks, tooth powder, tooth brushes, will sell fast. We can get rid of as many as we've got."

Mr. Lin stared. He didn't know what Shou-sheng was driving at.

"Look, this is a heaven-sent chance. The Shanghai refugees should have a little money, and they need the usual daily necessities, don't they? We ought to set up right away to handle this business!"

Shou-sheng poured himself another cup of wine, and drank, his face beaming. The two salesmen caught on, and they began to laugh. Only Mr. Lin was not entirely clear. He had been rather dulled by his recent adversity.

"Are you sure?" he asked, irresolutely. "Other shops have wash-cloths and wash-basins too —"

"But we're the only ones with any real reserve of that sort of stuff. They don't have even ten wash-basins across the street, and those are all seconds. We've got this piece of business right in the palm of our hand! Let's write a lot of ads and paste them up at the town's four gateways, any place in town where the refugees are staying — say, Ashi, where *are* they living? We'll go put up our stickers there!"

"The ones with relatives here are living with their relatives. The rest have borrowed that empty building in the silk factory outside the west gate." Ashi's face shone with satisfaction over the excellent result he had unwittingly produced.

At last, Mr. Lin had the whole picture. Happy, his spirits revived. He immediately drafted the wording of the advertisements, listing all the daily necessities which the shop had available for sale. There were over a dozen different commodities. In imitation of the big Shanghai stores, he adopted the "One Dollar Package" technique. For a dollar the customer would get a wash-basin, a wash-cloth, a tooth brush and a box of tooth powder. "Big Dollar Sale!" screamed the ad in huge letters. Shou-sheng brought out the shop's remaining sheets of red and green paper and cut them into large strips. Then he took up his brush and started writing. The salesmen and the apprentices noisily collected the wash-basins, wash-cloths, tooth brushes and boxes of tooth powder, and arranged them into sets. There weren't enough hands for all the work. Mr. Lin called his daughter out to help with writing the ads and tying the packages. He also made up other kinds of combination packages — all of daily necessities.

That night, they were busy in the shop late and long. At dawn they had things pretty much in order. When the popping of firecrackers heralded the opening of business the next morning, the shop of the Lin family again had a new look. Their advertisements had already been pasted up all over town. Shou-sheng had personally attended to the silk factory outside the west gate. The ad with which he plastered the factory walls struck the eyes of the refugees, and they all crowded around to read it as if it were a news bulletin.

In the "inner sanctum" Mrs. Lin, too, rose very early. She lit incense before the porcelain image of the Goddess Kuanyin and kowtowed for a considerable time, knocking her head resoundingly against the floor. She prayed for practically everything. About the only thing she omitted was a plea for more refugees to come to the town.

It all worked out fine, just as Shou-sheng had predicted. Mr.

Lin's shop was the only one whose trade was brisk on the first business day after the New Year's holidays. By four in the afternoon, he had sold over one hundred dollars' worth of merchandise — the highest figure for a day ever reached in that town in the past ten years. His biggest seller was the "One Dollar Package," and it served as a leader to such items as umbrellas and rubber overshoes. Business, moreover, went smoothly, pleasantly. The refugees came from Shanghai, after all; they were used to the ways of the big city; they weren't as petty as the townspeople or the peasants from the out-lying districts. When they bought something, they made up their minds quickly. They'd pick up a thing, look at it, then produce their money. There was none of this pawing through all the merchandise, no haggling over a few pennies.

When her daughter, all flushed and excited, rushed into the back room for a moment to report the good business, Mrs. Lin went to kowtow before the porcelain Kuanyin again. If Shou-sheng weren't twice the girl's age, Mrs. Lin was thinking, wouldn't he make a good son-in-law! And it wasn't at all unlikely that Shou-sheng had half an eye on his employer's seventeen-year-old daughter, this girl whom he knew so well.

There was just one thing that spoiled Mr. Lin's happiness — completely disregarding his dignity, the local bank had sent its man to collect eighty per cent of the sales proceeds. And he didn't know who egged them on, but the three creditors of the shop, on the excuse that they "needed a little money to buy rice," all showed up to draw out some advance interest. Not only interest; they even wanted repayment of part of their loans too! But Mr. Lin also heard some good news — another batch of refugees had arrived in town.

For dinner that evening, Mr. Lin served two additional meat dishes, by way of reward to his employees. Everyone complimented Shou-sheng on his shrewdness. Although Mr. Lin was happy, he couldn't help thinking of how his three creditors had talked about being repaid their loans. It was unlucky to have such a thing happen at the beginning of the new year.

"What do they know!" said Shou-sheng angrily. "Somebody

must have put them up to it!" He pointed with his lips at the shop across the street.

Mr. Lin nodded. But whether the three creditors knew anything or not, it was going to be difficult to handle them. An old man and two widows. You couldn't be soft with them, but getting tough wouldn't do either. Mr. Lin pondered for some time, and finally decided the best thing to do would be to ask the head of the Merchants Guild to speak to his three precious creditors. He asked Shou-sheng for his opinion. Shou-sheng heartily agreed.

When dinner was over, and Mr. Lin had added up his receipts for the day, he went to pay his respects to the head of the Merchants Guild. The latter expressed complete approval of Mr. Lin's idea. What's more, he commended Mr. Lin on the intelligent way in which he conducted his business. He said the shop was sure to stand firm, in fact it would improve. Stroking his chin, the head of the Merchants Guild smiled and leaned towards Mr. Lin.

"There's something I've been wanting to talk to you about for a long time, but I never had the opportunity. I don't know where Kuomintang Commissioner Pu saw your daughter, but he's very interested in her. Commissioner Pu is forty and he has no sons. Though he has two women at home, neither of them has been able to give birth. If your daughter should join his household and present him with a child, he's sure to make her his wife, Madam Commissioner. Ah, if that should happen, even I could share in the reflected glory!"

Never in his wildest dreams had Mr. Lin ever imagined he would run into trouble like this. He was speechless. The head of the Merchants Guild continued solemnly:

"We're old friends. There's nothing we can't speak freely about to each other. This kind of thing, according to the old standards, would make you lose face. But it isn't altogether like that any more; it's quite common nowadays. Your daughter's going over could be considered proper marriage. Anyhow, since that is what Commissioner Pu has in mind, there might be some inconvenience if you refuse him. If you agree, you can have real hope for the future. I wouldn't be telling you this if I didn't have your interests at heart."

"Of course in advising me to be careful, your intentions are the best! But I'm an unimportant person, my daughter knows nothing of high society. We don't dare aspire so high as a commissioner!" Mr. Lin had to brace himself up to speak. His heart was thumping fast.

"Ha ha! It isn't a question of your aspirations, but the fact that he finds her suitable. . . . Let's leave it at that. You go home and talk it over with your wife. I'll put the matter aside. When I see Commissioner Pu I'll say I haven't had a chance to speak to you about it, alright? But you must give me an answer soon!"

There was a long pause. Then, "I will," Mr. Lin forced himself to say. His face was ghastly.

When he got home, he sent his daughter out of the room and reported to his wife in detail. Even before he finished, Mrs. Lin's hiccups rose in a powerful barrage that was probably audible to all the neighbours. With an effort she stemmed the tide and said, panting:

"How can we consent? — hic — Even if it wasn't a concubine he wanted hic — hic — even if he were looking for a wife, I still couldn't bear to part with her!"

"That's the way I feel, but —"

"Hic — we run our business all legal and proper. Do you mean to say if we don't agree he could get away with taking her by force? Hic —"

"But he's sure to find an excuse to make some kind of trouble. That kind of man is crueler than a bandit!" Mr. Lin whispered. He was nearly crying.

"He'll get her only over my dead body! Hic! Goddess Kuanyin preserve us!" cried Mrs. Lin in a voice that trembled. She rose and started to sway out of the room. Mr. Lin hastily barred her way.

"Where are you going? Where are you going?" he babbled.

Just then, Miss Lin came in. Obviously she had overheard quite a bit, for her complexion was the colour of chalk and her eyes were staring fixedly. Mrs. Lin flung her arms around her daughter and wept and hiccuped while she struggled to say in gasps:

"Hic — child — hic — anybody who tries to snatch you — hic — will have to do it over my dead body! Hic! The year I gave birth to you I got this — sickness — hic — It was hard, but I brought you up till now you're seventeen — hic — hic — Dead or alive, we'll stick together! Hic! We should have promised you to Shou-sheng long ago! Hic! That Pu is a dirty crook! He isn't afraid the gods will strike him down!"

Miss Lin wept too, crying "Ma!" Mr. Lin wrung his hands and sighed. The women were wailing at an alarming rate, and he was afraid their laments would be heard through the thin walls and startle the neighbours. This sort of row was also an unlucky way to commence the new year. Holding his own emotions in check, he did his best to soothe wife and daughter.

That night, all three members of the Lin family slept badly. Although Mr. Lin had to get up early the next morning to go to business, he wrestled with his gloomy thoughts all night. A sudden sound on the roof sent his heart leaping with fear that Commissioner Pu had come to trump up charges against him. Then he calmed himself and considered the matter carefully. His was a family of proper business people who had never committed any crimes. As long as he did a good business and didn't owe people money, surely Pu couldn't make trouble without any reason at all. And now Lin's business was beginning to show some vitality. Just because he had raised a good-looking daughter, he had invited disaster! He should have engaged her years ago, then maybe this problem would never have arisen. . . . Was the head of the Merchants Guild sincerely willing to help? The only way out was to beg for his aid — Mrs. Lin started hiccuping again. Ai! That ailment of hers!

Mr. Lin rose as soon as the sky began to turn light. His eyes were somewhat bloodshot and swollen, and he felt dizzy. But he had to pull himself together and attend to business. He couldn't leave the entire management of the shop to Shou-sheng; the young fellow had put in an exhausting few days.

He was still uneasy after he seated himself in the cashier's cage. Although business was good, from time to time his whole body was shaken by violent shivers. Whenever a big man came in, if Mr. Lin didn't know him, he would suspect that the man had been sent by Commissioner Pu to spy, to stir up a fuss, and his heart would thump painfully.

And it was strange. Business that day was active beyond all expectations. By noon they had sold nearly sixty dollars' worth of merchandise. There were local townspeople among the customers too. They weren't just buying; they were practically grabbing. The only thing like it would be a bankrupt shop selling its stock out at auction cheap. While Mr. Lin was fairly pleased, he was also rather alarmed. This kind of business didn't look healthy to him. Sure enough, Shou-sheng approached him during the lunch hour and said softly:

"There's a rumour outside that you've cut prices to clear out your left-overs. That when you've collected a little money, you're going to take it and run!"

Mr. Lin was both angry and frightened. He couldn't speak. Suddenly two men in uniform entered and barged forward to demand:

"Which one is Mr. Lin, the proprietor?"

Mr. Lin rose in flurried haste. Before he had a chance to reply, the uniformed men began to lead him away. Shou-sheng came over to stop them and to question them. They barked at him savagely:

"Who are you? Stand aside! He's wanted for questioning at the Kuomintang office!"

## VI

That afternoon, Mr. Lin did not return. They were busy at the shop, and Shou-sheng could not get away to inquire personally. He had managed to conceal the truth from Mrs. Lin, but one of the apprentices let it leak out, and the lady became frantic almost to the point of distraction. She absolutely refused to let Miss Lin go out of the swinging doors.

"They've already taken your father. They'll be coming back for you next! Hic —"

She called in Shou-sheng and questioned him closely. He didn't think it advisable to tell her too much.

"Don't worry, Mrs. Lin," he comforted. "There's nothing wrong! He only went down to the Kuomintang office to straighten out the question of our creditors. Business is good. What have we got to be afraid of!"

Behind Mrs. Lin's back, he told Miss Lin quietly, "We still don't really know what this is all about." He urged her to look after her mother; he would attend to the shop. Miss Lin didn't have the faintest idea what to do. She agreed to everything Shou-sheng said.

Between waiting on the customers and thinking up answers to Mrs. Lin's constant questions, it was impossible for Shou-sheng to find time to inquire about the fate of Mr. Lin. Finally, at twilight, word was brought by the head of the Merchants Guild: Mr. Lin was being held by the Kuomintang chieftains because of the rumour that he was planning to abscond with the shop's money. Besides what Mr. Lin owed the bank and the wholesale house, there were also his three poor creditors to be considered. The total of six hundred and fifty dollars which they had put up was in jeopardy. The Kuomintang was especially concerned over the welfare of these poor people. So it was detaining him until he settled with them.

Shou-sheng's face was drained of colour. Dazed, he finally managed to ask:

"Can we put up a guarantee and have him released first? Unless we get him out, how are we going to raise the money?"

"Huh! Release him on a guarantee! You can't become his guarantor if you go there without money in your hands!"

"Mr. Guild Leader, think of something, I beg you. Do a good deed. You and Mr. Lin are old friends. I beg you to help him!"

The head of the Merchants Guild frowned thoughtfully. He

looked at Shou-sheng for a minute, then led him to a corner of
the room and said in a low voice:

"I can't stand by with folded arms and watch Mr. Lin
remain in difficulty. But the situation is very strained now! To
tell you the truth, I've already pleaded with Commissioner Pu
to intervene. Commissioner Pu only wanted Mr. Lin to agree
to one thing, and would be willing to help him. I've just seen
Mr. Lin at the Kuomintang office where I urged him to
consent, and he did so. Shouldn't that be the end of the
matter? Who would have thought that dark pock-marked
fellow in the Kuomintang would be so nasty? He still
insists —"

"Surely he wouldn't go against Commissioner Pu?"

"That's what I thought! But the pock-marked fellow kept
mumbling and grumbling till Commissioner Pu was very
embarrassed. They had a terrible row! Now you see how
awkward things are?"

Shou-sheng sighed. He had no idea. There was a pause,
then he sighed again and said:

"But Mr. Lin hasn't committed any crime."

"Those people don't talk reason! With them, might makes
right! Tell Mrs. Lin not to worry; Mr. Lin hasn't been mis-
treated yet. But to get him out she'll have to spend a little
money!"

The head of the Merchants Guild held up two fingers, then
quickly departed.

Though he racked his brains, Shou-sheng could see no other
alternative. The two salesmen plagued him with questions, but
he ignored them. He was wondering whether he should report
the words of the head of the Merchants Guild to Mrs. Lin.
Again they had to spend money! While he didn't know
whether Mrs. Lin had any private resources of her own, he was
quite clear as to the financial condition of the shop: After the
local bank got through deducting its eighty per cent from the
cash earned during the past two days, all that was left for the
shop was about fifty dollars. A lot of good that would do!
The head of the Merchants Guild had indicated a bribe of two

hundred dollars. Who knew whether that would be enough! The way things were, even if business should improve even more, it still wouldn't be any use. Shou-sheng felt discouraged.

From the back room, someone was calling him. He decided to go in and size up the situation, and then determined what should be done. He found Mrs. Lin leaning on her daughter's arm.

"Hic — just now — hic — the head of the Merchants Guild came — hic —" she panted. "What did he say?"

"He wasn't here," lied Shou-sheng.

"You can't fool me — hic — I — hic — know everything. Hic — your face is scared yellow! Hsiu saw him — hic!"

"Be calm, Mrs. Lin. He says it's all right. Commissioner Pu is willing to help —"

"What? Hic — hic — What? Commissioner Pu is willing to help! — hic, hic — Merciful goddess — hic — I don't want his help! Hic, hic — I know — Mr. Lin —hic, hic — is finished! Hic — I want to die too! There's only Hsiu — hic — that I'm worried about! Hic, hic — take her with you! — hic! You two go and get married! Hic — hic — Shou-sheng — hic — you take good care of Hsiu and I won't worry about anything! Hic! Go! They want to grab her! — hic — the savage beasts! Goddess Kuanyin, why don't you display your divine power!"

Shou-sheng stared. He didn't know what to say. He thought Mrs. Lin had gone mad, yet she didn't look the least abnormal. His heart beating hard, he stole a glance at Miss Lin. She was blushing scarlet; she kept her head down and made no comment.

"Shou-sheng, Shou-sheng, somebody wants to see you!" an apprentice came running in and announced.

Thinking it was the head of the Merchants Guild or some such personage, Shou-sheng rushed out. To his surprise, he found Mr. Wu, proprietor of the shop across the street, waiting for him. What does he want? wondered Shou-sheng. He fixed his eyes on Mr. Wu's face.

Mr. Wu inquired about Mr. Lin, and then, all smiles, said he was sure it was "not serious." Shou-sheng felt there was something fishy about his smile.

"I've come to buy a little of your merchandise —" The smile had disappeared from Mr. Wu's face and the tone of his voice changed. He produced a sheet of paper from his sleeve. It was a list of over a dozen items — the very things Mr. Lin was featuring in his "One Dollar Package." One look and Shou-sheng understood. So that was the game!

"Mr. Lin isn't here," he said promptly. "I haven't the right to decide."

"Why not talk to Mrs. Lin? That'll be just as good!"

Shou-sheng hesitated to reply. He was beginning to have an inkling of why Mr. Lin had been detained. First there was the rumour that Mr. Lin was planning to run away, then Mr. Lin was arrested, and now the competitor's shop had come to gouge merchandise. There was an obvious connection between these events. Shou-sheng became rather angry, and a bit frightened. He knew that if he agreed to Mr. Wu's request, Mr. Lin's business would be finished, and the heart's blood that he himself had expended would be in vain. But if he refused, what other tricks would be forthcoming? He simply didn't dare to think.

"I'll go and talk to Mrs. Lin, then," he offered tentatively. "But she only operates on a cash basis."

"Cash? Ha, Shou-sheng, of course you're joking?"

"That's the kind of person Mrs. Lin is. I can't do anything with her. The best thing would be for you to come again tomorrow. The head of the Merchants Guild just told me that Commissioner Pu is willing to take a hand in the matter. Mr. Lin probably will be back tonight," said Shou-sheng with cold deliberateness. He shoved the list back in Mr. Wu's hand.

His face twitching, the latter hastily forced the list on Shou-sheng again.

"All right, all right, if it has to be cash then it's cash. I'll take the goods tonight. Cash on delivery."

Scowling, Shou-sheng walked into the back room and told Mrs. Lin about the shop across the street wanting to gouge merchandise.

"When the head of the Merchants Guild was here, he really

said Mr. Lin was fine; he hasn't been through any hardships. But we'll have to spend some money to get him out. There's only fifty dollars in the shop. Now this fellow across the street wants goods — from the looks of his list, about a hundred and fifty dollars' worth. Why not let him have them? The important thing is to get Mr. Lin back as soon as possible!"

Upon hearing that they had to spend money again, tears gushed from Mrs. Lin's eyes, and her hiccups truly shook the heavens with their intensity. Beyond words, she could only wave her hand, while her head, which she rested on the table, resounded alarmingly against the wooden top. Shou-sheng could see that he was getting nowhere, and he quietly withdrew. Miss Lin caught up with him outside the swinging doors. Her face was deathly white, her voice trembling and hoarse.

"Ma is so angry she can't think straight," Miss Lin whispered urgently. "She keeps saying they've already killed Papa! You, you hurry up and agree to what Mr. Wu wants. Save Papa, quick! Shou-sheng, Brother, you —" At this point, her face suddenly flamed scarlet, and she flew back into the room.

In a daze, Shou-sheng stared after her for a full half minute, then he turned away, determined to take the responsibility for selling the merchandise to their competitor. At least Miss Lin agreed with him on what should be done.

The table had already been laid for dinner in the shop, but Shou-sheng had no appetite. As soon as Mr. Wu arrived with the money, Shou-sheng took one hundred dollars in his hand and concealed another eighty dollars on his person, and rushed off to find the head of the Merchants Guild.

Half an hour later Shou-sheng returned with Mr. Lin. Bursting into the "inner sanctum," they nearly startled Mrs. Lin out of her wits. When she saw that it was really Mr. Lin in the flesh, she agitatedly prostrated herself before the porcelain Kuanyin and kowtowed vigorously, pounding her head so loudly that it drowned out the sound of her hiccups. Miss Lin stood to one side, her eyes staring. She looked as if she wanted to laugh and cry at the same time. Shou-sheng took out a paper-wrapped packet and set it on the table.

"This is eighty dollars we didn't have to use."

Mr. Lin sighed. When he finally spoke, his voice was dull. "You should have let me die there and be done with it. Spending more money to get me out! Now we've got no money, we're all going to die anyhow!"

Mrs. Lin jumped up from the ground, excited and wanting to speak. But a string of hiccups blocked the words in her throat. Miss Lin wept quietly, with suppressed sobs. Mr. Lin did not cry. He sighed again and said in a choked voice:

"Our merchandise has been cleaned out! We can't do any business, they're pressing us hard for debts —"

"Mr. Lin!"

It was Shou-sheng who shouted. He dipped his finger in the tea, then wrote on the table the one word — "Go."

Mr. Lin shook his head. Tears flowed from his eyes. He looked at his wife, he looked at his daughter, and again he sighed.

"That's the only way out, Mr. Lin! We can still scrape together a hundred dollars in the shop. Take it with you; it'll be enough for a month or two. I'll take care of what has to be done here."

Although Shou-sheng spoke quietly, Mrs. Lin overheard him. She curbed her hiccups and interjected:

"You go too, Shou-sheng! You and Hsiu. Leave me here alone. I'll fight to the death! Hic!"

Mrs. Lin suddenly appeared remarkably young and healthy; she whirled and ran up the stairs. "Ma!" called Miss Lin, and dashed after her mother. Mr. Lin stared at the stairway, bewildered. He felt he had something important to say, but he was too numb to recall what it was.

"You and Hsiu go together," Shou-sheng urged softly. "Mrs. Lin will worry if Hsiu stays here! She says they want to snatch —"

Tears in his eyes, Mr. Lin nodded. He couldn't make up his mind.

Shou-sheng felt his own eyes smarting. He sighed and walked around the table.

Just then, they heard Miss Lin crying. Startled, Mr. Lin and Shou-sheng rushed up the stairs. Mrs. Lin was coming out of her room with a paper packet in her hand. She went back into the room when she saw them, and said:

"Please come in, both of you. Listen to what I've decided." She pointed at the packet. "In here is my private property — hic — about two hundred dollars. I'm giving you two half. Hic! Hsiu, I give you in marriage to Shou-sheng! Hic — to-morrow, Hsiu and her father will leave together. Hic — I'm not going! Shou-sheng will stay with me a few days, and then we'll see. Who knows how many days I have left to live — hic — So if you both kowtow in my presence, I can set my mind at ease! Hic —"

Mrs. Lin took her daughter by one hand and Shou-sheng by the other, and ordered them to "kowtow." Both did so, their cheeks flaming red; they kept their heads down. Shou-sheng stole a glance at Miss Lin. There was a faint smile on her tear-stained face. His heart thumped wildly, and two tears rolled down from his eyes.

"Good. That's the way it'll be." Mr. Lin heaved a sigh. "But Shou-sheng, when you stay here and deal with those people, be very, very careful!"


VII


The shop of the Lin family had to close down at last. The news that Mr. Lin had run away soon spread all over town. Of the creditors, the local bank was the first to send people to put the stock into custody. They also searched for the account books. Not one was to be found. They asked for Shou-sheng. He was sick in bed. They grilled Mrs. Lin. Her reply was a string of explosive hiccups and a stream of tears. Since she after all enjoyed the social position of "Madam Lin," there was nothing they could do with her.

By about eleven a.m., the horde of creditors in the Lin shop were quarrelling with a tremendous din. The local bank and the other creditors were wrangling as to how to divide the remaining property. Although the stock was nearly gone, the remainder and the furniture and fixtures were enough to repay the creditors about seventy per cent; but each was fighting for a ninety, or even one hundred, per cent for himself. The head of the Merchants Guild had talked until his tongue was a little paralysed, to no avail.

Two policemen arrived and took their stand outside the shop door. Clubs in hand, they barked at the crowd that had gathered to see the excitement.

"Why can't I go in? I've got a three hundred dollar loan in this shop! My savings!" Mrs. Chu argued with a policeman, twisting her withered lips. Tottering, she was elbowing her way through the mass. The blue veins on her forehead stood out as thick as little fingers. She kept pushing. Then suddenly she saw Widow Chang, with her five-year-old baby in her arms, pleading with the other policeman to let her enter. He looked at the widow out of the corners of his eyes, and while feigning to tease the child, furtively rubbed the back of his hand against the widow's breasts.

"Sister Chang —" Mrs. Chu gasped loudly. She sat down on the edge of the stone steps, forcibly moving her puckered mouth.

Tears in her eyes, Widow Chang took an aimless step, which brought into her line of vision Mrs. Chu panting on the edge of the stone stairs. She practically stumbled over to Mrs. Chu and sat down beside her. Then, Widow Chang began to cry and lament:

"Oh, my husband, you've left me alone! You don't know how I'm suffering! The wicked soldiers killed you — it was three years ago the day before yesterday. . . . That cursed Mr. Lin — may he die without sons or grandsons! — has closed his shop! The hundred and fifty dollars that I earned by the toil of my two hands has fallen into the sea and is gone without a sound! Aiya! The lot of the poor is hard, and the rich have no hearts —"

Hearing his mother cry, the child also began to wail. Widow Chang hugged him to her bosom and wept even more bitterly.

Mrs. Chu did not cry. Her sunken red-rimmed eyes glared, and she kept saying frantically:

"The poor have only one life, and the rich have only one life. If they don't give me back my money, I'll fight them to the death!"

Just then, a man pushed his way out of the shop. It was Old Chen. His face was purple. He was cursing as he jostled through the crowd.

"You gang of crooks! You'll pay for this! One day I'll see you all burning in the fires of Hell! If we have to take a loss, everybody should take it together. Even if I got only a small share of what's left, at least that would be fair —"

Still swearing vigorously, he spotted the two women.

"Mrs. Chang, Mrs. Chu, what are you sitting there crying for!" he shouted to them. "They've finished dividing up the property. My one mouth couldn't out-argue their dozen. That pack of jackals doesn't give a damn about what's reasonable. They insist that our money doesn't count —"

His words made Widow Chang weep more bitterly than ever. The playful policeman abruptly walked over to her. He poked her shoulder with his club.

"Hey, what are you crying about? Your man died a long time ago. Which one are you crying for now!"

"Dog farts!" roared Old Chen furiously. "While those people are stealing our money, all a turd like you can do is get gay with women!" He gave the policeman a strong push.

The policeman's nasty eyes went wide. He raised his club to strike, but the crowd yelled and cursed at him. The other policeman ran over and pulled Old Chen to one side.

"It's no use your raising a fuss. We've got nothing against you. The Merchants Guild has ordered us to guard the door. We've got to eat. We can't help it."

"Old Chen, go make a complaint at the Kuomintang office!" a man shouted from the crowd. From the sound of it, it was the voice of Lu, the well-known loafer.

"Go on, go on!" yelled several others. "See what they say to that!"

The policeman who had mediated laughed coldly. He grasped Old Chen by the shoulder. "I advise you not to go looking
for trouble. Going there won't do you any good! You wait
till Mr. Lin comes back and settle things with him. He can't
deny the debt."

Old Chen fumed. He couldn't make up his mind. The
idlers were still shouting for him to "go." He looked at Mrs.
Chu and Widow Chang.

"What do you say? They're always screaming down there
how they protect the poor!"

"That's right," called one of the crowd. "Yesterday they
arrested Mr. Lin because they said they didn't want him to
run away with poor people's money!"

Almost involuntarily, Old Chen and the two women were
swept along by the crowd down the street to the Kuomintang
office. Widow Chang was crying as she walked, and cursing
the wicked soldiers who had killed her husband, and praying
that Mr. Lin should die without sons or grandsons, and reviling
that dirty dog of a policeman!

As they neared the office, they saw four policemen standing
outside the gate with clubs in their hands. The policemen yelled
to them from a distance:

"Go home! You can't go in!"

"We've come to make a complaint!" shouted Old Chen, who
was in the first rank of the crowd. "The shop of the Lin
family has closed down, and we can't get hold of the money
we put up —"

A swarthy pock-marked man jumped out from behind the
policemen and howled for them to attack. But the policemen
stood their ground, restricting themselves to threats. The crowd
in back of Old Chen began to clamour.

"You cheap mongrels don't know what's good for you!"
screamed the pock-marked man. "Do you think we have nothing better to do than bother about your business? If you don't
get out of here, we're going to fire!"

He stamped and yelled at the policemen to use their clubs.
In the front ranks, Old Chen was struck several times. The

crowd milled in confusion. Mrs. Chu was old and weak, and she toppled to the ground. In her panicky haste, Widow Chang lost her slippers. Pushed and buffeted, she also fell down. Rolling and crawling, she avoided many leaping and stamping feet. She scrambled up and ran for all she was worth. It was then she realized that her child was gone. There were drops of blood on the upper part of her jacket.

"Aiya! My precious! My heart! The bandits are killing people! Jade Emperor God save us!"

Wailing, her hair tumbled in disorder, she ran quickly. By the time she fled past the closed door of the shop of the Lin family, she was completely out of her mind.

*June 18, 1932*

# WARTIME

After four in the morning, the rifle and artillery fire ceased. Slowly getting up from the floor, Mr. Li put his right hand behind his back and lightly punched his stiff spine. He groped his way to a chair and sat down. With his head cocked to one side, he fell into a bemused trance.

Following his example, his seven-year-old son got up too, his small behind rising first, then the rest of him. The child's very first step brought him tripping over his little sister's fat leg. He thumped to the floor, emitting so lusty a howl that Mr. and Mrs. Li jumped with fright.

"This place is pitch dark! I don't suppose it would matter if I turned on the light now," Mr. Li said half to himself. Without waiting for his wife's consent, he flipped the switch.

At the sudden flood of light, the little five-year-old girl, who was only half awake, rubbed her eyes with the backs of her chubby hands and began to cry. Mrs. Li glanced at the two-year-old little boy sleeping in her bosom, then reached out a hand and patted her small daughter.

"Don't cry, little sister. We won't let the Japanese soldiers get you! . . ."

The seven-year-old stood before his father, intending to play their old game of riding papa's knee. But seeing how solemn and preoccupied his father looked, the child only leaned lazily against him and imitated the way he cocked his head to one side.

The parents were conversing in low tones.

"We can't hear them any more. Does that mean they've stopped fighting?" asked the mother.

"Who knows! I think I'll go out and take a look."

"No, please don't!"

"It won't hurt to have a little look. I won't go far."

"Don't go, I tell you! Why don't you ever listen to me? All during the daylight hours, people were leaving this part of the city; the foreign concession districts shut their big iron gates. On top of all that, the maid kept insisting she had to get away from here too — I was nearly frantic by the time you came home from the office. But you — free and easy — guaranteed nothing was going to happen! If the maid wants to go, you said, let her go!"

"We should have kept her. Then you wouldn't be afraid of the Japanese."

"Aya! Do you have to try and be funny? You see how nervous I am! Three little tots; somebody has to help carry them. If the maid were here she could carry at least one. Of course we won't be able to take our things —"

"So you still haven't given up the idea of moving away!"

"And you only want to go out and take a look! What good is just looking going to do?"

Mrs. Li was a little angry. The heaving of her breast awoke the two-year-old and he cried. She patted him, crooning, "Mama's here, precious, Mama's here." She shot her husband an aggrieved glance.

Mr. Li hung his head. Frowning, he rubbed his hand on his knee.

"What a mess! If we don't move, we won't feel safe. If we do move, we'll have to spend a lot of money. I never thought they'd really fight. . . ."

"I'm afraid to spend the money too. That's why, even though it was still daylight, I agreed we should stay. We can just count ourselves lucky some shell hasn't hit us!"

Seeing her husband's mournful expression, Mrs. Li regretted she had spoken so sharply. Forcing a smile, she continued, "There hasn't been a sound for a long time now. There probably won't be any big battle. You'd better get some sleep. In a while, you still have to go to the office."

Mr. Li looked at his wife and he too managed a smile, which

he followed with a large yawn. He felt his wife was right. The Japanese soldiers were very fierce and cruel. When they were attacking Shenyang in the Northeast provinces, even though they hadn't met with any resistance, reports said they laid down a huge machine-gun and artillery barrage. Very likely all that firing just now was the same sort of thing. In that case, everything would be peaceful as usual. There wouldn't be any serious clash. The office would be open for business and he would go. Staying home a day he'd lose two silver dollars and fifty cents. What for!

"I'll lie down for a while. Then we'll see."

Mr. Li's wife agreed, and he walked up the stairs, patting his stiff thighs. The seven-year-old boy wanted to follow, but Mrs. Li called him back. She kept the child beside her on the quilts they had spread on the floor, covering him with a blanket.

At the top of the stairs, Mr. Li again became worried. In front of him was a short ladder leading to a small open porch a few feet higher than the level of the upper storey but lower than the roof. He decided he'd better go up and see how things really stood.

No sooner had he opened the porch door than — ping! ping! — two sharp reports. Mr. Li shrunk back and peered through the door crack. Frigid clouds filled the sky; here and there a few cold winter stars glimmered. The wind blowing through the crack was icy. Someone seemed to be standing on the porch of the house next door, surveying the darkened city. Mr. Li took a grip on himself and pulled the folds of his felt hat down over his face until only his eyes were visible. Thus fortified, he eased himself out of the door, crouching and sticking close to the wall. Once outside, he immediately squatted, his ears listening intently.

He thought he heard shouts in the distance, but perhaps it was only the wind. The sky was free of any red glow or black smoke. It was just like any other winter night in the last month of the year. Mr. Li slowly rose to his feet and walked to the low cement railing of the porch to get a better view.

"Is that you, Mr. Li? A little while ago you could see lots of red flashes from up here. Must have been the Japanese artillery, the bastards!"

Mr. Li turned a startled face in the direction of the voice. Only when the man finished speaking did Mr. Li identify him as the fellow who lived in a cramped little room in the house next door. His name was Hsiang and he was a typesetter in the publishing company where Mr. Li was employed. They were both in the same line, so to speak.

"Been up here long?" Mr. Li asked casually, frowning slightly. He strained his eyes, looking in all directions for any sign of a red flash. Although Hsiang was a neighbour and they both worked for the same firm, since one was a "gentleman" in the editorial department and the other only a worker in the printing press, the two seldom met. When they did, an exchange of glances substituted for hailing each other by name. Mr. Li was replying now only out of common politeness; he was not intending to enter into conversation. To his surprise, Hsiang responded with enthusiasm.

"We beat the Japanese!" Hsiang said joyfully.

Mr. Li was electrified. What? Were the Japanese actually beaten? That was rather hard to believe. He turned to face Hsiang. The worker's big white teeth flashed in a grin; he was swinging a clenched fist high.

"We licked 'em. They all ran back to the Japanese concession in the Hongkew district!"

It sounded convincing, but Mr. Li had to ask, "How do you know?"

"The cop on the corner outside our lane said so. Besides, I saw —"

"You saw what? What did you see?"

"I saw lots of 19th Route Army men going north. People said they were going to help the soldiers holding the railway station at Tientungan. The Japanese attacked at Paoshan Road, and they were knocked back there too. They had to retreat to Fusheng Road and take cover."

"Oh? Well. . . ." Mr. Li was still a little sceptical. But

he finally knew why the artillery had seemed to be coming from all sides a few hours ago. He and his wife and kids had tumbled out of bed and rushed downstairs to the parlour to sleep on the floor. Their house was directly between two lines of fire! Controlling himself with an effort, Mr. Li sighed.

"It's turned into a big affair. The Japanese certainly won't be willing to quit. . . ."

"Then we'll fight the sons of bitches!"

The words had just left Hsiang's mouth when two sharp reports split the air, followed by the crack of other rifles returning the compliment. Mr. Li froze for an instant, then quickly squatted low, his legs trembling.

"Hah! They've started again," he heard Hsiang shout. "Let 'em have it! Kill the Japanese dogs!"

But after a brief exchange, silence again reigned in the night. To Mr. Li the quiet was like an iron slab pressing down on his heart. Still squatting, he shifted his feet uneasily and rose a little. The best thing to do, he thought, was to hurry back down the stairs and talk to his wife about getting out in the morning. Just then, a gust of wind struck his face. Overwrought, he stifled a cry and dropped back to his squatting position. A machine-gun began chattering to the north. Even though Mr. Li's ears were covered by the thick felt of his pulled down hat, the sound nearly deafened him. He was sure the machine-gun was very near. And the porch had to face north, of course! In a cold sweat, Mr. Li squatted motionless. He didn't dare move, but he was afraid that if he didn't move he'd be killed on his own porch. Rat-ta-ta-ta, boom! boom! Wrapping his arms around his head, Mr. Li leaped up, but immediately fell forward like a log. Frantically, he crawled through the porch door and tumbled down the small ladder. He uttered one loud squawk, then seemed to lose consciousness.

"Ayo, my poor husband! Ayo, ayo! . . ."

The wails from downstairs shocked Mr. Li's numbed senses back to life. The machine-gun was silent now; there was only occasional scattered rifle fire. Feeling his head, Mr. Li found it intact. He clutched the banister and staggered down the stairs. Sobbing tragically, his wife threw herself on his bosom. He held her a moment, then sat down gingerly on the lowest step.

"My dear, what happened to you? Where were you wounded? Where were you wounded?"

"I'm all right," Mr. Li replied in a shaking voice.

A single question was nipping at his heart like a bedbug — How can we get away from here in the morning?

## II

It was almost daybreak. The five-year-old and the seven-year-old were curled up under the blanket sleeping peacefully. The two-year-old baby, lying in his mother's arms, began to gurgle and sing. He obviously enjoyed the whole family sleeping on the floor together. It made such a nice big bed!

Outside in the compound, the cockerel they were keeping for their New Year's Day dinner, crowed loudly.

Mr. Li lay on his back, staring with red-rimmed eyes he hadn't closed all night. He frowned but did not speak.

The tramping of footsteps on the street beyond the lane's high solid iron gate didn't stop for a single second. The floor beneath Mr. Li's head seemed to vibrate with their tread. Noisy conversations drew abreast of the big gate, drifted past it.

Mrs. Li sat up, holding the two-year-old. Too listless to respond to his chortles, she automatically rocked back and forth. After a minute, she turned to Mr. Li.

"Have you figured out how we'll travel?"

"Wait till it's light, and I'll ask. There's bound to be at least one road open from this part of the city to the foreign concessions."

Mr. Li's voice was hoarse. He rolled over and faced his wife. "There hasn't been any shooting for an hour. Maybe they'll talk peace today," he said with a wry smile. "If the British or the American Consul comes out and mediates, there's a good chance the fighting'll end."

"Weren't you saying all day yesterday there wouldn't be any fighting? Then last night it started!"

"Well, all right. As soon as it's light, we'll move to the foreign concessions for a few days."

Mr. Li was already calculating how much it would cost to live in a hotel. Two adults and three children — one small room at a dollar or so a day would be enough. They'd probably spend another dollar a day on meals. He had over sixty dollars on hand; they could easily get by for nine or ten days. Anyhow, Mr. Li was sure the fighting would be over long before then. Shanghai was a big cosmopolitan city, and the eyes of the whole world were on it now. Would a battle be allowed to go on in a place like this for as long as nine or ten days? Mr. Li just couldn't believe it.

He kept his conviction to himself, however. Yesterday's prediction had discredited him badly. This "new" hope he retained as a private consolation.

Having reached this point in his rationalization, Mr. Li felt somewhat better. Exhausted by his sleepless night, he groggily closed his eyes.

Less than ten minutes later, he woke with a start. Voices were clamouring in the lane; a deep powerful sound droned almost directly overhead. Mr. Li and his wife exchanged a frightened glance, unable to imagine what new disaster had struck. They heard people running and shouting in the street, right outside the gate of their lane.

"Japanese bombers coming! Go home and take shelter!"

"Take shelter! Scatter! Bunching together you're sure to be bombed!"

Wildly running footsteps, followed by several loud bangs, very close by. People were slamming their doors and gates shut, but Mr. and Mrs. Li mistook the noise for exploding bombs, and their faces went green.

Nearer and nearer came the planes, engines throbbing. Now they were right overhead. Except for the roaring engines, alternately increasing and fading in volume, the lane was deathly quiet. Mr. Li and his wife sat back to back on the bedding spread on the floor. Stretching his neck, the two-year-old baby was listening too, his eyes frightened and staring. The two older children still slept peacefully beneath the blanket. Mr. Li's whole family was here before him, all in one tight little group. If a bomb should drop now —

His blood froze in his veins. He didn't dare think any further.

It was already quite light, though there was no sun. Rain had fallen the night before and a pale grey curtain was stretched across the sky. The planes had gone, apparently. Only their faint droning could still be heard in the distance. After a while, that was gone too. Mr. Li heaved a sigh, again listened carefully. Those machine-guns and artillery pieces that nearly scared the life out of him the previous night were completely at rest. A babel of voices again rose in the lane, and on the street beyond the big gate footsteps resumed once more.

"What shall we do? I wonder what it's like, travelling on the streets? . . ." Mrs. Li said to herself, but aloud. She looked at the baby in her arms and the two children sleeping beneath the blanket.

Mr. Li stood up. "The only thing to do is go out and see. Nobody'll come and tell you, just sticking in the house!" His eyes seemed to be pleading for his wife's consent. He patted the long fleece-lined gown he was wearing and got ready to leave.

Mrs. Li could think of no better alternative. Her only answer was a sigh. She shut her eyes to hold back the tears.

Afraid to wander too far, Mr. Li made a brief tour of the lane. Last night his neighbours, like himself, had not intended to run away either. Now many of them, carrying children and bundles, were moving out. Someone said the Taiyang Temple Road was still open, and Mr. Li felt much better. He walked to the lane's entrance. The big iron gate was already closed, but the small door through it remained open. Two policemen standing in the street raised their faces from time to time to peer at the sky. Many were leaving the lane; practically none

were coming in. People walked along the street in twos and
threes — from the looks of them, all on their way to the
"foreign concessions." Standing in the doorway of the iron
gate, Mr. Li called to the policemen.

"Are the streets from here passable?"

"Sure!"

"Not dangerous, is it?"

"Hard to say."

"Have they stopped fighting?"

"Just listen!"

Mr. Li's heart leaped. He strained his ears. There were
a few faint rifle shots. He listened again. Only silence. He
looked up at the sky. High to the north were three tiny planes,
chasing each other in a circle like mating dragonflies. Then
they formed a straight line and slowly grew larger. He could
hear the sound of their engines now. Soon he could see the red
dots on each of their silver wings; their ominous droning was
terrifying. A detachment of marching soldiers immediately
scattered and pressed themselves close to the walls of the houses
lining the street. Mr. Li turned and ran. Just as he reached
his own front door, he heard the first distant explosion.

Boom!

"Go, go, go!" Mr. Li chattered to the frightened wife
rushing to meet him. He was very pale. His legs suddenly
went soft and he sank to the floor in a heap, panting hard.

Mrs. Li could no longer restrain her tears. Picking up the
baby, she burst into muffled helpless sobs.

In the distance, they heard it again.

Boom! Boom!

Mr. Li jumped up, his face as white as a sheet. Silently he
picked up the older boy and the little boy. Mrs. Li carried the
girl. They ran into the lane. When they reached the entrance
way, it was jammed with people. Both the big iron gate and
the small door were shut tight. Outside, the policeman was
shouting:

"Don't get excited! Stay in your houses! Running around
in the open is just asking for it!"

At the gate, men were yelling, women screaming. A plane, its engine thrumming, appeared over the rear end of the lane and flew towards two rising columns of black smoke in the north. After circling the smoke, the plane suddenly plummeted downwards. The crowd inside the gate set up a cheer. But in another instant the plane came out of the smoke in a steep climb and turned east. And immediately following — Boom!

Mr. Li was panicky, irresolute. His children cried and complained they were hungry. Putting them down, he conferred with his wife. Better go back to the house and wait a while. If they were killed it would be because Fate intended it that way! He asked people about the Taiyang Temple Road and was told it was blocked. The only route open to the "foreign concessions" was a wide detour via Tsaochiatu, a ten-mile trip. Steeling himself, Mr. Li decided to risk it.

Bringing the three children into the house, Mr. Li told his wife to feed them. He himself went upstairs to pack some of his books and clothing. He was thinking more clearly now. With no means of transport but his own two legs, he would have to cover ten miles, carrying three kids besides. He decided he had better leave the books behind and just pick out a few changes of clothing. At first he packed all his better clothes in a large bundle, but after weighing it in his hands, came to the conclusion that it was too heavy. With a sigh, he selected only enough to tide him over a few days and made a parcel of it. Even so, it still seemed heavier than his five-year-old daughter. There were ten miles of difficult road ahead of him. For the third time he sorted his clothing. In the end, he picked only a few shirts and sets of underwear and the gown which his wife liked the best. The bundle now was no bigger than a pillow.

Wiping the sweat from his face, Mr. Li went to close the window. The sun shone weakly through the pall of black smoke that covered the sky. He was sure there must be a big fire somewhere, but his mind was too dull to give it much thought. Taking his small bundle, he went downstairs.

The three children had already eaten their fill. Holding on to a chair for support, the youngest was chattering animatedly in a language all his own. The two elder children were out playing in the courtyard, chasing things that flew like small black butterflies. As Mr. Li watched his three lively little youngsters, he was oppressed by the thought that this happy home which he had spent ten difficult years building might be blotted out in an instant by a shell or a bomb. Tears came to his eyes.

Suddenly, Mrs. Li came running out of the kitchen, a dish-cloth still in her hand.

"Do you know what happened? Do you know?" she cried, distraught. "The Commercial Press was bombed! The whole plant is in flames!"

"What! Then that big fire is at the Press? Who says so?"

"Hsiang's wife, next door!"

The seven-year-old boy bounded into the parlour with the little black things he had caught in the courtyard, his little sister right behind him. Mr. Li's eyes opened wide. Those black butterflies were bits of burnt paper! It was all clear to him now. His heart beat fast. The Japanese had smashed his livelihood, they had broken his rice bowl! Destroying China's biggest publishing house, they had broken the rice bowls of thousands of workers and employees! A savage laugh burst from Mr. Li's lips; his pale face became tinged with an angry purple.

"Those Japanese have gone too far!" he cried.

He forgot all about the danger of bombs. His "rice bowl" was broken. What more was there to fear! He rushed out of the door, why or where he had no idea, nor did he care.

Mrs. Li ran after him. "Don't go out!" she wailed. "Where are you going?" But the howls of all three kids bawling in unison pulled her back to the house.

Mr. Li ran to the entrance of the lane in one breath. Hsiang and another printing-press worker were just coming in. Mr. Li greeted Hsiang like a long-lost friend.

"What's the fire like at the Press?"

"Dozens of big blazes!" Hsiang retorted angrily. He was in the uniform of the plant's fire-fighters. His clothing was half drenched, his face brick-red. On his head was a bright brass helmet. Wiping his mouth with the back of his hand, he said hotly:

"Japanese bombs fell like rain. Wherever they burst, fires started. There were fires all over the place. Our fire-fighting squad couldn't handle them all. And the Japanese wouldn't let fire-engines through from the concessions. The dirty bastards! I'm going to show those dogs a thing or two!"

"Plant Five is the only one left now," put in Hsiang's workmate, "but sooner or later the Japanese'll bomb that too!"

Mr. Li didn't know the man's name but recognized him as another typesetter. Mr. Li's heart was pounding hard. It seemed to grow bigger with each beat. Standing with these two valiants, Mr. Li felt like a new man.

"The Japanese planes take off from Hongkew Park," he grated. "We ought to smash into there. Then we'd fix 'em!"

Hsiang was confident. "That's just what we're going to do! Today, the 19th Route Army'll drive the Japanese back to their ships!" His big teeth flashed in a laugh.

"And the Army doesn't have to worry about men," said Hsiang's friend. "We'll all join! The plant's burned down and we're out of work. But we're not leaving Shanghai. We're going to fight the Japanese!"

Mr. Li's thumping heart grew larger still; the blood rushed to his face. At that moment his wife arrived, leading two children by the hand. Hsiang's wife was carrying the baby. Mr. Li frowned, then he sighed. He looked at the muscular physique of Hsiang and his workmate, then at his own white hands. The difference was too great. "Each must go his own way in life." Recalling the old axiom, Mr. Li felt much less ashamed.

His only problem now was how to travel down Chungshan Road and get across Tsaochiatu. Plane engines, now near, now far, could still be heard overhead.

## III

Although the second and third Japanese assaults were defeated, it became more obvious daily that the enemy would not be driven back to their ships as Hsiang believed. The Chinese troops held only the Chinese section of the city, while enemy soldiers swaggered about Hongkew, the Japanese concession, and awaited reinforcements from Japan.

One day, Japanese planes bombed the Chapei district. A dozen fires sprang up in the neighbourhood of Paoshan Road; by nightfall, they still crimsoned half the sky. This bombing enraged Hsiang much more than the destruction of the Commercial Press. He and his workmate Chun-sheng felt like throwing themselves into the blaze and beating out the fires with their bare hands. They had no fire hose, no pump, no water. Flames spread to the most densely populated section of Paoshan Road and consumed the hovels of the workers. None of them had that essential qualification for finding shelter in the "foreign concessions" — money! Countless refugees had to sleep in the streets on the perimeter of the blaze. The Japanese planes bombed every place that was thickly congregated. Chapei was turned into a field of rubble, Chapei was turned into a hell on earth!

Though the section where Hsiang lived did not catch fire, it was without water or electricity. He had also run out of food. None of these problems disturbed him, however. He and Chun-sheng were busy loading trucks with ammunition and gifts from the people for the 19th Route Army. Hsiang almost forgot that he had a wife waiting at home with nothing to eat.

Every day there was news of ships arriving with fresh Japanese reinforcements. But no reinforcements came for the Chinese troops. When a man was killed they were just short one more soldier. Hsiang and the other workers nearly went mad with rage. They realized it was a pure daydream to think the Chinese forces could drive the Japanese back to their ships. Now it would be a miracle if the defenders could even hold on to Chapei.

But the workers were not downhearted. Though their bellies were half-empty, they put everything they had into their jobs.

The day of the four-hour armistice, early in the morning, Hsiang went running to find Chun-sheng.

"I'm sending my wife away!" Hsiang announced resolutely.

"She'll starve to death, you nitwit! Out by herself like that, she'll be helpless."

"I've asked a friend from my old village to take her back there," said Hsiang. He spat angrily.

Chun-sheng silently looked up at the sky. The men were sitting by the wall of the flame-blackened shell of a house. A truck heavily laden with furniture and household goods rolled past them down the street. The wealthy took refuge in the "foreign concessions" in proper style. Hsiang spat again.

A soldier on leave from the front had wandered over while the two workers were talking. Munching a large wheatcake, he joined in the conversation.

"Got any other relatives in your village?" he asked Hsiang.

"Not a one."

"Hah! Then you're practically telling your wife to shift for herself."

"I can't help it. Chapei's been burned to the ground, tens of thousands of poor people have been killed — didn't they all have mothers and fathers who loved them? Who can worry about a wife at a time like this? I hate those rotten Japanese! I'll fight them to the death — it's them or me!"

The soldier nodded solemnly.

"Do you think we can get into your outfit?" Hsiang asked him. "We can fight the Japanese together!"

The question had been on Hsiang's mind for several days. He and Chun-sheng had discussed it a number of times and had asked the man in charge of their work brigade about joining the army. He told them it wasn't as simple as all that; you couldn't just join whenever you felt like it. They then barged in and made application at a branch of the Shanghai Volunteers, but were rejected because they hadn't brought any letters of identification from their factory or union. They hadn't followed up on this however because they learned the Volunteers were not to be sent to the front. It came as a surprise to them that men who were willing to risk their lives fighting the Japanese needed to go to so much trouble, and even required a special introduction.

"Know how to handle a rifle?" the soldier asked Hsiang and Chun-sheng.

"We were a couple of months in the workers' detachment in '27!" Chun-sheng replied excitedly. "— When we fought off the warlord army of Chang Tsung-chang!" Beside him, Hsiang was grinning with satisfaction.

"I'll speak to my platoon leader," said the soldier.

That afternoon, Hsiang and a few dozen other workers were sent to the town of Miaohong, a few miles out of Shanghai, to dig trenches. This hardly satisfied Hsiang's thirst for action, but he worked hard, ripping out great shovelfuls of earth. Pausing to wipe the sweat from his face, he noticed something in the sky.

"Planes!" he said to Chun-sheng. "Are they Japanese or ours?"

Five black dots circled buzzing overhead. As they flew lower, the red suns on their silver wings became visible. Japanese, of course. They were directly above the workers now. The men glanced up at them, then went on with their digging.

Working vigorously, Hsiang was soon dripping sweat. He rested the shovel against his leg and spat on his hands.

"Son of a bitch!" he swore. "Why did we wait till they got all their troops in position before starting to dig trenches out here?"

"The idea now is to hit 'em so hard they'll never come back!" a worker beside him laughed, giving Hsiang a wink.

"If we'd pushed on through Hongkew that day and driven them to their ships, we could've saved ourselves lots of grief," Chun-sheng put in. "Chapei wouldn't have been burned down and thousands of people'd still be alive today!" Angrily he tossed a shovelful of earth out of the trench.

"Chapei's in ashes now and all those people are dead," said

Hsiang bitterly. "The rest of us'll be dead too if we don't kill the Japanese!" He picked up his shovel.

A raucous voice above the trench suddenly barked:

"Stop your blasted gabbing!"

It was the overseer of the labour gang, carrying a long bamboo switch. He glared at them a few seconds, then stamped away. The workers continued digging, digging, digging. Sweat rained from their foreheads, soaking into the grey-brown clay, but their arms never stopped.

When the battle at Miaohong started, Hsiang and Chun-sheng both had an opportunity to go to the front. But they were ordered to carry the wounded, not guns. Artillery shells whistled over their heads, they could see the flame spat by coughing machine-guns. They made trip after trip, carrying wounded soldiers to the rear and loading them on to trucks.

"What does it all add up to, Hsiang?" Chun-sheng asked during an enemy artillery barrage. "A shell lands and bang! — a man is finished!"

"As long as you help beat the Japanese, and stop them from getting through, it adds up to your being a blinking hero!"

Hsiang had become friendly with the soldiers. He saw that they had no thought of retreat, and weren't afraid to die. The Japanese would never pierce our lines! Feeling quite assured, Hsiang was even a little less angry about not having a chance to shoulder a gun.

In several days of fierce fighting, Japanese artillery virtually levelled the town of Miaohong. But the Chinese soldiers stuck to their posts. Their lines seemed to be made of iron. Hsiang and Chun-sheng were especially happy because their sweat had watered the digging of those trenches. Their efforts had not been in vain. What's more, they were almost certain they would be called to take direct part in the fight; for casualties were mounting by the day and our ranks had thinned out considerably.

In their dreams the two workers saw murderous Japanese tanks come rumbling towards them, and themselves, leaping out of the trench, throwing hand grenades. The tanks were blown to smithereens, and they would wake up smiling.

But the fighting around Miaohong gradually died down. The Japanese, having been knocked back with heavy losses each time they attacked the town, changed their tactics. Hsiang and Chun-sheng were happy, but a little disappointed that their dreams about the grenade throwing couldn't come true for the time being. They were transferred to another sector — Patsechiao. The situation was tense there and a great many workers were needed. Hsiang and his mates were put to carrying food and ammunition.

The battle grew fiercer every day. It was rumoured that a Japanese general, Shirakawa, had arrived with three full divisions, supported by a fleet of over a dozen war vessels. The Japanese attacked on all fronts, laying down a heavy artillery barrage against the Chinese lines. The Chinese stuck to their positions, their casualties mounting by the hour. Taking ammunition to the front and carrying the wounded back, Hsiang and his mates hadn't slept for several nights. They didn't even have time to think. They worked mechanically with only one idea in their minds — die but never retreat!

Hsiang was in a labour detachment of fifty or sixty men. One night, laden with artillery shells, they followed the march of the army unit to which they were attached. They walked very quickly. A sickle moon hung in the sky; there were a few stars and grey drifting clouds. Travel was difficult over the bumpy road. Following in the wake of the troops, the workers mechanically kept pace as usual. But gradually they began to feel that something different was in the air. The thunder of the big guns was growing fainter; it required a real effort to hear them at all.

Conscious of the peculiar atmosphere, Hsiang was puzzled. After marching a little longer, he couldn't contain himself. He poked Chun-sheng, who was walking beside him.

"What's up?" Hsiang asked in a whisper. "Have we taken the wrong road? I can't hear the artillery any more!"

"I've just been wondering about that myself! We seem to be going towards the rear, not forward."

"They must be sending us to another front," a porter behind Hsiang interjected.

Hsiang wasn't so sure and only made a noncommittal sound. A man in front of him laughed shortly. Turning his head, he said:

"You're all way off the track! I've heard something, only I don't know whether it's true or not. — The Japanese are too strong for us. We can't hold this line any more. We're retreating to our second line of defence!"

Hsiang was shocked.

"Second line? Where's that?" Chun-sheng demanded.

"Not far, but not exactly near either. I heard it's Kunshan!"

Hsiang snorted. He was speechless and his face was pale. His red-rimmed eyes looked ready to drip blood. Just then seven or eight mounted men came galloping up from behind and clattered past the work detachment. They were followed by rumbling artillery caissons and hundreds of foot soldiers, marching in close formation.

Hsiang knew the score now. He flung his porter's pole to the ground. The whole detachment of workers halted to look at him. His eyes big with anger, Hsiang shouted:

"Retreat? Chapei's been gutted; Kiangwan and Woosung have been burned to the ground. Are we going to let the Japanese get away with that? We can't retreat! We have to hold on if it kills us! We're going to fight the Japanese, we're not going to run!"

Still yelling, he rushed after the retreating soldiers. Chun-sheng hadn't been able to restrain him, and now, also shouting, he started to follow. But before Chun-sheng had taken five paces, the labour detachment leader caught him and flung him to the ground.

"Are you tired of living!"

As Chun-sheng rolled to his knees, he was struck a hard blow on the head. His ears rang and everything went black. He heard loud angry voices in the distance, then a few sharp reports of a pistol. Chun-sheng lost consciousness.

## IV

After all Chinese soldiers within a radius of twelve miles of Shanghai had withdrawn, the fighting stopped. Innumerable meetings were held to discuss terms for ending the war; finally a draft agreement was signed. Chapei lay in ruins; from all over the city came cries, varying in degree of enthusiasm, calling for the restoration of Shanghai. China's losses had been severe. Reams of statistics were published in the local newspapers. The Commercial Press alone had been damaged to the extent of sixteen million dollars.

In any event a large institution like the Commercial Press — a publishing enterprise, a cultural institution — simply had to be put back into operation. It ran an announcement in the newspapers: The Press was discharging all its old employees; it would begin hiring, on a new basis, after repairs were completed. As to "retirement bonuses" for those being discharged, because of "the heavy losses the Press had suffered in the nation's time of trial," it would not be able to pay on the originally agreed terms.

This brought an immediate response from the more than five thousand former employees of the Press, including Mr. Li, who was now living in a small rented room in the French Concession. Mr. Li became very busy. His fellow employees formed an organization to demand payment of the retirement bonus in full. Mr. Li naturally took part. They inserted an announcement in the press denouncing their employer's unilateral action, they sent representatives to confer with officers of the company, they tried to enlist public support, they gave press conferences, they petitioned the Social Bureau of the municipal government. . . . In all of this, Mr. Li participated. He had been with the Press for over ten years and had a retirement bonus of more than a thousand dollars due to him. He was so busy

running around that he didn't have even a moment to help his
wife with their two-year-old.

After two months of wrangling the Press offered what it
described as a magnanimous concession. It knocked a tiny
fraction off the huge cut it had already decided to make in the
bonuses; beyond this it positively would not go. Now, even
if Mr. Li wanted to be busy, he had nothing to occupy him.
He could only sit in the dark damp of his narrow little room
and sigh. His wife berated him for having wasted his time
and money on missions for the discharged employees'
organization.

Mr. Li stamped. "What do women know anyway!" His
temper wasn't too good lately.

Again the company published an announcement. On a
certain date, at a certain address on Szechuan Road, it would
begin paying the retirement bonuses. The money would be
waiting.

The union countered with its own announcement, stating that
the dispute had not yet been settled and warning its members
not to draw the money at Szechuan Road. Moreover, it decided
to post a few men near the place to stop any of its members
who might weaken, and persuade them to change their minds.

Mr. Li was sure he was not one of those who would need
persuasion. But when asked to serve as a persuader of others,
he was afraid he couldn't measure up to the job. He spent his
time, therefore, sitting in the cramped little room, waiting for
news of the outcome.

Mrs. Li was fully occupied with cooking and washing, and
the three children tumbled riotously on the room's only bed.
Too dispirited to bother about them, Mr. Li borrowed a newspaper from his next-door neighbour to read the advertisements.
Blurbs about new books and magazines of the small publishing
houses spread over a page and a half. The publishing world
had made a lively come-back once the fighting stopped — or
so it seemed to Mr. Li. The thought comforted him. But his
hand instinctively moved to his much flattened wallet, and
Mr. Li frowned. He skimmed idly through the pages of the

newspaper, then turned back to the company's "money waiting" announcement. . . .

Three days later, the company inserted another announcement in the press. It said that it had already paid out many thousand dollars, and gave the figure; it hoped that the few who had not yet drawn their money would do so immediately; it was extending its offer one final week. . . . When he read this, Mr. Li's heart leaped; the newspaper fell to the floor. It seemed to him that he was the only one holding out so stubbornly. What for? He had five mouths to feed, the landlord wanted his rent, and here he was, flat broke! Raising his head, he looked at his wife, cleaning vegetables in the family washbasin.

"I suppose I'd better go and pick up that money. What do you say?"

"I'm a woman. What do I know anyway!" She hadn't forgotten the remark he had made a few days before. Lately, her temper hadn't been too good either!

Mr. Li smiled a lonely smile, then took their last twenty cents and went out.

An hour later, he was at Szechuan Road, furtively entering the company's temporary office.

When he came out, there was a little over a hundred dollars in his wallet. His hand pressing his pocket, he stepped briskly, his backbone a bit straighter. He could see that Szechuan Road was still the gay colourful street it had always been.

Suddenly, from behind, a tragic voice assailed his ears.

"Give me back my Hsiang!"

Mr. Li automatically stopped and turned around. There stood a woman, oddly dressed, her hair wildly awry, ashenfaced, the whites of her rolled-up eyes gleaming. It was the wife of his former neighbour Hsiang! The events of those two frightening days of the bombardment flooded back to him.

"Give me my Hsiang," the woman cried piercingly. "You know where he is!"

"But I don't —"

The woman bared her teeth in a terrifying laugh that made Mr. Li's heart race. Staring straight ahead, she began to wail.

"You do know! You're in the gang that schemed against him! You got your share, don't deny it! You know! Ha-ha, I know you do!... Hsiang, they all want to suck up to the Japanese, they made a fool of you, you died for nothing! ... I know you all ganged up on Hsiang, don't deny it! You're in it too. Today I've found you out, don't deny it!"

Mr. Li shuddered, his heart pounding. Hastily he turned and walked away, not daring to look back.

"You all plotted against him! You can't deny it!..."

*September 8, 1932*

# BIG NOSE

Of the three million people in Greater Shanghai our hero probably ranked the lowest of all.

We used to see him sneaking through the big, darkly gleaming iron gates of some expensive housing development, some "Heights" or "Village" of three-storey buildings that boasted of "modern plumbing." He'd steal to the big cement garbage bin, along with the stray dogs, and search its mildewed contents for anything of "value." If he could snatch a bone with a bit of meat on it before the dogs got it he would examine it carefully. Usually it was so filthy he had to throw it back to the dogs — who had much higher capabilities of self-preservation. On rare occasions he might find a rotten apple or half an old turnip — things which the dogs scorned. These would delight him so, his thin dirty little fingers would tremble.... Like the dogs he too would crouch and peer into the small door at the bottom of the cement garbage bin. Perhaps he might catch a glimpse of something glittering — an old bottle, or a broken toy that a rich child had discarded. Then he would even forget his hunger for the moment and stretch his thin little arm into the bin and claw and dig, wishing he could shove his whole body through the small door in his eagerness. But usually at that time his backside would receive a kick from a thick leather sole, which experience had taught him probably belonged to the watchman of the "Heights" or the "Village." And so, together with the dogs with their tails between their legs, he would scurry out of the darkly gleaming big iron gates, and look for another place to continue his risky occupation.

When he was lucky, he might avoid the eye of the watchman and slip to the back door of one of the three-storey houses with their "modern plumbing." And if the door were open and the cook happened to be coming out to dump last night's left-overs into the refuse pail, he would try to speak to her. Though his voice would be so low that it was almost inaudible, the cook would understand what he wanted. Then he would either get half a bowl of thin gruel, or a dirty look, or a sympathetic — yet to him quite useless — remark:

"Run along! I can't give you anything. People pay money for this stuff. They sell it to farmers for swill."

All these events took place as a rule in the early morning while rich little boys and girls were still asleep in their cosy beds.

Later in the day we might see him on a busy corner, following some big-bellied gentleman and his sleek lady, stepping smartly on her high-heeled shoes. In a low quavering voice, the child would be pleading:

"Mister, Mrs., do a good deed. . . ."

Or at the approach to the bridge that spans Soochow Creek we might observe him suddenly shoot out from the crowds like a little mouse and dash to the rickshaw straining up the incline. And as he helps the rickshawman pull to the top of the rise, he turns to the passenger and entreats:

"Please, do a good deed!"

For this labour he might get a copper at most, or perhaps nothing at all.

But even such attempts to work for a living were dangerous. If a policeman saw the child he might educate him with his club. Or if the policeman decided to "do a good deed" and pretended not to notice, other children at either end of the bridge might not be so conciliatory. Older than our hero and more experienced, they would swear at him and hit him. This then was his "freedom to work"!

Even in this risky occupation there were those who had "exclusive franchises" in fixed sections of the commercial territory, and behind the scenes each of them had his boss. There was no free competition in this business!

Yet there were other times when our hero was extremely successful.

Usually that was when only the red and green neon signs still gleamed on the main thoroughfares, and the sole illumination of secluded little alleys were small dim street bulbs coldly gleaming at their entrances. Then our hero, perhaps by coincidence, would join forces in one of the dark alleys with five, six, or even ten comrades of the same age, and lie in wait. They would wait and wait until a bus-boy went by, carrying dishes back to his restaurant from some late supper customers. Like his ambushers, the boy seldom was more than twelve or thirteen years old. Most of the time the dishes he carried were empty and the dark bronze rice bucket hadn't enough left in it to fill one small stomach. If luck was good, however, there still might be a little gravy in the bowls or a few bones and some wilted vegetables; maybe the bucket actually contained enough cold rice to appease the appetite of a healthy dog. Because superiority rested with our hero and his comrades, the boy never resisted. Our hero could then partially satisfy his hunger. After licking the oily dishes clean, he would run off, cheering in triumph.

But mostly our hero's daily fare consisted of curses, beatings and kicks. No stray dog suffered a harder lot.

## II

How many children like our hero lived among the three million population of Greater Shanghai we don't quite know.

Or, to put it another way, among the three million population of Greater Shanghai, how many children were comfortably sleeping in their cosy beds while our hero was being kicked by a watchman because he was scrabbling through a rubbish heap to get hold of one of their discarded toys — of this we're not sure either. Nor need we concern ourselves for the moment with whether there was not much difference between the two numbers, or whether the children peacefully sleeping in their beds were somewhat in the minority.

But one thing we know beyond any doubt: Of the three million population of Greater Shanghai there were three to four hundred thousand children about the same age as our hero working in silk factories, in match factories, in electric-light bulb factories and various other kinds of factories. From six in the morning to six at night the machines drank their blood! And it is no exaggeration to say that their blood was the food and nourishment of the peacefully sleeping rich little children, as well as the slumberers' fathers and mothers.

When our hero watched the shrivelled youngsters slowly emerging through the gate of some bulb factory or other, if his stomach was rumbling with hunger, he might envy them. He knew they had a home to return to, even if it were only a matshed. At least they would get a rough bran cake of some sort, at least they could sleep under something that passed for a roof until five the next morning.

Of course it never occurred to him that in another few years, after the machines had drained dry the blood of these children he so envied, they would be spewed out on to the streets, without even the ability to battle with the dogs for bones, without even the strength to help push a rickshaw over the bridge.... But why talk about that? Let us get back to our hero.

Though he had a home when he was born, he didn't remember it clearly. He had a faint recollection of the year war came to Shanghai and "iron birds" dropped incendiary bombs. Some fell on the high buildings, but many more fell on the quarter where the poor people lived. And then he didn't have any home.

His papa and mama disappeared then too — where, he didn't know. He couldn't remember what they looked like; he was only about seven when he lost them. But even while they were still around, he had never got a good look at them. They always left before daylight and returned after dark. They too fed machines somewhere.

He could never forget however that he once had a papa and mama, nor could he forget the disaster that took them away, and who was responsible for it. He also remembered how, after papa and mama were gone, he and a large crowd of old women and children were sent to a place where they were given a bit of thin gruel or, at times, mouldy bran cakes. After six months or so, a pompous gentleman suddenly called them all into a room and questioned them one by one. He remembered being asked, when his turn came:

"Do you have a home?"

He shook his head.

"Do you have any relatives?"

Again he shook his head.

Whereupon the pompous gentleman shook his head too, made a mark on a sheet of paper and called the next number.

A few days later, our hero dazedly found himself on the street. With no clear purpose in mind, he joined a gang of other children in the same condition. Sometimes they got along well, sometimes they fought among themselves. At times he teamed up with wild dogs, at times he fought against them. That was how he had been living for several years, and he had grown used to it. He had a vague feeling that people like him probably were intended to exist like that.

## III

And so we can see that our hero's life, while apparently most unusual, actually was quite ordinary. Every day he had great adventures, but no reporter of even the most sensation-mongering paper ever considered them of any news value.

Well then, let us pick an "extraordinary event" ourselves from his most unusual and yet quite ordinary life.

What month or year it was we cannot say for sure. Anyhow it was on a day that was neither hot nor cold, a fine day without wind or rain and not too much sun.

The reason why that day is worthy of being designated an extraordinary one in his life is due to the following circumstances:

About two in the afternoon of the day in question he sat dozing in the sun against the wall of a small brick building — one of Shanghai's public toilets. This was his place. He had found it and shed blood to establish his right to it. There's a little history connected with his discovery. When he saw this lovely public toilet for the first time many months before, he was surprised. Being illiterate, he couldn't read the sign it bore. He wondered whether this neat little building was someone's home or the office of a business corporation. A fat man in a long black gown went in, then a policeman with a pistol belt, then a gentleman in European dress — ho! all important people, high society people who had the right to kick him any time they felt like. Afraid of drawing too near, he decided the building must be at least an office, and he gazed at it with profound respect. But suddenly from another door a woman emerged who didn't look wealthy at all. Next a child went in who appeared no more prosperous than himself. Outraged, he gathered his courage and edged forward to have a look. Only then did he understand the nature of the "business" all those important people were transacting in the little building!

He felt cheated. He had been frightened for nothing and he wanted revenge. His first thought was to go in and relieve himself all over the place. But then he noticed a new arrival giving a copper to the old woman sitting at the doorway, and this immediately led him to conclude that there must be something "special" about the place which he still hadn't discovered. Not daring to plunge ahead blindly, he spat insultingly at the little structure instead, then picked a spot against the wall not far from the entrance and sat down.

At that moment he wasn't yet thinking of reserving the spot as his special domain. But when the child he had seen going in emerged, and came and sat beside him, legs sprawled out, back against the wall, just like him — that was going too far.

"Hey! Where did this little turtle-bastard come from?" he asked himself aloud.

"Who're you swearing at? Stinking scab-head!"

The battle started. Both contestants were evenly matched, but somehow our hero's head was knocked against the brick wall and blood flowed. The other lad, perhaps fearing that he had gone to extremes, or perhaps considering himself already victorious, scooted off like a streak. Our hero was left in control of the field. From then on that spot against the wall of the public toilet remained his private domain.

By the day in question he had long since become thoroughly versed in the intricacies of the public toilet. The beginnings of a friendship were growing between him and the old woman who sold toilet paper at the entrance. And so on this day that was neither hot nor cold, a fine day without wind or rain and not too much sun, as he sat on his private spot, dozing against the wall, he seemed very satisfied with the world.

It was not one of the toilet's "rush hours" and the old woman munched her gums as if she were chewing something. Then she munched out a few words, directed at the lord of the spot beside the wall:

"Hey, Big Nose! Take over for me, will you? I'll be back in a little while."

What? Big Nose! Who was Big Nose? The boy, awakening, raised his head and looked around, unable to believe that she was addressing him. Again the old woman spoke:

"Take over for me, Big Nose, please. I'll be back soon. If you don't mind. . . ."

When he realized that by Big Nose she meant him, he was much incensed. He had a very respectable given name when his mama and papa were still alive; he was able to say it too. After he began roaming the streets, however, he had no definite name. At first, he told his name to his pals; to his surprise they twisted it and made fun of it. Later, he forgot it. But even his pals had never called him Big Nose. Perhaps his nose was a little bigger than the other boys'. Still, it wasn't so big that it caught people's eye. Among his pals the giving of a nickname to a boy that stressed one of his physical attributes was an insult. For instance when they were down on a child whose scalp had a skin ailment they called him "scab-head."

Our hero was therefore annoyed to hear the old woman hail him as Big Nose. Yet in spite of his displeasure he felt a certain amount of satisfaction. This was the first time anyone had ever considered him human enough to entrust him with a job.

"Take over for you? All right, but don't be long. I'm very busy," he replied, trying to look like a man of affairs as he stretched and rose to his feet.

The old lady gave him a pile of toilet paper sheets and departed. Before she had gone very far, she turned her head to remind him:

"There are twenty-five sheets, Big Nose, twenty-five!"

"I'll have to count them," he retorted without looking up. And he actually did count them.

After ten minutes on the job, he was bored. He could stand aimlessly on some street corner or squat idly on a road curb for half an hour without becoming restless. But now his "responsibility" weighed on him heavily.

"That old hag," he muttered. "She's got me tied here hand and foot!"

Weary of this curtailment of his freedom, he was just getting up to leave when a customer approached and threw down a copper.

Handing over a sheet of toilet paper, Big Nose was conscious of a new sensation. He was really "in trade"! He felt rather important. No one could go in and transact any "business" without first taking a sheet of paper from him.

With solemn respectability he placed the copper beside the pile of paper, then carefully straightened the sheets into neater order.

The public toilet seemed to have its rush hours and this, apparently, was one of them. Persons of every description arrived in a steady stream and coppers rained down on the box of toilet paper. Soon there were five or six coins. The sales representative was rather flurried. In the first place he was new to the world of commerce. Secondly he had never possessed so many coppers before.

Taking advantage of a temporary lull, he began arranging

them in a pile. He looked at the first three he had just stacked
and weighed the fourth coin in his hand as though loath to part
with it. But in the end he added it to the pile, and then a fifth
and then a sixth coin.

Customers continued to arrive until the number of coppers
reached twelve — a new high. After that, the sales representative was again able to relax.

Twelve coins! They stacked into a copper pillar over an
inch high. Like a cat toying with a mouse, our hero picked
up the stack, weighed half in each hand; then as one hand
returned one half to the box, the other hand — naturally
holding the other half of the coppers — edged close to the
pocket of his tattered shirt. But then with a sudden movement — the cat drops the mouse from her mouth again — he
added those coins to the pile too, re-forming the copper pillar.

The second time he nipped off half the pile, his hand didn't
pause to weigh the coins but with a practised movement went
directly towards his pocket. At the pocket his hand stopped as
his eye fell on the coppers remaining in the paper box. He
might have returned the coins he was taking if the old lady
hadn't come back just at that moment.

Startled, he greeted her, while the hand with the coins slowly
slipped into his pocket.

The old lady had hurried back and she was panting for
breath. Her lips moving, she looked at the reduced pile of toilet
paper and the coppers resting on top of it.

"See, haven't I done well? You ought to thank me!" He
stood up, blinking his eyes, and started to walk away.

After a few steps he turned around. The old lady had
counted the coppers and was counting the paper. He was
about to run, but then decided it wasn't necessary.

"The wind blew a few sheets into a puddle," he shouted.
"Take them out and dry them and they'll be as good as new!"

The old lady finally recognized the discrepancy between the
coins and the paper. She moved her lips with a great effort.

"You're not honest, Big Nose!"

"What do you mean? I tell you the wind blew them!" he

retorted as if offended, and trotted off. Then he stopped and
raised a clenched fist.

"Guess what I've got in this hand, old woman! Guess right
and it's yours! Ha, ha, ha!"

Laughing, he flew across the street.

### IV

After a while our hero slowed down, his fingers counting the
coins in his pocket.

There were five altogether. It was the first time he ever had
five coppers at once. He felt he could put this not incon-
siderable capital to a great many uses. Walking still slower, he
pondered: Buy a little something to tickle the palate? ... He
considered candy. With regard to filling his stomach with food,
he shared the view of his pals. That problem could be solved
by begging or by more effective means (such as waylaying a
bus-boy from a restaurant). Only a nitwit spent money on
food!

Candy — now that was different. If you tried to beg candy
from a person, you'd more likely get a punch in the nose. And
there certainly wasn't any candy among late supper-leavings
being brought back to a restaurant. Our hero had once eaten a
bit of candy, and now with five coppers in his pocket the thought
of it was most attractive.

At the entrance to a wide clean lane he saw a few children
gathered in front of a stand, and he halted beside them. Here
no candy was sold, but picture-story books were rented to youngsters to read on the spot and return.

Our hero had been avid to get a look at books of this sort for a
long time, and had peered at them over the shoulders of other
children. But whenever he was beginning to understand a
picture, the reader always turned the page. He decided to rent
a few books and enjoy them at his own pace.

"Twenty for a copper, isn't it?" he asked with an experienced
air. "I'll read them here and give them right back."

The book pedlar glanced at him and said contemptuously, "Run along, little scab-head!"

"What! Who are you calling names? I've got money, look!" He opened his hand to reveal five coins gleaming with sweat.

"Five books for a copper," said the stall-keeper, reaching for the money. "For five coppers I'll give you a bargain — thirty books."

"Nothing doing! Fifteen to a copper then. You mean to say you won't even give fifteen?" He thrust the coins back in his pocket and craned his neck to peer at a book another child was reading.

The deal was closed at ten. He only handed over two coppers for which he received twenty books. All were about Taoist monks who were formidable swordsmen, and bold women warriors.

Not being able to read the words, he put his own interpretation on the pictures. The books were in series, but because the pictures weren't too well drawn, plus the fact that he was illiterate, he couldn't tell which followed which.

However, he went through the books patiently.

One picture showed a woman with a small child fighting off a ring of fierce-looking attackers (among whom was a monk). A large double-edged sword was sweeping towards the woman and child. Our hero ordinarily had the greatest admiration for weapons like double-edged swords, but here it roused in him a feeling of repulsion.

"Like beating a drowning dog — any bastard can do that! The dirty cowards!"

He turned the page to find the woman and child fleeing towards a forest, pursued by the fierce-looking men brandishing their swords. Worried, he quicky turned another page. Not bad. The woman had stopped to give battle at the edge of the forest. And in this picture another monk, wielding a knife, was seen running up, obviously to join the fight.

Who is he coming to help? our hero fretted, and turned another page. He felt that if the monk were a good monk he'd certainly have to help the woman and child. That's what he himself would have done. But in the next picture, while the same people were shown, they had stopped fighting. Everyone seemed to be standing around talking, including the monk.

Had he been able to read he would have known what they were talking about and whom the monk was helping. Obviously the monk was speaking — for a kind of balloon was coming out of his mouth and within the balloon were words.

He puzzled over the words of the next picture, but of course he couldn't make anything out of them. The battle was definitely finished. A balloon was here emerging from the mouth of the woman.

The following picture also showed the woman and child, but all the others (the fierce men, the two monks) had disappeared. And the woman was no longer in the forest; she was in a house. She wasn't holding a sword now, but sat on the edge of a bed, hanging her head as if very weary and perplexed. The child stood before her, and from his mouth came a balloon with more of those hateful written words.

Our hero hadn't the faintest idea what was happening and was very annoyed with the artist. "Can't draw the most important parts," he muttered. "Just uses a lot of words to get by." It seemed to him that the woman and child couldn't be of much use — having to hide at home like that. Still, he was glad they had finally reached home safely. He supposed that was where they were going in the first place.

In a word, he was quite concerned about the welfare of the woman and child. Though he knew nothing of their background, he decided they must be good people. Very anxious to learn their ultimate fate, he chose only books with pictures of them and scanned the drawings carefully. In some places they battled against enemies. Using his imagination he connected this with the earlier part of the story. Before long he finished all of the twenty books.

"Here, I've brought 'em back, twenty! Got any more about

the woman and the kid?" he asked the stall-keeper. He placed a hand on his stomach. It was beginning to rumble.

Busy with another young reader, the stall-keeper carelessly picked up a set of books with a picture of a woman on the cover and gave them to our hero.

He could see from her costume that she wasn't the same woman. She carried neither sword nor spear. But she seemed quite an impressive personage, striking poses all over the place.

Flipping through the pages, our hero was very disappointed with the contents. He suddenly recalled that he hadn't yet paid the fee for this set and quickly placed it back on the stall. "Not much good," he said casually, turning to leave.

"You haven't paid yet," said the stall-keeper. He counted the books in the set. "This'll cost you two coppers too."

"What! I just examine the merchandise and you want money?"

"You didn't say that's what you wanted to do, did you? If you only wanted to see what they were like, you could have looked at one book. You went through the whole set! Don't cheat now, let's have those two coppers!"

"Who's cheating?" Our hero was rather embarrassed, but the more he thought about it the less he felt like giving up the two coppers. "All right, mark it up then. I'll pay you tomorrow —"

"I don't know you from a hole in the ground. No credit."

"You don't know me? I'm Big Nose. Just ask that old woman who looks after the public toilet; she'll tell you!"

With these last words our hero rapidly departed. He was very skilful at this sort of thing.

He had kept his two coppers and had admitted that he was Big Nose. Not a bad name, he thought. When any of the boys in his gang boasted of his prowess didn't he always point at his own nose? (The way a Western child would thump himself on the chest. — Translator.) It was a precious part of the anatomy.

## V

Our hero — or rather Big Nose, since that was what he wanted to be called — had other, even more interesting escapades.

As usual, we cannot confirm exactly the date when this one occurred. In any event it was not long after the adventure just described — one year, perhaps — on a muggy day that alternated between sun and showers.

It was lunchtime and the streets were crowded. Our Big Nose was standing in an advantageous location with an eye peeled for affluent people, hoping to convince them to bestow on him a bit of their "affluence."

Springing forward lightly, he began to follow a handsome young couple.

"Miss, young sir, please give a copper," he wheedled in a soft voice. He knew from experience that if you trailed people of this sort long enough, you got results. Sooner or later the young lady would pout and say something about "annoying little wretch!" and the young man would give him a copper to buy his ears a rest — and purchase the favour of the young lady.

But today he followed for a long time, to no avail. Arm in arm, the couple were deeply engrossed in their own conversation. They turned a street corner, and there stood a policeman. Big Nose stopped and let the couple draw well ahead, then, after strolling past the policeman, he hastened to resume the pursuit. They were already a long distance away and he wasn't sure he could catch up. The chase wasn't hopeless yet, however, for he could see that they had stopped.

Big Nose broke into a sprint. Another woman had joined the couple and was talking to them. Suddenly the two women began to quarrel and hit each other. The young man, frantic, tried to get between them, pleading with each in turn. As Big Nose drew near, a crowd had already formed around the contestants and was offering a variety of conflicting advice. Someone in the jostling crowd dropped a small packet of coppers, which the sharp eye of Big Nose immediately noted.

Unwilling to entrust the task to anyone else, he gallantly retrieved the packet and firmly placed it in his pocket. Then, slipping out through the legs of the watchers, he walked to the opposite side of the street, whistling jauntily.

Big Nose was always bold on such occasions, though he hadn't yet reached the stage of dipping into people's pockets. On such occasions he was also very decisive. If he appeared to have been vacillating in the past — as when he took only five coppers from the old lady who looked after the public toilet — it was not due to any childish weakness on his part, rather that he was unwilling to betray a trust. The old lady had given him the job as a friend. He couldn't very well take her entire proceeds.

## VI

When the weather was warm, Big Nose could make his "home" anywhere. There was something rather mysterious about him and his kind. During the day we seemed to keep meeting him on the street wherever we went; at night we seldom knew where he slept. Yet he certainly still was in Greater Shanghai. He couldn't have sprouted wings and flown — we can say that with assurance.

Did he burrow into the ground like a field mouse? Never having investigated, the author is forced to leave this question open.

However, the author can bear the responsibility for saying that at least one of Big Nose's many temporary "homes" was neither in the sky nor beneath the earth.

As our readers probably know, in the northern section of Greater Shanghai, just where the Chinese quarter meets the foreign concessions, there is a field of rubble overgrown with weeds, which stands as a reminder of the baptism of fire bestowed on this sector by the Japanese Imperial Army in January 1932. Within this honourable battle-scarred area a number of high walls still remain erect, as if nothing could ever bring them down. Against one of the walls is a cement garbage bin, a relic of Shanghai's "prosperity" era. Now covered by broken brick and earth, from a distance the bin looks only like a mound of rubble. Big Nose discovered this special "accommodation" — we can't say how or when — and was immediately much taken by it. Probably by exerting a little effort, he cleaned it up a bit and converted it into his winter billet.

We make these statements not without foundation. Someone actually saw him debonairly emerging from this "home" — which was neither in the sky nor beneath the ground — one day towards the end of January.

It wasn't very cold that day though the sky was overcast. That's right, there was no sun. Since early morning the heavens wore a mournful expression.

That morning, in certain quarters of Greater Shanghai, prosperous respectable gentlemen were sure to have risen from their sagacious contemplations and stood in "three minutes' silence" before departing for their government departments, their business offices. . . .

And that morning along one of Shanghai's principal avenues a huge column of people of every description flowed like an angry tide. Their earth-shaking shouts thundered an answer to the artillery of four years before.

Our friend Big Nose had just left his "home" and was setting out in search of breakfast. When he first saw the marchers he thought they were part of a funeral procession. "Damn Little Wu-tse," he muttered. "Here was a chance to get hired as a professional mourner, and he never let me know!" He stood on the curb, looking to see whether he could spot Little Wu-tse bearing a paper floral wreath or some other item of funeral paraphernalia.

But none of the marchers were dressed like mourners. There were people in Chinese gowns, people in Western clothes, students, workers, apprentices . . . and most of them carried small banners.

The ranks flowed on without end. No, rather say that the end of the column kept growing longer as people left the sidelines to join the procession, hundreds and thousands of people, men and women, young and old.

Walking along with the demonstration (or riding beside it on bicycles) were people distributing handbills to the spectators who lined the roadside, and speaking a few words to them. Suddenly, from the line of marchers came a tremendous roar:

"China must be free!"

The cry rose from thousands of throats, thousands of voices shouting in concert!

While Big Nose didn't understand the cry, it was obvious to him that this was no funeral procession. A little disappointed, he still couldn't help being interested. Someone shoved a sheet of paper into his hand and said:

"Come with us, youngster! Join the patriotic parade!"

Big Nose didn't know what was required of him. There were no mourning wreaths for him to carry. . . . But Big Nose was always bold where there were crowds and excitement. He went along.

The demonstration continued its march. Directly ahead of Big Nose were two young men and a girl. He didn't understand what they were talking about, particularly since their conversation was interspersed with foreign words. Big Nose had always hated foreign words, for foreigners had often struck him, and Chinese who used foreign words frequently struck him too, the only difference being that the Chinese hit him harder.

The head of the column seemed to have run into an obstacle. Shouts were heard up front and everyone halted. On all sides of Big Nose, angry voices were raised in protest.

"Forward! Smash the traitors!" was the cry that swept up from the rear.

And from the vanguard came a roar like a clap of thunder on a clear day:

"Down with all traitors!"

"Long live the spirit of the twenty-eighth of January, 1932!"

"Down with —"

Something happened up front that cut the cry short, but the rear ranks shouted it in full, and with double militancy:

"Down with Japanese imperialism!"

Big Nose joined in the cry. Then he noticed that a student beside him had neglected to button his overcoat. The handle of a small purse was sticking out of an inner pocket. Inspired by a newly acquired skill, Big Nose could clearly see the handle of the purse beckoning to him. Still shouting "Down with — son of a bitch!" he edged closer to the student.

But just when Big Nose felt the opportune moment had arrived, the marchers were savagely charged from the side by police who snatched their banners and yelled:

"You're not allowed to call slogans! It's forbidden!"

Frightened, Big Nose scooted out between a pair of long legs. He saw the student and one of the girls being beaten by the police. They refused to give up their banners!

Many people rushed to the aid of the student and the girl. Bicycle riders, ringing their bells, came speeding towards them. Marchers in the front turned to their rescue. They immediately became the centre of a whirling battle.

"Hit back!" rose the cry, and Big Nose joined in with a will. This was something he thoroughly understood. His mind worked out a formula on the spot: He himself was always being beaten by the police. Now the student and the girl were being beaten. He was a good person, therefore they must be good too. And good people ought to help one another!

Someone had dropped a banner. Big Nose snatched it up and waved it for all he was worth.

Finally, the fighting stopped and the march resumed. The student and the girl had lost one of their banners in the struggle, and they now marched side by side with Big Nose. He offered his banner to the student.

"Don't worry! I've got another one here. Take it!"

The student grinned at him amiably, then said something which Big Nose didn't understand to another student. Annoyed, Big Nose suddenly thought of something.

"Where are we going?"

"To Miaohong."

"Why? What are these banners for?"

"Do you remember four years ago, little friend?" the girl interrupted. "Shanghai was bombarded by big guns and planes, Japanese planes! Many, many houses were burned down."

"I remember!" said Big Nose.

"It's good that you remember. Don't you want revenge?"

Big Nose could comprehend this kind of talk. He grimaced to indicate his agreement.

"China must be free!" Another thunderous roar shook the heavens. Big Nose immediately, if not quite accurately, echoed it.

"Down with Japanese imperialism!"

"Long live the spirit of the twenty-eighth of January, 1932!"

On all sides the cries swelled like tides of fury. He could understand something of the anger against Japanese imperialism and he lustily shouted the slogan opposing it. The student in the open overcoat waved his arms as he yelled. Only Big Nose saw his purse fall to the ground. Nimbly picking it up, Big Nose weighed it in his hand. Then:

"Down with the traitors!"

"On to Miaohong!"

With a deft twist of his practised fingers, Big Nose returned the purse to its owner's pocket. His spirits suddenly soared, and swinging his arms, he shouted:

"Down with — son of a bitch! On to Miaohong!"

He didn't know where or what kind of a place Miaohong was, but he had confidence in the student and the girl. He felt he ought to go, that something good was sure to come out of going!

"China must be free!"

The demonstrators marched past the field of rubble where Big Nose had his "home." The sight struck them like a charge of electricity. In one voice they shouted again:

"China must be free!"

*May 27, 1936*

# SECOND GENERATION

He smoothed the sheet of paper and picked up his pen. Although he couldn't see the door from where he sat, he heard it open quietly. From the sound of the footsteps he knew that his son Hsiang had come into the room.

The clock on the chest of drawers opposite the desk said only twelve or thirteen minutes past eleven. Is it running slow again? he wondered, and put down his pen.

"Papa, I have to go to the Chamber of Commerce Building this afternoon."

"Oh," he replied, his mind on the article he was writing. A phrase occurred to him and he pondered over it. His son, getting no response, turned to leave.

To the Chamber of Commerce, eh? he thought, his son's remark finally registering. His wife had complained yesterday that Hsiang was always going off with his schoolmates. Sometimes they even walked as far as Wen Miao Park — nearly seven miles, there and back. She thought it was too much for a boy his age.

"What are you going to do at the Chamber of Commerce?" asked the father.

"Have a meeting." An irrepressible suggestion of a smile tugged at the corners of the boy's mouth.

Ah, he remembered now — today was May Thirtieth.*

So you've reached the stage of taking part in campaigns already, he mused. He scrutinized his son's face.

"I'm going with two others. They're both in my class," said

---

*On May 30, 1925, workers and students, demonstrating in Shanghai's British concession in support of striking textile workers, were fired upon by British police. Many were killed or wounded.

the boy. He wouldn't have told even this much had he not been afraid that his father wouldn't let him go alone. He had always been very close-mouthed about his "private affairs."

"Do you know the way?"

"Yes. At least the boys I'm going with do."

"All right. But you're not to walk. Take the bus both ways. I'll give you fare money." He returned to his article. Only a few words were needed to finish the paragraph. Then he could have lunch.

As he wrote, he could hear his son take a book from the shelves in the next room and walk down the stairs.

The paragraph concluded, he read it through. He shook his head and put his pen on the desk.

Taking twenty cents to give Hsiang for fare, he also went downstairs.

Hsiang was sitting in the wicker chair with the shrewd smile he always wore when he thought adults were making too much fuss.

The boy's mother was ironing clothes. "Hsiang wants to go to a mass meeting outside the Chamber of Commerce. Did you give him permission?" she asked. "He knew you wouldn't refuse him, so he spoke to you first. I think he shouldn't go; it'll be dangerous. But he says you've already agreed."

"I don't think it'll be very dangerous." The father walked up to his son as he spoke and looked at him carefully. So you've reached the stage of taking part in campaigns, he thought. Is it just as an amusement or do you really . . . ?

"Suppose they arrest you?" the mother asked Hsiang. "What will you say?"

"I'll say I only came to watch," replied the boy. Again he smiled shrewdly.

"You see!" the mother turned quickly to the father. "They have their alibis all prepared. They're organized I tell you. They even expect a clash with the police."

The father said nothing. His son broke the silence.

"They told us not to carry much money. They said don't bring any paper or pencil."

"You mean the school told you to go?" asked the father.

"No."

"Well then, who did? How do you know there's going to be a mass meeting at the Chamber of Commerce today?"

"The school hasn't formally told them to go," said the mother, "but it's encouraging them. They won't be marked absent. Some of the teachers are going too."

"But we're not going together. Our teachers will be in a different group."

"Ah!" The father looked at the mother. Evidently she had guessed right. The students expected a clash with the police. And how could it be otherwise? This was Kuomintang China, 1936!

Her ironing finished, the mother disconnected the electric iron. "I still feel he shouldn't go," she said. "He's too young!"

"Make me some fried rice and eggs, will you?" the boy urged. "My group is meeting at twelve."

"Isn't it twelve yet?" asked the father. Hsiang usually didn't come home for lunch until noon.

"They let them out an hour early today," said the mother. "It doesn't count as a cut either." She went into the kitchen.

Staring at his son, the father recalled that May Thirtieth eleven years ago. Hsiang was only two then. He had just learned to walk. The evening of the day Nanking Road was dyed with blood, Hsiang's mother and two of her girl friends went to a mass meeting outside the Chamber of Commerce to demand that all shops close in protest against the massacre. When she returned, she threw her arms around the baby.

"There were elementary school students in the rear of our detachment," she said agitatedly. "The mounted police broke through our front ranks; many children were ridden down. I saw one little boy — he couldn't have been more than twelve or thirteen — fall beneath a horse's hoofs. Luckily one of our flying squads picked him up in time. I thought of our Hsiang. Let's hope when he grows up the world will be different!"

Thereafter every time there was a demonstration, every time school children were struck with whips and trampled under horses' hoofs, the mother would come home and crush Hsiang to her bosom. Each time she would passionately repeat the same prayer.

Recently, she saw some pictures of students who had been wounded in the demonstration in Peking on December 16, 1935.* She showed the pictures to Hsiang.

"Look at that boy with the bandaged arm, Hsiang," she said. "He's not much bigger than you! Ai! How can they treat children so brutally?"

And now Hsiang too was taking part in campaigns. Countless children who were no older than Hsiang eleven years ago, today like him, curious and full of excitement, were about to join in a demonstration for the first time.

Though the thought disturbed the father, it somehow gave him a certain amount of comfort.

He and the mother sat watching Hsiang wolf down a bowl of fried rice and eggs. The father felt he ought to say something to the boy, but he didn't know where to start. How could he make him understand? Hsiang was only a child after all.

The boy's mother spoke first. "If there's a parade after the meeting I don't want you to go along. Do you hear, Hsiang?"

Hsiang concentrated on shovelling down his rice.

"Your mother's right," the father agreed. "Your lungs have only just recovered. Too much walking is bad for you. If they rush you and scatter the parade in some part of town you don't know, you'll get lost. How will you find your way home?"

The boy had been eating quickly, with a shrewd look in his eyes. But at this point he retorted in an aggrieved tone:

"What are you afraid of? If I don't know where I am I can ask! I can take a rickshaw!" Then he held out his hand. "My fare money?"

The father gave him the twenty cents and Hsiang left. The mother stood at the door until Hsiang went through the gate at the end of the lane.

---

* On December 16, 1935 over 30,000 Peking students, led by the Chinese Communist Party, staged a gigantic demonstration demanding that Chiang Kai-shek "stop the civil war; unite to resist Japan!"

"You shouldn't have let him go," she said reproachfully as she came back into the room.

"If we didn't let him go this time, next time he'd go without telling us."

"But he's so young," she sighed.

The father shook his head and lit a cigarette. His mind went back to that unfinished article. He had to hand it in tonight.

The house seemed unusually quiet as they ate their lunch.

"At first I was thinking of going with him," said the mother, half to herself. "I figured if there was a parade after the meeting I'd bring him home. But then I decided I'd better not go. I'd be sure to meet a lot of people who know us, and he probably wouldn't agree to come back with me anyway. . . ."

The father laughed loudly. "Of course not. He wants to go with the masses — not be tied to his mother's apron strings!"

"But he doesn't understand anything. He's just thinking with his heart. It's blind courage. You ought to teach him."

"How? Teach him what? Shall I tell him to avoid useless sacrifices? He's too young. He probably wouldn't understand that." Again he gave a loud laugh, but the skin of his face was taut.

They talked no more of Hsiang during the remainder of lunch.

After he had lit a cigarette and was slowly pacing the floor, he stopped several times to glance at his wife. There was an excited flush on his cheeks. Finally he came and stood before her.

"I'm afraid it won't be until Hsiang has a son of his own in school that mass meetings will stop being dangerous. China's revolution is a long hard struggle."

"I know Hsiang is going to be very brave. I wouldn't worry a bit if he were twenty. But he's only thirteen! I wish he were twenty right now!"

"Don't worry. Sometimes the days go very quickly."

The father and mother smiled at each other, their eyes a bit moist. Then their smiles became happier, more natural.

The afternoon was over before they knew it, but after six time started to act very peculiarly again — now dragging, now fairly racing. The boy's mother began considering where to make inquiries and wondering whom she should ask for help.

By eight p.m. the father was worried too. A friend came to call, bringing with him a number of leaflets he had received at the mass meeting. He said there hadn't been any clashes. Hsiang's mother felt somewhat relieved.

But then she thought of other things to worry about. "Did he get lost? Suppose he was run over by a car?" To a mother a child is always as helpless as a new-born lamb.

It wasn't until about nine fifteen that the boy finally returned. "Where did you get these?" he cried the moment he came in the door and saw the pamphlets lying on the table. He quickly brought his own set out of his pocket.

His parents burst into laughter and his mother took him by the arm.

"How was the parade? Tell Mama all about it."

"We marched to the graves of the May Thirtieth martyrs. Then we wanted to go to the North Railway Station, but troops blocked our way and we broke up. My feet don't hurt a bit." He produced a slip of paper printed in words of red.

"These are our slogans. We really shouted them today!"

*Shanghai, June 1936*

# THE BEWILDERMENT OF MR. CHAO

Mr. Chao not a capable operator? That would hardly be fair to say. In the Stock Exchange he was considered one of the best.

He had eyes like a hawk. No matter how many hands were wildly signalling bids, no matter how many fingers were being held up on each hand, he could take them all in at a glance. At once he could calculate the total number of fingers; he could fill in on his mental chart how many hands were raised palm up, how many palm down. Nine cases out of ten, he could even guess the brokers to whom the hands belonged.

His ears were first rate too. From the babel of numbers he could pick out a quietly mentioned figure — for instance, three dollars and sixty cents. "Ah, a new quote!" he would immediately say to himself.

But in spite of all these excellent attributes, Mr. Chao had a fatal weakness. From the time he was in his mother's womb, he was constantly "looking for a fall." On certain occasions others also looked for a fall, but they had their reasons, their private information. With Mr. Chao, looking for a fall seemed to be a kind of principle. News that made others in the market "look for a rise" — not merely rumours — was never acceptable to Mr. Chao. He would purse his mouth, wrinkle his nose and spit. "Bah! Just talk!" Yet he readily believed any rumour, however incredible, that the market would fall. At such times, his eyes glowed with excitement, his short pudgy fingers trembling, the fleshy folds twitching beneath his eyes. He would speak more tersely than usual, as if breathing was difficult. Should anyone happen casually to offer a contrary

view, Mr. Chao would take it as an insult, and argue
vehemently.

Anyhow, you have to admit that Mr. Chao's principle of
looking for a fall was profitable at times. He had some glorious
days between the Japanese invasion of the Northeast provinces
in September '31 and their attack on Shanghai in January '32.
But lately he had begun stumbling in the market quite frequently. The funny part was that the more he stumbled the
more he looked for a fall.

One evening about six o'clock he came rushing out of the
main entrance of the Stock Exchange, all in a sweat. A large
stone pressed on his heart — he had taken a loss of fifty-seven
hundred dollars. Usually he went home by rickshaw, but today,
in view of the financial blow he had suffered, he decided to
walk. To no avail; his legs wouldn't obey orders! He would
have to go by rickshaw after all. He haggled unsuccessfully
right down the row of rickshaws lined up at the curb, moving
along like a general reviewing his troops. Fortunately, the
eighth rickshaw puller he confronted was a thin dried-out opium
addict who needed cash badly. Mr. Chao triumphantly beat
him down several pennies, then, with an air of generous
majesty, seated himself in the rickshaw.

The fifty-seven hundred dollar loss pressed on his heart
like a stone. Perhaps because of this additional weight, the
rickshawman travelled at a snail's pace. It was under trying
circumstances like these that Mr. Chao demonstrated his kindly
disposition. He just sat with his eyes closed and let the loss
oppress him, refusing to think of anything for the time being.

Making a turn, the rickshaw tilted a bit and Mr. Chao
opened his eyes. There, about thirty or forty houses away,
stood the large gate of his compound. Suddenly he grew very
agitated. "Faster, faster!" he cried, drumming his feet on the
floorboard so vigorously that he almost dashed the shafts from
the hands of the rickshaw puller. Mr. Chao had seen in the
distance the glimmer of the electric bulb over the gate of his
compound. Sheer wastefulness!

Leaping from the rickshaw, he thundered the knocker against

the gate. As soon as the gate opened a crack, he charged against it, flinging it wide. In three strides he reached the door to the parlour and flicked off the switch for the gate light. As he turned around, he saw that the room in the wing was blazing with all six bulbs of the chandelier aglow. Uttering a cry, he reached his hand in and swept down all the switches controlling the chandelier. Only then did he hurry back to the gate and pay off the rickshaw puller.

But as Mr. Chao returned towards the parlour, the six bulbs in the wing again were shining brightly, and the electric fan was going in addition. The room was occupied!

There were two people in the wing, and they were quarrelling. Mr. Chao recognized the voices of his younger son and his eldest son's widow — a girl of only nineteen. The quarrels of this pair kept the household in a perpetual turmoil. Mr. Chao sighed. Feigning deafness, he walked into the wing, frowning. Those six bulbs worried him. "Always arguing, always arguing," he muttered, and turned off five lights.

"Who's arguing?" retorted the son. "I'm asking her for a measly fifty dollar commission, and she's making a big fuss over it!"

At the word "commission" Mr. Chao's heart skipped a beat. He promptly stepped forward, his eyes bulging at his son. But then his gaze slid to the lit bulb of the chandelier. It was the biggest of the six. Mr. Chao quickly went to the switches, turned on a small bulb and extinguished the large one. He sighed, feeling better.

"How that man can lie!" the young widow was exclaiming. "He's lost money at gambling and now wants to pawn things that don't belong to him. He just brought someone to look at it. No shame at all!"

"Look at what?" asked Mr. Chao as he turned off the electric fan. He couldn't make head or tail of this dispute.

"Papa, let me tell you. Not long ago didn't sister-in-law say it was a pity that her redwood furniture was just lying around gathering dust? That she wondered whether anyone wanted it. Well, today I just happened to meet a customer —"

"When did I say I'd sell my furniture? When did I ever say that?"

"— I just happened to find a customer and I brought him home to have a look. Of course, it's up to her whether she sells or not.... Dear little sister-in-law, that's the truth, isn't it? What's there to get so upset about?"

"Thank you very much! In the future, please don't concern yourself so much about my affairs. Bringing home any old cat or dog and claiming he's a real buyer!" The girl giggled in spite of herself. "Saying he's come to look at the furniture! A drifter like that. I wouldn't waste my time on him!"

"Ai, ai!" Mr. Chao shook his head impatiently and turned to leave. Then he stopped abruptly, his attention arrested by a whirring sound. The young people had turned on the electric fan again.

"He only came to see your things," the son said with a laugh, "not to see you. What do you care what kind of a cat or dog he is!"

"I'll thank you to keep a decent tongue in your head!" the young widow said sharply, her eyes shifting in the direction of Mr. Chao. But it was difficult to tell whether she hoped he hadn't heard or was looking at him as if to say — "Did you hear that!"

The only sound in Mr. Chao's ears at the moment however was the whirring of the electric fan. Solemnly, he walked over to the fan; carefully, he turned it off. "It's not hot. What do you need this thing for?" he muttered, and hurried from the room.

"I won't forget your dirty mouth!" the young widow said, glancing sideways at the son. Her small white teeth bit into her lower lip.

"Aiya, dear sister-in-law, darling benevolent sister, may my tongue rot if I ever say anything to offend you again!"

Twisting her waist, the girl kept her face averted. "Of all the nasty tricks!" But again she burst into laughter.

The son quickly came closer and made her an obeisance.

"Angelic saviour, you must lend me fifty dollars. Tomorrow I'll invite you out to dinner."

"Who needs your invitations! Besides, where would I get the money to lend you?"

"I know, dear sister, I know. Why not ask a certain Mr. Sun?"

The face of the young widow flushed, then turned pale. She pouted. Laughing softly, the son watched her, his eyes crafty. After a pause, the girl said with mock severity:

"Just say that again and see how fast I lend you anything!"

"May my tongue rot in my head!"

She opened her purse slowly and took out three ten-dollar bills. Without looking at the son, she placed the money in his hand. "That's really all I have," she said, and fled from the room.

The son then also left the wing and wandered aimlessly about the parlour like a headless fly, unable to decide to what use he could best put the thirty dollars he had just received. His father entered, intently listening for any possible resumption of the electric fan. But the fan was silent! As Mr. Chao continued towards the wing to switch off the light, he asked his son:

"Who did you bring to look at the furniture?"

"A customer from a Szechuan business group."

Ha, a Szechuan business group! That reminded Mr. Chao of something. He stared at the ceiling, his mouth half open, tapping his right forefinger and thumb together in a nipping motion.

Mr. Chao had a Szechuan friend, manager of the Shanghai branch of a big Chungking firm. This friend had told him that the cost remitting currency from Szechuan to Shanghai had taken a steep rise; his main office had just sent him a telegram to buy nothing more, to hold whatever merchandise he had on hand, to re-route to Hankow any goods already cleared through local Customs. This was not some fairy tale the friend had invented! Mr. Chao was the very first to hear this news, without a single detail omitted. And he wasn't dreaming

either!  He had learned the news at one o'clock at night.  As
soon as the market opened the next morning, he naturally
began "looking for a fall."  There were a lot of rumours going
around too.  Mr. Chao heard them with his own ears.  And
in the financial column — though it wasn't set forth very
clearly — reading between the lines, he found plenty of evi-
dence to support his expectations.  And yet, forty hours later,
Mr. Chao's heart was weighted with a big stone — a fifty-seven
hundred dollar loss!

He had been wrong to anticipate a drop in the market, yes,
wrong.  But all his experience had taught him that the grass
doesn't move unless there's a wind blowing.  At a time like
that what is a man supposed to do?  Not look for a rise, that's
sure!  It wasn't as if he had been daring to hope for a two or
three point fall.  Even one point, more or less, would have
satisfied him.

Puzzled, Mr. Chao shook his head, then brought his eyes
back into focus and looked around the room.  His son had
disappeared.  The small parlour light cast only his own lonely
shadow.

What would he do when the time came for him to pay off
the loss?  Mr. Chao wondered about the next step.  By the
time he paid his debts, he probably wouldn't even get back
his original investment.  He recalled his daughter-in-law's redwood furniture.  That ought to be worth a little money.  After
all she was a member of the family.  It would be better to seek
help from her rather than from some outsider.  But perhaps
that wouldn't be too easy.

Mr. Chao wasn't very clear about what kept his daughter-in-
law occupied all day, nor did he know how his son spent his
time.  He knew exactly, however, why he himself was so busy.
During the day, he was busy at the Stock Exchange looking
for a fall; in the evening when he came home, he was busy
with electric lights and other incidentals — in a word, "pre-
venting waste."

The same night, about two in the morning, when Mr. Chao
returned home again, he was a little tipsy.  By coincidence, a

few minutes later, his daughter-in-law also came home. That Mr. Chao should actually know that the young widow returned after midnight is worth noting here, because this unusual circumstance led them to discuss family affairs — a thing they seldom did.

"I don't quite understand why that man came to see your furniture today," Mr. Chao said with studied casualness.

Apparently reluctant to talk about the matter, the girl pursed her lips. But after examining her manicured nails a moment, she laughed and said:

"Really now, that furniture of mine — what do you think it's worth?"

"Thirteen or fourteen hundred?"

"Oh? Then an offer of fifteen hundred isn't bad."

"What? Has someone quoted you a price already?"

"Uh-huh, a girl friend of mine. Wants the furniture desperately. Talked to me about it several times. She wants to sell it for me — the price she gets is none of my business — and give me a promissory note for fifteen hundred at fourteen per cent annual interest. Pay me off in two years."

Daughter-in-law chattered along airily, but Mr. Chao, his eyes bulging, could hardly wait for her to finish.

"Fourteen per cent a year!" he cried. "Not enough, not enough! Let me have the furniture and I'll give you sixteen!"

"All right," replied the girl, with a calm smile. "But we'd better let my friend pay the sixteen per cent, and you lend her fifteen hundred dollars. She needs the money badly. I've already promised to help her."

Mr. Chao frowned, speechless. There was absolutely no hope. He had some inkling before he started, but he hadn't suspected it would be so completely hopeless.

"They're coming for the furniture in a day or two," added his daughter-in-law. She went up the stairs.

His face a mask of bitterness, it seemed to Mr. Chao that several pounds had been added to the stone on his heart. Had he been able to foresee that a few days after the removal of the furniture his daughter-in-law would also vanish, he might have attempted other expedients. But as it was, he only sat woodenly.

He didn't think of the furniture for long, however. Just before coming home, he had heard some remarks at the house of a friend, and now he carefully chewed them over. The friend was also a "bear" who played for a fall in the market. Quite a number of Mr. Chao's friends had speculated on a drop this time. All of them had taken a tumble, and they scratched their heads in bewilderment. Just bad luck? Not quite as simple as that. After everyone had had a couple of drinks and tongues began to wag more freely, a confidence was revealed that turned the wine in the drinkers' stomachs into cold sweat: *The big bankers were buying in, they were holding on, they were supporting the market, they wouldn't let it fall!*

Mr. Chao's face tightened as he thought of this, his hands were clenched and trembling. He knew such things had happened in the past, and on more than one occasion. But he couldn't understand. Market prices had reached the very pinnacle. Why should the bankers buy in now? They all had millions in reserves. Why couldn't they let Mr. Chao sell short and earn a point and a fraction? Surely a tiny profit like that wouldn't affect the market! But no, they immediately had to buy in, give support; within forty hours they had raised prices even higher! Really, really, he didn't know what they could be thinking, what they were after! It was as if they were deliberately out to make a fool of Mr. Chao personally!

Maybe it was wrong to sell short, but Mr. Chao would never admit it. Many people were defaulting on their taxes, rumours were everywhere, and the market had already reached its peak. Who could look for a rise? Mr. Chao had a friend who once bought for a rise. Fine! He got caught just as some big outfit was unloading the same stock; and his nose was rubbed in the dust!

There was only one explanation — they say "in the national interests" the big bankers were "taking a loss to uphold financial stability." But if he lived another twenty years, Mr. Chao could never get through his hundred per cent commercial head how it was that the bankers were always "taking a loss to uphold financial stability" yet ending up every year with a surplus.

The clock struck three. The house was very silent. In another hour, Mrs. Chao would rise for her morning prayers. Still confused, Mr. Chao fell into a troubled doze. The big stone continued to weigh on his heart, but gradually it eased off. When the time came to pay, maybe his creditors would look ugly, but Mr. Chao would sigh and press into their hands promissory notes for instalment payments. He would have guarantors whose guarantees would be worthless. As to what would happen when the date of the first instalment rolled around, Mr. Chao naturally didn't have to worry about that in advance. There were plenty of financially embarrassed operators like him in the market.

Several days later, his daughter-in-law slipped away. Mr. Chao merely sighed and sent out people to search for her. After another short interval, he acted as if the thing had never happened.

In addition to keeping a meticulous watch on the electric lights and the cooking coke, and always choosing the seediest-looking rickshaw pullers, Mr. Chao probably continued forever after "looking for a fall." And forever after he no doubt went on living dully in his financially embarrassed state, always puzzled and bewildered.

But to say that Mr. Chao was not a sharp capable operator — that would be doing him a great injustice!

*October 24, 1934*

# "A TRUE CHINESE PATRIOT"

He started the day with hot milk, at seven a.m., as per schedule. Madam personally put in the two and a half lumps of sugar and delivered the cup to his bedside. On the gilded Fukien lacquer tray also lay the morning newspaper.

Madam sat on the edge of the bed — according to schedule — and smilingly watched her husband sip the milk as he skimmed through the paper. According to schedule, he first read the advertisements, then the local news, and finally the important national and international news. By this time the cup of milk was empty and the Master put down the newspaper and looked at Madam with a smile (also according to schedule).

After stretching lazily, or massaging his temples with his index fingers, he usually sank his head back into the down-filled pillow and closed his eyes. This was in order to think over the things he had to do that day. Then Madam would ring the bell, and the maid, who had been waiting for the signal, would glide in like a shadow, and remove the cup, the tray and the newspaper. Madam would follow her out, softly shutting the door behind her.

All this was the result of the scientific orderliness which the Master had been introducing into their daily routine over the past two years. These household rules didn't exist when the Master first began "serving society" through his activities in the commercial world. He drank milk then too, but not necessarily in bed. Nor did Madam have to put the sugar in herself and deliver it to him personally. Even less did she have to sit on the edge of the bed and watch him drink it. In those days the Master usually got up first and opened the window himself. Then the maid timidly came in and with quick light steps began tidying up the room while Madam, lying on her side, watched through half-closed eyes.

The innovations began with the expansion of the Master's commercial enterprises, when he changed from merely "serving society" to "serving the nation." In order to sacrifice his personal pleasures for the nation's sake, he decided to put his family life "on a scientific basis." The busier he became the more rules he brought into their home, so that every precious minute might be fruitfully utilized. Among other things, he asked Madam to go "back to the kitchen." In the course of a year the Master ate lunch at home only two or three times; only one day in ten did he return home for dinner. But every morning he did have breakfast at home, and it was then, with the hot milk, that Madam could demonstrate her respect for the "back to the kitchen" decree. Her personal attention to the sugar and the delivery of the milk became an impressive ceremony.

But why did she have to sit on the edge of the bed and watch him drink it? The reason is that in addition to having a "scientific" side, the Master was possessed of "tenderness"; he was a careerist with a "poetic" nature. His every nerve fibre was devoted to the service of the nation. "I have long since cast aside any thought of personal enjoyment," he was fond of saying. The morning milk time, however, was a bit of private life he felt he ought to retain. He rationalized this in keeping with the romantic-poet side of his nature:

"Of the twenty-four hours in a day, we have only these few moments to partake of a little sweet intimacy, and it is only right that we should do so. Our connubial bliss, the union of our souls, when expressed in that wordless exchange of glances, attains life's rarest and truest flavour!"

"But why do you want to read the newspaper at the same time?" Madam asked him jokingly when he first offered the romantic-poet rationalization.

The Master's answer was extremely reasonable. "Ah, my dear wife!" he exclaimed. "That's because my time is so precious. But though my eyes are on the paper, I am looking at you with my heart!" He squeezed Madam's hand affectionately.

Madam couldn't fail to be satisfied with this explanation. But as time went on she found it difficult to concentrate on blissfully gazing at him in silence. At times she drifted off into a reverie, at times she watched his facial expressions reflect what he was reading in the newspaper. She was even reminded occasionally of their eldest child — how bad tempered he had been as a one-year-old. He refused to sleep unless she lay beside him where he could nestle against her bosom. But whenever this thought occurred to her, Madam quickly drove it from her mind. Looking at her husband with an apologetic smile, she would say to herself: He's so busy all day — for the nation. Why shouldn't I indulge him in this one little quirk if it gives him comfort?

Today all the scheduled matters were performed according to schedule, except for one deviation — the Master opened his newspaper directly to the national news section.

Seated beside him, Madam was involved in her own thoughts. Although she continued to smile at him out of habit, she did not observe the change of expression on his face. It was only when he noisily flung the newspaper aside that she was startled into attentiveness.

"Ah —" All of Madam's unreserved humility was expressed in the single syllable. Her eyes, though still tender, were a bit frightened.

"Aw!" said the Master, as if in answer. But Madam, who understood every one of the Master's "Aws" and "Ohs," knew that it was not an answer; what's more, he was frowning.

Caressingly, almost lying against him, Madam placed her lovely hand on the Master's forehead. It seemed a little hot. Her eyes went wide and she opened her lips in exaggerated alarm. Before she could speak the Master pushed her hand aside and took up the glass of milk.

"Ai!" exclaimed the Master, rather impatiently. He drank a sip of milk. "I'm all right. Perhaps it's because you put too much sugar in the milk?"

"I only put in the usual amount!" Startled, she stared at him and assumed a hurt expression. Then she laughed gaily. "Don't try to fool me. Something's troubling you. It isn't that the milk's too sweet. I'm afraid you've found something in the paper too bitter!"

The Master smiled wryly and took another sip.

Madam wanted to look at the newspaper, but the Master stayed her hand. He drained the glass, put it down and leaned wearily back against the pillows.

"Why take it so hard? After all, what does it matter if affairs of state —" Madam cut herself short with a hasty laugh. She had almost forgotten that the Master had dedicated every one of his nerve fibres to the nation.

Fortunately he hadn't noticed. His gaze remained calm — an unmistakable sign of the profundity of his meditation.

With no regard to the schedule, Madam personally carried the glass and the Fukien lacquer tray to a table before the window, then stood looking irresolutely at her reflection in the mirror of her dressing table.

"Then yesterday's rumour was true!" mused the Master. "Settle with the Communists peacefully! Goddam nonsense!" Catching himself, he shot an awkward glance at his wife. He never swore in the presence of ladies of her calibre, though he was free enough with his language at the factory. He rubbed his face and said fretfully:

"You don't understand. National principles are what count. Losing ten thousand men in a battle — what does that matter? Yet there are some among us who insist on coming to terms with the Communists. Even our friend Chien the banker wants peace. It's enough to make anyone furious!"

"Yes, yes, of course," said Madam soothingly, walking back to the bed. She remembered her husband often saying that to lose one's temper right after eating was bad for the digestion, and she felt he ought to preserve his strength for the nation. Tenderly seating herself on the edge of the bed, she said, "Of course you're right. But if it's already been decided to make a peaceful settlement, there's no use your getting excited. We

have a woollen factory.  No one needs wool to fight a war and
you're not a munitions broker, so why get all upset over peace?
When the Japanese attacked Shanghai in 1932 didn't you keep
hoping for peace —"

"Bah!" The Master's impatient exclamation frightened his
spouse into silence.  Hesitantly she again stretched her hand
towards his forehead, but he brushed it aside.

"I have no fever.  For heaven's sake stop mothering me.  My
dear wife, how can you be so addle-pated?  'Nothing is more
precious than peace among those living together' — true.  But
that doesn't apply to everyone.  Suppose our cook or our maid
started getting cheeky?  Would you make peace, or would you
put them in their place?"

Madam nodded.  The mention of the cook made her a bit sad.
Ever since the Master had sent her "back to the kitchen" the
cook always consulted her before going out to buy food.  He
offered it for her inspection on his return from the market and
requested her supervision when it was ready for the pot.  All
this was in accordance with the Master's "law."  Out of respect
for her husband's will, Madam could not say to the cook, as
she wished — "Don't bother me.  Do as you think best."  The
whole thing gave her a headache.

Now, smiling her agreement, she nodded again.

But the Master had just got into stride.  Taking Madam for
one of the proponents of peace, he drove ahead relentlessly.

"And another thing — Isn't there a proverb which says that
one who fails to see far will court immediate danger? The question has to be considered from all sides.  Our Japanese neighbours have offered to form an anti-Communist front with us, to
help us clean out the rebels.  How can we make peace with the
Communists at a time like this? If the Japanese decide to crack
down on us, if they send a couple of divisions and a few hundred
planes — what will we do then?  Do we dare go to war with such
a powerful enemy? Ha, my dear wife, if that day ever comes,
not only will our woollen factory be smashed to dust, but you
and I won't be here any longer, chatting in our comfortable
bed!"

Round-eyed, Madam admitted complete defeat, but it gave the Master no joy. While blasting Madam as a peace proponent, he had frightened and depressed himself by his own eloquence. Sinking his head deeper back into the pillow, he wearily shut his eyes.

Madam heard a noise outside the door. She tiptoed from the bed and called softly:

"Who's there?"

"It's me," answered the maid. "I've been waiting for the bell a long time. I came to see. I was afraid it's broken."

Madam was reminded of the daily schedule. "It's not broken," she replied, automatically pressing the button.

When the maid left with the empty milk glass and the tray, Madam followed and gently closed the door behind her. But she forgot to take the newspaper; it was still lying on the bed.

*

At eight thirty the Young Master and the Elder Young Mistress left for school in the car. The car returned at nine, and the Master departed for the office. After that, Madam and the Little Young Mistress took over as guardians of the mansion. At four in the afternoon Madam telephoned the Master to ask whether the car should go and pick up the children at school. If the Master needed the car, Madam notified the school, then sent the maid to call for the children in a taxi. This was also in accordance with the Master's law.

After the children returned they were served an afternoon snack which the cook had already prepared. Madam had to go to the kitchen to examine it first because, as the Master often said, people like the cook had "no conscience." Unless you watched them carefully they served you food that was dirty and unsanitary. Five o'clock was Madam's busiest time of the day. While listening to the children tell what happened in school that day (she later had to report this to the Master), Madam kept at the telephone, trying to locate the Master and ask him if he were coming home for dinner. This procedure too had been fixed by the Master.

Only during the period when she and the Little Young Mistress were alone guarding the mansion did Madam enjoy any quiet.

Madam used to have many friends, her own as well as her husband's. But ever since the Master put their life on a scientific basis, Madam's friends found them rather dull and seldom came to call. Although there were no restrictions on Madam's going visiting, she first had to notify the Master by telephone, and this she felt to be too much of a nuisance. Therefore except for shopping and absolutely obligatory social events, she seldom left the house.

As the Master had put it: "In the course of a week there are at least two functions you must attend; sometimes three or four. Then you have to go shopping once or twice a week. It seems to me that keeps you busy enough. You can't have much time or energy left for silly amusements."

As a well-educated person, naturally, Madam was quick to grasp a lofty principle. She acquiesced without a word of complaint.

One day Madam thought of a pastime: She decided to knit a sweater for the Little Young Mistress. When still a girl at school, Madam had seldom been seen without her knitting bag after September. Crocheted bags were all the rage then and hers was made of silk, with a pair of well-worn bamboo knitting needles sticking out two inches, like a set of horns. The whole school knew about those needles, because once a near-sighted old teacher of Chinese, seeing them on her desk and mistaking them for some new type of pencil, had picked one up and tried to mark the attendance roll with it. The needles had long since disappeared and Madam bought new ones. But these, somehow, weren't pliant enough; Madam was probably out of practice too long. Before she had knitted a strip an inch wide all the joints of her fingers ached. Just when she was ready to give up knitting for good she received unexpected encouragement from the Master.

He happened to be home for dinner one night and picked up and examined the unfinished masterpiece. "Wife!" he said earnestly. "You're amazing! This is much better than the imported sweaters. It's so soft and light and warm! Cheaper too, I suppose?"

"I'll use half a dollar's worth of yarn at most," Madam replied with a laugh.

"Ah! Make me one too. I can wear it instead of a flannel shirt."

"You're much bigger. Wool for you would cost about four dollars."

"That's still very cheap!" said the Master, stroking the knitted piece with his hand.

Madam was in a dilemma. While she didn't think she'd have the patience to knit a sweater requiring two large hanks of fine yarn, she was not in the habit of refusing the Master anything. After pondering a moment, she said:

"I hear that this kind of yarn is made in Japan. It probably wouldn't be right for you to wear it."

"What difference does that make?" The Master was surprisingly forthright. "When we buy imported sweaters aren't we sending money out of the country too?"

Madam nodded, but she obviously wasn't happy. Actually the Master was very understanding. If she had told him frankly that knitting him a sweater of fine yarn would make her too tired, he would have smiled and told her to forget about it. But instead she had chosen the boycott-Japanese-goods argument, as though it wasn't just as unpatriotic to buy from Western countries. The Master never could agree with that kind of talk. He often argued with those who held the same views as his wife.

"Buying articles is a small thing," he would say. "But to claim that Japanese goods should be boycotted and only Western goods allowed means that you're merely preferring one foreign country over another and diverting attention from the main problem — building up China's own industry. That kind of thinking is the whole root of our country's inability to become self-sufficient!"

In his opinion any useful article — no matter where it came

from — was worth dealing in. "If the tiger on the east mountain is a man-eater, can the tiger on the west mountain be a vegetarian? The Western countries are just as bad as Japan." This was his answer to those who would boycott Japanese merchandise.

Now the Master felt that Madam, as a proponent of the theory that the only choice was between Japanese and Western goods, simply had to be chastened.

"An imported sweater would cost twenty dollars at the very least, wife," he explained, "whereas knitting one yourself needs only four dollars' worth of wool. Twenty dollars as against four — either sum going out of the country in any event. Wouldn't it be better if we could keep sixteen dollars more here? That's why I always say those people who won't buy Japanese goods are swayed too much by emotion. Emotion won't build the nation's economy."

Madam hastily nodded her agreement. She hoped the Master wouldn't overdo it, that he'd stop here and rest; besides, it was time for her to supervise the cook. The Master was warming to his subject, however, and had just thought of a new and crushing argument. He didn't want to miss this chance to use it.

"Fine woollen yarn now — what is it?" demanded the Master with a twist of the eyebrows. He faced his wife and waited for a satisfactory answer.

"Fine woollen yarn is two-strand wool."

"Aiya, wife!" The Master was disappointed. "Fine woollen yarn is a semi-finished product — a semi-finished product. It's quite different from sweaters. When a country imports more semi-finished products that's a very good sign! . . ."

Madam hurriedly nodded and rose to go "back to the kitchen."

"I'll buy your wool tomorrow," she said.

As a well-educated person, quick to grasp a lofty principle, Madam decided that for the sake of helping the Master serve the nation she would have to be more patient even in matters which tried her patience sorely.

*

Any pastime which is converted into an obligation loses its taste. That was how Madam had felt about mahjong in the days before her life was put on a scientific basis. And if you top off the obligation with a pompous high-sounding title, it becomes not just tasteless but downright obnoxious. Although Madam respected her husband, she was a woman of delicate sensibilities.

One day while she was forcing herself to carry out his latest edict, the madam of another family came to call on her. On learning why she was knitting, the aristocratic visitor laughed heartily.

"You *are* patient, my dear, and *so* thrifty. But really, for the sake of a few old dollars, why work yourself to the bone?"

Madam blushed. As hostess, she couldn't very well trot out the Master's theories on the matter. She mumbled something about it being a pastime; it wasn't that they were trying to save money.

The next day she took the bit of sweater she had started and hired someone to finish it for her. Of course she didn't tell the Master.

And so when Madam kept vigil with the Little Young Mistress, she had to find some other way to occupy her time.

Every morning, after the Master left for the office, she telephoned to various friends and relatives. Nothing was sacred in their conversations, there was no matter which they didn't discuss. With these useless amenities, Madam was able to spend half the day. If, on any given day, there was no little boy's head cold to chatter about with one family, or no quarrel between the Young Master and Young Mistress of another family to chatter about, Madam found it extremely difficult not to become bored.

Occasionally, while still desperately struggling to keep busy, Madam would discover that the children had already returned from school. Then she would heave a deep sigh, as if she had just been relieved of a heavy burden.

Fortunately this sort of thing seldom happened more than once or twice a month.

The day the Master broke with precedent to expound upon a political theme during the morning milk also turned out to be one of those days when Madam could find nothing to do. None of the ladies she tried to reach on the telephone were at home. She decided to see what was new in the department stores and instructed the cook to serve lunch half an hour earlier.

After lunch she dressed and leisurely put on her make-up. The Little Young Mistress, having learned that a trip was in the offing, had long since persuaded the maid to dress her for the street. She sat waiting for her mother.

Just as Madam was about to summon a taxi, the Master's car was heard pulling up to the door. Madam hurried downstairs and found the Master reclining on the sofa, a half-smoked cigar between his fingers. Remembering how he had excited himself that morning she approached quickly to feel his forehead.

He caught her hand in mid-air and with studied casualness pushed it aside.

"I'm all right," he drawled. "I was having lunch with a few friends at Maury's when I felt a kind of pressure on my heart. It's nothing. It'll pass."

Madam sat down beside him on a small stool. "Shall I ask Dr. Huang to come and have a look at you?" she inquired hesitantly.

"It's not necessary." The Master closed his eyes. After a moment, he laughed coldly. "Damned peculiar. Even a big businessman like Lu is opposed to fighting! At lunch today all four of them were against me. . . ."

Madam's plucked brows drew together. But seeing that the Master's forehead was smooth, she immediately erased her frown and forced a laugh.

"You haven't heard the worst!" the Master continued. "They quoted an editorial in the British *North-China Daily News*. I have it here." He patted his pocket. "Wait till you see. Damned strange!"

The Little Young Mistress tugged Madam's hand and looked up with bright black eyes which obviously were asking why Mama was delaying the visit to the department store. Unconsciously, Madam pulled the little girl close, then called to the maid:

"You take her. If she likes any toys buy a few of each kind, but don't let her eat any candy."

"Oh, were you going shopping?" asked the Master. It was only then he noticed that they were dressed to go out. "Go ahead then. I need a little quiet for my letter to the *North-China Daily News*. . . ."

"Aiya! What do you want to write a letter for? You're not feeling well. Why should you tax your brain now?"

"I'll feel better when I get it off my chest. Writing won't do me any harm. You just run along."

Madam's eyes were large. She couldn't understand how it was that the Master, who had always despised "scribblers," should have such a change of character. It also occurred to her that if the letter were not published — or worse still, was published with some satirical comment by the editor — the Master would be greatly embarrassed. After all the paper was run by very influential foreigners. She couldn't let him risk it.

"Better not write," she pleaded. "You're a man of position. Why should you lower yourself to quarrel with a lot of ink slingers? It's not worth it!"

"Don't interfere!" the Master retorted sharply. "Just run along to your department store!" Then he added in a softer tone, "Don't worry, I won't use my real name. . . ."

"Then what will you use?"

"Go ahead. And bring me two boxes of cigars." The Master stood up. "I've already thought of a pen name. I'll sign myself: 'A True Chinese Patriot'!"

*February 5, 1936*

# FRUSTRATION

The April weather really was going too far. Within thirty-six hours it changed drastically. People had no sooner shed their furs than they had to dig out their summer clothing. This sudden attack by Heaven caught Mrs. Chang completely unawares. She was furious. As she sorted through her trunks she cursed everything she could think of.

The first trunk mainly contained her husband's winter clothing, made at a time when he wasn't quite so stout. You can't beat those Hankow tailors, mused Mrs. Chang, absently turning up a few garments. There's real skill! Her face was hard. Praising the Hankow tailors was equivalent to reviling their local brethren. Although she had been living in Chungking for more than four years, she had never been without Shanghai servants, many of whom had also moved west up the Yangtse River when the government transferred its wartime capital to Chungking. Actually she had nothing against the local tailors, but when she was in a temper no one could escape her ire. Suddenly, she frowned. Abandoning the poor tailors, she directed her wrath against a new target.

Those rice-stuffing policemen! She vigorously shook out a garment, as if shaking from it something unclean. They act so important. First they come and make me fill out a Stolen Property List. Then two days later they come again and make me fill out another. Then they disappear like a rock dropped into the sea — not a word out of them. You'd think their only job was recording thefts — not catching thieves!

Mrs. Chang giggled, puncturing her rage. Wearily, she sat down on a chair. To the Chungking maid servant who had been watching her, expressionless, she said:

"Open the Young Master's trunk."

Probably out of sympathy or, to be more accurate, because she thought she ought to say something to indicate her concern over her mistress' predicament, the maid, while hastening to comply, remarked with a smile:

"The thief who stole your trunk ought to be shot! Of all the trunks, he would pick the one with Madam's spring gowns!" She was an honest woman of about forty who was quite anxious to learn to speak like some of those clever maids she knew.

Mrs. Chang apparently didn't hear her. She was still muttering about "rice-stuffing policemen," and her eyes were fixed on the open trunk with her husband's winter suits. It was bad enough losing the trunk, but worst of all the trunk was full of spring clothing, and it was all *her* clothing, and now the weather had suddenly turned warm. If tomorrow were just as hot and she had to go into town, what could she wear? And she positively had to go into town tomorrow. . . .

I had a couple of beige gowns in another trunk, but which trunk was it? brooded Mrs. Chang. She began to feel very warm. She hated the police for delaying her. If they hadn't been so confident in their assertions that they would recover the trunk, she would have had new spring clothes made already.

Bolt after bolt of material paraded past her mind's eye, trailed by a row of prices. When she had spoken to her husband about it, he had heard her out, only to say negligently, "It's still cold anyhow and money's a little tight this month. . . ." Now that remark again flashed through her brain.

"I'm suffocating!" she cried angrily, leaping to her feet. In three steps she rushed over to the maid, snatched the Young Master's trunk from her hands, dumped it like a Customs inspector, then stirred through the pile of clothing on the floor with her toe.

Stormily Mrs. Chang tore through all the trunks, her rouged face bedewed with perspiration. But at last she had to admit defeat. "That means I've left two items off the Stolen Property List. . . ." she muttered weakly. She didn't have the courage to think any more about the miserable affair. Mrs. Chang looked at the tumbled disorder of the trunks and smiled a cold smile.

She went back to her own room, determined not to waste any more energy. When her husband returned, she would see about the next step. To amuse herself, she opened her case of cosmetics. By various clever means she had managed to obtain quite a good deal of this precious imported merchandise, most of it before the Pacific War started in 1941. In other words, she got it cheap. Her slim fingers nimbly arranged the paints and powder in neat ranks, and the sight of them comforted her. Gradually the round, square, oval, many-angled, flashing crystal bottles and jars transformed themselves into little zeros that streamed from the end of a number in a long train, making quite an astronomical figure.

If I tried to buy this now at present market prices.... A faint smile appeared at the corners of Mrs. Chang's mouth. Even if I had the money, there's no place to buy it! Of course we have everything here in the interior, but even with a wad of money you have to know where to look. A merchant is doing you a big favour just to admit he's got the stuff....

The practical problem of the moment, as if jealous of her satisfaction, again thrust itself into her consciousness, and her brows abruptly puckered into a frown. Mrs. Chang's face became very grave. Quite a number of her stolen gowns could not be replaced at any price — or at least it would require an enormous amount of prestige and pull to buy others like them, to say nothing of the long row of digits that would be needed to make up their purchase figure.

The wealthy young girls and matrons of her acquaintance used many devious methods and expended much effort to get their hands on adorable items like Mrs. Chang's cosmetics. She recalled the eldest daughter of the Wang family. The girl was an expert at the game; she could give lectures on the subject. The tricky business deals that Miss Wang had personally handled could fill a book. It had never been necessary for Mrs. Chang to engage in such activities. She had a substantial reserve of "merchandise" to begin with. What's

more, her husband as an industrial engineer had good connections, and had been able to replenish her stock from time to
time when the international lines were still open. But now a
wretched thief had collapsed a big corner of the material goods
edifice Mrs. Chang had been so carefully building the past four
years!

Other things he didn't touch. No, he had to take all my
spring gowns, fumed Mrs. Chang. May he die a lingering
death!... But she no longer hated the thief so much that she
could have swallowed him down in one gulp. Her mood was
now tinged with melancholy.... And the Old Lord of the
Sky is adding fuel to the flames — turning the weather so hot
all of a sudden. Aiya, it's enough to suffocate a person!...
Through the window she could see a fiery sun blazing down
with a menace that seemed to be directed at her personally.

Mrs. Chang closed her eyes. Better just stay in bed all day
and pretend to be ill, she thought. The black flower embroi-
dered on the border of the somewhat worn nightgown in which
she was clad winked at her insultingly. Mrs. Chang sighed.
Her eyes drifted back to the array of cosmetics on the table.
She remembered how Mrs. Li had been attracted by one of her
lipsticks and hinted at it several times; but she had pretended
not to understand. If the acid-tongued Mrs. Li should learn
of the fix she was in, the remarks she would make would be
just too horrible to imagine!

The heavy steps of the Chungking maid entering the room
startled Mrs. Chang from her contemplations. Annoyed,
almost distracted by the problems confronting her, she only
glared at the maid, but said nothing.

"Shall I put these things back, Madam?" asked the maid in
a loud coarse voice, poking her toe against the trunk heaped
with Mr. Chang's winter clothing.

"Mm," assented Mrs. Chang listlessly. She closed her eyes
in vexation, but the troublesome problems continued to press
down on her relentlessly, this time in the form of zeros, now
big now small, one within the other, flying wildly in all
directions, till Mrs. Chang was quite breathless. Three thou-

sand? Not enough?... an imaginary opponent argued with her. Well then, how much altogether? What! Why that's enough for a four-foot lathe!...

Mrs. Chang's eyes flew open. What ever made her think of that? That was what her husband had said ten months ago when they estimated the value of her collection of cosmetics. Of course he was being a bit sarcastic.

It was at this moment that the maid set up an excited cry, "Madam, Madam! I've found one! Isn't this one?" She thrust a kingfisher blue gown under Mrs. Chang's nose.

Mrs. Chang couldn't restrain a smile of joy. She forgot that she shouldn't act like a poor relation in the presence of the maid, and seized the gown eagerly. Controlling herself with an effort, she assumed an indifferent air, shook out the gown and carefully examined it. Her face fell. Any theatrical company's wardrobe mistress could tell in an instant what year the gown was made.

"Where did I ever get a gown like that?" Mrs. Chang started to say, then corrected herself, "What's it doing in his trunk, wrapped so carefully, as if it were something precious?"

"Madam," persisted the tactless maid, anxious to display her zeal, "what do you call this material? It has a beautiful sheen!"

Ignoring her, Mrs. Chang smiled bitterly. That gown had its memories. Usually her recollections went against the stream — from the present back to the past. But today she started from the beginning. She remembered when she got married, right after the Japanese attack on Shanghai in January 1932. The next few years passed quickly, then the fighting began again. Step by step her little home had retreated with the government west up the Yangtse. Finally, four years ago, they had settled here in Chungking. . . . The gown had been made for her trousseau but the tailor had cut it poorly and so she had never worn it.

If I hadn't been in such a whirl the past few years, I'd have given this antique away long ago, thought Mrs. Chang. With a sigh she tossed it back into the trunk.

But when the lid of the trunk banged shut, Mrs. Chang turned quickly to the maid.

"You'd better take it out again. Put it on the bed."

Perhaps she could have it altered and get by with it for the next few days while she was having new gowns made, thought Mrs. Chang. Her nose tingled and tears came to her eyes. She was suffering, really and truly suffering for the first time since the war began.

That evening, after Mr. Chang came home, they were visited by their neighbours Commissioner Li and his wife. From the difficulty of buying pork their talk rambled to prices in general. It seemed to Mrs. Chang that Mrs. Li's sharp eyes were ceaselessly examining her from head to toe as if seeking a flaw. What's more, Mrs. Li was dressed in sharkskin. Was she showing off especially for Mrs. Chang's benefit?

"It was hard to get toothpaste in the city yesterday," said Mrs. Li, her eyes sweeping from the faces of the two gentlemen to Mrs. Chang's profile, then travelling downward. "Today every single shop, big and small, tells you flatly — Sorry, all sold out! Those merchants are a shrewd lot. They won't sell a scarce item till its price goes sky high!"

"Oh," said Mrs. Chang. She was quite upset. Maybe she's going to ask me if I don't feel warm, wearing such heavy clothing, worried Mrs. Chang.

Commissioner Li laughed. "But when someone they know comes in, they always manage to produce some — for a consideration, of course."

"Everyone knows that," Mrs. Li glared at her husband. "It's just such a nuisance finding someone they know!" Then she smiled and asked Mr. Chang, "Why doesn't someone open a toothpaste factory here? Unfortunately that's not in Mr. Li's line, otherwise —" She smiled again.

"It's not so simple," Mr. Chang replied thoughtfully. "You have to have lead-foil tubes, and for that you need lead. But by the time your machines are ready to go into operation perhaps you find it more profitable to sell the lead than to make tubes out of it."

"I don't believe it!" Mrs. Li's eyes again darted to Mrs.

Chang. "Boats rise with the tide. Why can't you do the same?"

Mr. Chang only smiled bitterly and looked at Commissioner Li.

The official nodded his head. "It's not simple," he confirmed with the utmost gravity, "not at all simple. The world of commerce is in a state of constant fluctuation."

But Mrs. Li was never one to concede anything. She laughed coldly. "Constant fluctuation, piffle! The market's always going up. That kind of fluctuation any idiot can understand. It's not like our April weather. Now there's something that really fluctuates!" She turned to Mrs. Chang with a smile. "Don't you agree, Mrs. Chang? Cold one minute and hot the next, changing a dozen times a day. You go mad trying to keep up with it."

Mrs. Chang's nerves were ready to snap when Mrs. Li addressed her. It wasn't until Mrs. Li finished that Mrs. Chang was able to relax. Strange. She was like a soldier going into battle for the first time; after the initial volley she became calmer. And with her mind under control, she could make her mouth obey her will. Her reply was quite casual.

"Yes, indeed. The best thing to do is just ignore it. Mark my words — tomorrow will be cold as usual."

"Aiya, what am I going to wear!" cried Mrs. Li with unexpected vehemence, as if flinging down her last card.

Startled, for the moment Mrs. Chang didn't know what to say. Fortunately, Commissioner Li changed the subject.

"Do you hear any news from your home town?" he asked Mr. Chang.

"Nothing lately."

"Who controls the town now?"

"First it was occupied by the Japanese. Then the guerillas took it back." His head to one side, Mr. Chang reflected, then continued, "It must have been six months ago, the enemy moved in again. Probably it's still in their hands."

"Was any of your property damaged? What about your house?"

"I think it's still intact."

"Then you've got nothing to worry about," Commissioner Li said firmly. "What's already been destroyed — well there's no use talking about that. But from now on you can be sure of what remains."

"Oh?" Mr. and Mrs. Chang exclaimed together, the wife with joy, the husband rather sceptically.

Commissioner Li smiled. Before he could elaborate, Mrs. Li took the floor.

"It's something he's heard. The Japanese devils know they're going to lose in the end, that at the peace conference we're sure to present them with a big damage bill. If they burn anything else now they'll just be making things worse for themselves. Even the Japanese devils can figure that much out."

"Of course that's only an opinion, but it's not without reason." Again Commissioner Li smiled. "Otherwise why do you people in industry keep talking about taking over the enemy factories in China? After all the damage they've caused don't you think we're going to make them compensate you?"

"Naturally we want to be compensated." Mr. Chang's voice rose a little with excitement. "There are figures to prove how much public and private enterprises have been damaged. There are even approximate figures on the extent of damage to the ordinary people's homes and property. But the fact that we want·compensation is one thing; whether the enemy feel they'll have to pay the bill and so stop acting like barbarians is another. I think the Japanese devils won't quit until we drive them into the sea. The Japanese warlords will be savage to the end. They'll burn and steal and loot, they'll behave worse than ever. They know that they, the handful of warlords, won't have to foot the bill. It's the Japanese people who'll be made to pay."

"Won't quit until we drive them into the sea — Ha, ha, ha!" Commissioner Li burst into hearty laughter. No one understood what was amusing him, but as usually the case when loud laughter is suddenly injected into a conversation, the serious atmosphere eased. Mrs. Chang added a finishing touch.

"I don't know what those Japanese warlords can be thinking," she said with a lazy sigh. "They're sure to lose. Why do they insist on dragging the thing out?"

"It won't be long now," Mrs. Li assured her. "Do you know, Mrs. Chang, there's a new game that you play with numbers and the alphabet. If you do it with 1943, the word comes out in English — 'Victory.' We're going to have victory this year and everybody can go home!"

Mrs. Chang was delighted. She insisted that Mrs. Li demonstrate immediately, and promptly produced the necessary matchsticks. Standing beside the table, the two ladies manipulated the matchsticks in a demonstration of their deep concern over the outcome of the war.

The two gentlemen began to chat about the present state of industrialization.

"China must industrialize, no question about it," said Commissioner Li in a burst of enthusiasm. "State-owned heavy industry, privately-owned light industry — that's the only answer. We must make a long-range plan, the sooner the better. One of the most cheering symptoms today is that everyone's eyes are looking towards the future, everyone is talking about national construction! Everyone is planning how to make China completely industrial. . . ." Counting on his fingers, he enumerated the number of articles dealing with "National Construction" in recent newspapers and magazines — at least fifty in the past two months.

In a low voice, he continued solemnly, "That's not to be sneezed at! It's the biggest fruit the war has brought us. If it weren't for the war there wouldn't be nearly so much enthusiasm for industrialization. . . ."

Mr. Chang listened in silence, thinking of the many difficulties that harassed him — the shortage of raw materials, of capital, of technicians, heavy taxes, how to keep production going. . . . And so Commissioner Li's beautiful picture of the future didn't glow before Mr. Chang's eyes with quite the same lustre.

"But we have problems," he muttered, almost to himself. "How do we solve them? . . . Everybody ought to concentrate on that."

"Ah — yes, that's as it should be," Commissioner Li said quickly. Mr. Chang wasn't sure whether he was referring to having problems or the need for everyone to concentrate on solving them. But the Commissioner then switched back to the April weather and Mr. Chang had to shelve the case as unsettled.

By the time the minute hand of the clock had moved another four or five numbers, both hosts and guests felt they had nothing more to say. The visitors took their leave.

It was still only about eight p.m. and Mr. Chang took from his portfolio a large pile of letters and charts. He studied them, raising his head from time to time to stare into space while tapping the table lightly with a crayon pencil. He always did this when wrestling with knotty problems, and a technician not particularly skilled in administrative matters is very likely to run into problems, extremely troublesome problems. After tapping the pencil a while, Mr. Chang slowly shook his head, pushed the sheet of paper in front of him away and stood up with a sigh.

He looked around the room, as if searching for someone whom he could talk to. At times like this he always wished there was someone to whom he could unburden himself; but there never was, or by the time someone showed up he had already lost the desire. Today, however, perhaps his opportunity had come. Just as he began looking around, his wife entered. He put down the crayon pencil and, drumming on the table with the knuckles of his left hand, said:

"When Mr. A recommends raw materials, Mr. B says they're no good. When Mr. B recommends raw materials, Mr. A finds fault. When we go out and buy materials on our own, the two of them jump all over us. . . ."

Mr. Chang sighed and rubbed a hand across his face. He was about to go on when his wife interrupted.

"What's that noise? Can it really be rain?"

There was indeed a sound like rain pattering against the tile roofs, rising and falling in intensity. Mrs. Chang was beside herself with joy. "Good, it's raining! Good!" she kept repeating. "Now it'll turn cold. . . ."

"It'll turn cold," Mr. Chang echoed. He smiled a lonely smile and sat down again at the table. He didn't know or care why rain should make his wife so happy, nor was he interested in whether it was actually raining or not. All he knew was that his wife's mention of rain had washed away the words he had been about to speak.

Mrs. Chang's joy was short-lived, however. The pattering noise she had heard through the window had already changed to a series of hard sharp taps. "Oh," she said, disappointed, "it was just neighbours shuffling their mahjong pieces!" Only then did her husband's previous remark register in her mind. Turning to him, she asked, "Who jumps all over you?"

Mr. Chang grinned weakly. "People with too much energy."

Mrs. Chang seemed to be listening with only half an ear. Her eyes gazed vacantly. After a while she queried softly, "Will there really be victory this year so that all of us can go home?"

"Naturally that's what everyone hopes."

"Then it's not definite?"

"I'm afraid it won't be so soon."

"Next year, maybe?"

"That's more likely. But it's no use asking me. I don't know any more about it than you do. The optimists figure it shorter, the cautious ones think it'll take a little longer. Actually, they're just like you and me. No one can predict for sure. It isn't some tangible object that we can measure exactly."

Mrs. Chang listened silently. Then she sighed and said, "If I knew that we had to spend the rest of our lives here, I could settle down to it. But we don't know how long we'll be here. I'm always thinking about going home, but nobody knows when that day will come. That's the hardest part of all. Every day is harder to face. Even the weather tortures you here. One day you're sopping wet, the next day you're scorched."

"We've stuck it out so long. Just be patient a little longer —"

"Everyone is trying to be patient," Mrs. Chang interrupted. "It's easy enough to say, but when it affects you personally, how can you help being aggravated? Like the weather, for instance — turning so hot all of a sudden. Is it any wonder I'm upset?"

Mrs. Chang felt she had made her meaning sufficiently clear. It was now up to Mr. Chang to offer the solution voluntarily. She was thus retaining her self-respect while at the same time giving Mr. Chang a chance to display his sense of responsibility. But this time she miscalculated. Mr. Chang failed to respond. Again he picked up his crayon pencil and drew a fat envelope out from the sheaf of papers. The envelope contained a large blueprint which Mr. Chang spread on the table. Mrs. Chang had no choice but to set forth — in a detailed manner with figures attached — the proposal she felt should have come from Mr. Chang.

Noting the figures on a sheet of paper with his crayon pencil as she spoke, Mr. Chang silently waited until his wife finished, then added and checked the column.

"Why," he laughed, "that's enough to buy a four-foot lathe!"

These words, although spoken in jest, cut Mrs. Chang to the quick. The aggravation she had suffered all day brimmed to her eyes, but she managed to retain her control. Turning her face away from him, she said hotly, "Again that four-foot lathe! Very well, what if it is? If those clothes hadn't been stolen at least I wouldn't have kept them idle, and paid rent besides for a place to keep them idle in! And tell me this — did your precious lathes ever make you rich? You were running your own business three years ago, but what are you doing today? Playing messenger boy for someone else!"

When she was angry, Mrs. Chang didn't care how her words

stung. Of course the cataclysmic change that had taken place, the difference between their position three years ago and now, was certainly no less painful to Mr. Chang than to her. But that was her way of expressing herself, and whenever she mentioned their decline, there was always a note of reproach in her voice — no, say rather a cold outright sneer.

But her husband would not strike back and Mrs. Chang couldn't work herself into a real fury. She looked at him. He was still bent over his blueprint. It seemed to Mrs. Chang that she was losing ground.

"What about it?" she demanded formally. "Am I right or aren't I? Did your lathes ever make you rich?"

Mr. Chang raised his head and faced her helplessly. "You're quite right." His smile was bitter. "But what I did was also right! It wasn't the fault of the lathes that I didn't get rich. The reasons were quite complicated. But you wait and see. Sooner or later those lathes will make a big show again."

"Fine. I'd like nothing better. But when that happens I don't want them, and you, to be earning money for somebody else."

"What's the difference?" Mr. Chang forced a laugh. "We'll still be increasing national production."

His self-mockery displeased Mrs. Chang — if it was self-mockery; and if he were talking seriously, she was even more revolted. Glaring, she stabbed again:

"I'll wait and see. But I'm afraid by the time your lathes finally make a big show they'll be ready for the scrap heap!"

The shot went home. Mr. Chang sighed deeply and crouched closer to his many lined blueprint. The lathes that were the only vestiges of his glory of three years before had been idle for more than six months — that was a fact. Rather than sell them at a sacrifice he was paying rent for storage space — that was a fact too. And finally, though he would never admit it, the dismal thought his wife had just so poisonously expressed often stole like a black shadow across his heart — that was even more of a fact. The lines of the blueprint danced and wavered. Mr. Chang strained to keep them steady. Things are sure to get better, he thought. They must get better. They will, I'll stake my life on it. It's only a question of time. . . .

A slip of paper attached to a corner of the blueprint caught his eye. In addition to some numbers, the slip bore five or six bright crimson signature seals attesting the importance of the document. They also showed that the blueprint had been travelling for a long time from department to department through miles of red tape. The time it had spent touring from the bottom to the top and then back down again to Mr. Chang was already longer than it would have taken to build the object shown in the print. How long a road still lay ahead of it before it passed through the hands of a certain engineer to the workers and shop technicians Heaven only knew!

Some day there'll be fewer people putting seals on blueprints and more people drawing them, thought Mr. Chang, his heart beating steadily. There's sure to be a day when specifications won't have to make so many detours, when the big wheels of industry will turn day and night, turn in an orderly co-ordinated way. That day must come. I'd give my life to make it come, no matter when. . . . His heart seemed to be pumping with increased vigour. Slowly he raised his head and took a breath.

He met his wife's eyes, only this time he read her involved thoughts with the same keenness that he read a complicated blueprint. "The weather's warm," he said slowly. "You'd better make some clothes quickly. We'll manage about the money somehow."

"It's all right," she replied. "I've found a gown that I've never worn. I can get by with it for a while if I have it altered." Though she spoke without rancour, she couldn't control a sudden tickling in her nose. She quickly turned her head to avert her husband's eyes. She felt frustrated. There was an empty and yet comfortable sensation in her heart. Her urge to weep mingled with a sensation of relief. It was rather like her feeling when they left their comfortable home in Hankow's "foreign settlement" and started up the Yangtse towards the interior.

Once more a pattering could be heard through the window. But now besides the neighbours' mahjong pieces, something else was contributing to the sound. After listening carefully for a moment, Mrs. Chang laughed with innocent pleasure.

"It's really raining! Oh, this April weather!"

She lightly flitted to the window and closed the shutters to keep the rain from blowing in on her husband.

*April 26, 1943*

# FIRST MORNING AT THE OFFICE

Miss Huang had guessed that she wouldn't be too happy working in an office, but she never imagined the things which were to make her life so miserable.

At eight thirty in the morning Miss Huang stepped into the Company's general office. The first line of the first page of her life as an employee opened with the hushed giggles of several people talking in low tones. The light in the general office was rather poor. Although the windows facing east and north both were large, the view was blocked by buildings rearing into the sky. Instead of sunlight through the window panes came only the glow of electric bulbs in the offices opposite. A chandelier, big as a wash-basin and shaped like plum blossom, hung from the ceiling, all its five bulbs ablaze. But to Miss Huang, who had just left the brilliant May sunshine, everything suddenly seemed to go dark. For the moment she couldn't see what new and remarkable things were awaiting her in the large room.

She could hear the giggling clearly however. And one sentence emerged which sounded as if the speaker was holding his nose: "She's coming!" Though not an over-sensitive person, Miss Huang couldn't help thinking that the soft giggles were directed at her. With sinking heart she automatically turned her eyes in the direction of the laughter. She wanted to see what these rude people looked like.

Miss Huang stood awkwardly, not two feet from the office door.

Then someone approached her. "Huang, your place is over there."

It was the familiar voice of Miss Chang, her old schoolmate.

219

Chang was the only one she knew in the office. But now,
Heaven knows why, Chang suddenly appeared quite unfamiliar.
Miss Huang had visited her only the evening before, and Chang
had been her usual simply dressed self. Yet the girl walking
towards her in the light of the chandelier was swathed in flashy
reds and greens!

What's she all dressed up for? wondered Miss Huang.
Startled, she forgot to greet her. "Oh," she replied mechanically, and mechanically she followed Miss Chang past row after
row of empty desks to a windowless corner on the western side
of the room. Here Miss Huang could finally see half a dozen
people standing in a group beside the windows. There were
both men and women, and they gazed at her from a distance
as though she were some kind of interesting specimen.

Very uncomfortable, Miss Huang forced herself to concentrate on finding her desk — in the corner of the west wall that
had no windows. The desks here faced the entrance. There
was one against the wall which differed from the others, for
there were only three things on it — a bottle of ink, a pen and
a tiny piece of brand new blotting paper. Miss Huang realized
that this must be her desk.

"I'm two rows ahead of you, to the right." Miss Chang
pointed as she spoke, then glanced quickly towards the group at
the windows and gave an affected laugh.

Miss Huang couldn't resist following her friend's gaze. She
saw two men ogling Miss Chang quite openly, while two women
and another man chattered in whispers. The man's oil-slick
haircomb above a white European style collar and the two
women's frizzy permanent waves formed a close triangle.

"Oh," Miss Huang responded listlessly, and sat down at
her desk, feeling very lonely. No, just feeling lonely wouldn't
be so bad. The worst of it was that she was gripped by
nausea — as if she had got a whiff of raw fish. Dully, she
stared at the bit of new blotting paper on her desk. This is
one of the leading companies in Shanghai, she thought. Why
do those clerks behave like a bunch of third-rate actors and
actresses?

Her reflections were interrupted by a clear male voice rising above the babel at the windows and saying, "Not at all, not at all." Miss Huang looked up to see Miss Chang leave the group, a half smile on her face, and come gracefully swaying through the rows of desks.

"Huang, I want to introduce you to the people here," Miss Chang said formally. Her head cocked to one side, she flipped her hand towards the group at the window, twisting her waist and casting her eyes in their direction.

Miss Huang virtually had to push herself up from the desk in order to stand. Her body weighed a ton, her legs were particularly heavy. It was only about twenty feet from her desk to the window, but to Miss Huang it seemed miles. The office was cluttered with desks, and she nearly tripped over someone's cute pink parasol.

"This is Miss Li... Miss Chou... Mr. Chao... Mr. Wang —" Miss Chang burst into laughter. At each name Miss Huang murmured "Ah, ah," and made a deep bow, to which the others responded with a ninety-degree bend of the torso, highly ceremonious.

"And my name is Shao," a man about thirty introduced himself. He was elegantly dressed in a Chinese silk gown.

"Ah, ah." Miss Huang couldn't think of any conventional phrases to say to these creatures. They seemed to be of another world. She thought "Ah, ah," and deep bows were quite enough.

As she was being introduced to a Mr. Tsao, the last of them, and saying "Ah, ah," and making a ninety-degree bow, someone in the group echoed softly — "Ah, ah...."

For three or four seconds there wasn't a sound in the room. Then everyone burst out laughing. Though Miss Huang kept a firm grip on herself, she flushed, following which she turned pale — pale with anger. The elegant Mr. Shao quickly created a diversion.

"Lovely weather we're having," he prattled. "Don't you think so, Miss Huang?"

With a bitter smile she nodded and fled back to her desk.

She hadn't liked the desk the first time she sat behind it, but now it felt like her only refuge. Unconsciously, she picked up the pen and tested its point on her finger tip. If only it were time to start work! But there were still twenty minutes to go.

Fortunately, during that long twenty minutes, people arrived continually, most of them men. Miss Huang kept her head down and clung to her sanctuary in the corner. The later arrivals were a different type. With much clearing of throats they rang for the office boy and asked inconsequential questions in loud voices. Among themselves, they discussed the latest results of the "Champagne Stakes" races. These were the higher-ranking members of the staff. They didn't appear to notice the new little clerk in the corner.

Miss Huang finally ventured to look up. The windows were already deserted. Everyone was properly seated at his or her own desk. The elegant Mr. Shao was respectfully listening to the pronouncements on the Champagne Stakes of a fat middle-aged man in European dress. Both feet propped up on his desk, a cigar in his hand, Fatty talked in a shower of spittle. He suddenly straightened his pudgy neck, threw back his head and laughed uproariously. Mr. Shao hastened to share his mirth. Then the leather shoes scraped down from the top of the desk and the swivel chair whirled smoothly a half turn to the right. There the desks of Mr. Chao and Mr. Tsao stood face to face. Both gentlemen were leaning forward, conversing in low tones through a ledger rack. Startled by the unexpected appearance of the fat visage, their heads separated. Because they had heard laughter, they immediately realized that this was the time to join the chorus. Whereupon Mr. Chao and Mr. Tsao emitted noises resembling the quacking of ducks.

But no sooner had they managed to inject a natural tone into their laughter than they were compelled to stifle it. A white-uniformed attendant came rushing into the office and plumped a bulging leather portfolio down on a huge desk. He was the "Steam Roller," who every day paved the way for the appearance of the office manager. A hush fell on the room, broken only by the faint creaking of Fatty's swivel chair. The hoarse voice of the manager in the outer office shouted for an attendant, and many others cried, "He's come!" Amid a flurry of footsteps, leather shoes clumped nearer, then the office door with its frosted glass was thrown open. Seated diagonally opposite the entrance, Miss Huang was able to see very clearly. Another white-uniformed attendant, straight as a rod, was holding the door open with one hand, while with the other he supported a broad hat curled up at the edges in a Napoleonic twist. A moment later, a tall florid-faced individual, chest high and belly protruding, swept into the room. Behind him trailed the attendant who, with the utmost veneration, placed the Napoleonic hat on the left-hand corner of the huge desk.

So that's the manager, thought Miss Huang. She wondered if she ought to wait for him to give her work, or go up and ask him for some. She looked around the room to see whether there was some ceremony her colleagues had to perform upon the arrival of this impressive manager. Apparently none. The higher-ranking staff members were following his every move with their ears. The smaller fry had long since become busily engaged in writing or, with pens stuck behind their ears, were turning the pages of the big ledgers.

The manager seated himself. One hand rested on the bulging leather portfolio, the other drew out a snuff box.

Middle-aged Fatty sat in front of the manager, but he seemed to have eyes in the back of his head. No sooner had the manager taken his second pinch of snuff and directed his gaze forward than Fatty rose very nimbly. Carrying a sheaf of papers, he advanced on tip-toe to the manager's desk. His shoulders drooped servilely as he whispered a few words. He then placed the sheaf of papers before the manager.

"Ah —" rasped the manager. Miss Huang felt he was looking at her. She lowered her head, a bit flurried. The sight of her desk, empty except for the pen, the ink bottle and the blotter, made her squirm. She didn't know what to do with her hands.

The interval probably wasn't very long, but Miss Huang thought it would never end. Suddenly a hand fell on her shoulder and she looked up with a start. Fatty stood beside

her, smiling faintly. Her work had come! Miss Huang relaxed.
As Fatty pointed out various items on the document he was
giving her, his beady black eyes travelled up and down her
body. Appraising her clerical ability, no doubt.

"You understand it all?" Fatty asked formally, in conclusion. Then, still smiling faintly, he suddenly inquired, "Tell
me, Miss Huang, are you living alone or with your family?"

Taken by surprise, she didn't know what to say. Fatty
laughed and resumed his high pitched official voice. "Please
finish it this morning."

At last he left. But as he passed Miss Li's desk he stopped
and picked up a document she was copying. He held it so
close to his nose that it was difficult to tell whether he was
reading or smelling it.

Timidly, Miss Huang concentrated on her job, not even
daring to raise her eyes. She was only less than half way through
her work when her hand became stiff. She put down the pen
and wiped her forehead with her handkerchief. From the right, a
woman's low voice reached her ears: "The things you say!" Miss
Huang instinctively turned. There was Fatty, a large buttock
spread on the edge of Miss Li's desk, talking in whispers.

The florid-faced manager had left the huge desk in the
centre of the office, but his Napoleonic hat still rested exactly
on the desk's left-hand corner. The hands of the electric clock
pointed to ten past eleven.

Ten past eleven! Miss Huang's heart leaped. There was no
time for gazing around. She bent her head over her work.
But the more upset she felt, the less her hand obeyed orders
and the more acute her ears became. The whole office was
humming with low voices and soft seductive laughter. She
saw a girl three rows ahead stretch lazily, gracefully rise to her
feet, then lean over the man sitting in front of her and say,
"This account is killing me! Please help me with it, Mr. Chen,
won't you?"

Mr. Chen's only reply was a broad grin. Pouting, the girl
placed her unfinished document down on his desk, the man
taking this opportunity to pinch her arm playfully. "Oh!"

cried the girl in exaggerated pain, pressing her dainty handkerchief against the injured spot with excessive care.  But at
the same time, twisting her waist, she gave the man a mean-
ingful glance out of the corner of her eye.

Miss Huang saw it all, and it made her sick.  Sighing, she
was about to resume her work when she noticed Miss Chang.
Her old schoolmate was holding a handkerchief against her
mouth to stifle a laugh.  A higher-ranking staff member stood
before her.

How can an office be like this?  Miss Huang asked herself.
She gritted her teeth, determined to see and hear nothing —
just do the job at hand.

At that moment, she was probably the only one in the office
who thought the clock was moving too fast.  Her work — the
work she was told to finish that morning — was only half done
when chairs began to scrape.  In her haste, Miss Huang spattered a little ink on the paper.  Quickly, she applied the blotter,
worried that Fatty might come and examine her work.  But he
seemed to have completely forgotten what he had said to her
earlier.  He stood with his hat in his hand, his jacket draped
over one shoulder, waiting impatiently beside Miss Li's desk.
Miss Li was carefully making up her face with the aid of a
small hand mirror.

"Fatty and Miss Li are having lunch together again today,"
one of the clerks sneered to another, eyeing the departing
couple.

Then the noon bell rang.  Miss Huang dejectedly put down
her pen and supported her head with both hands, somewhat
dazed.

"Huang, let's go and eat!" called Miss Chang, looking at
her in surprise.

Miss Huang slowly rose to her feet and smiled bitterly at
Miss Chang, then went with her out of the office.  Before they
reached the restaurant, Miss Huang couldn't help asking in a
low voice:

"How can they act that way?  I — I find it a little hard to
take."

"Oh, you'll get used to it after a while," said Miss Chang lightly.

Miss Huang looked her friend over. It seemed to her that all those bright colours didn't blend very well. She noticed that Miss Chang had also rouged her cheeks.

"When in Rome, do as the Romans do," Miss Chang suddenly said rather sadly. Her eyes were earnest. "You can't get along if you're always going against the tide."

Viewing her own simple dress, Miss Huang thought of the elaborate finery of the other girls in the office. She couldn't imagine how they managed, since the best paid of them only got sixty or seventy dollars a month, while some received no more than thirty odd. Even if she spent her entire pittance of a salary on clothing she couldn't keep up with them. Besides, she needed it all to help the family. Miss Huang felt like crying.

I knew I wouldn't be very happy at this kind of a job but — but I never dreamed I'd be so miserable.... Tears rose to Miss Huang's eyes.

*1935*

# GREAT MARSH DISTRICT

For seven full days the autumn rain had been falling without cease. The previous night a big wind rose and raged so violently it threatened to blow the tents down. And when it subsided a little, moaning like a distant mournful pipe, the temporarily cowed rain raised its head and again stampeded, pounding like a thunderous war-drum.

Interspersed, there were other sounds, queer sounds — dismal, piercing sounds, rising and falling like human voices. They began in the midst of the storm two or three days ago. Some said they were the cries of foxes.

Camp had already been shifted to a rise. There, at least, the nine hundred conscripts could sleep on pallets of dry rice-straw. That was the only solution the two officers — leading the men to guard duty at a distant frontier post — could contrive. The officers were besotted with drink all day long.

They hadn't always been so dull. Although they themselves couldn't boast of many battles, their fathers and grandfathers had been bold generals in the iron cavalry which ravaged the land for ten years, defeating the kingdoms of Wei, Chao, Han, Chu, Yen and Chi and uniting them under Chin, the First Emperor. They had heard the beat of the war-drums while still in their mothers' wombs; they had grown up on the backs of spirited chargers. They were the descendants of generals, well-to-do landowners. To wear soldier's armour was their special privilege. Usually the men they led were landowners like themselves, youths from their own village, bound together by class loyalties. But today they were commanding mere conscripts, contemptible slaves who never before had the right to serve as soldiers, rabble with no feeling for their officers' class at all!

In this unaccustomed and even hostile company, on running into an endless downpour of depressing autumn rain, the two officers slowly drank themselves into a stupor. They were as bedraggled as muddy cats, but they were cats of whom the mice were no longer afraid.

Awakening in the middle of the night, the officers heard the piping sound of the wind and the drumming beat of the rain and felt the icy cold of the autumn wind bite into their bones. For the moment they had a vague feeling that they had already reached the endless sands of the northern frontier post. Their destination was Yuyang. Yuyang — how easily it rolled off the tongue! Could it be the same Yuyang to which the great general Meng Tien once led three hundred thousand men? Three hundred thousand men who never returned, whose bones are fertilizing the wild grass!

Away, cursed thought! After drink the mind is dark and morbid. Their orders were to arrive at the border post before the end of the eighth lunar month. Although the month was almost over they had only reached Great Marsh District, and now the infernal rain was holding them up. Military law dealt harshly with those who failed to carry out commands within the prescribed time.

There was a rumour that the day before a fish had been caught with a piece of white cloth in its stomach. Three vermilion words were written on the cloth: "Chen Sheng — Emperor!"

Chen Sheng? One of the two camp leaders was named Chen Sheng. He was a big man, unusually handsome for a peasant. But what was all this about "Emperor"?

Suddenly a strident cry rang from a distant height, so powerful that it drowned out the noise of the wind and rain. Paling, the officers looked at each other in the dim lamplight. The cry was breath-taking; it made your heart stop beating; it froze the blood in your veins. Foxes had been howling every night, but this was the howl of a fox-demon, a howl that shattered your heart. On and on, wailing, accusing, threatening. Words could be discerned clearly:

"Restore the Kingdom of Chu!"

"Chen Sheng — our Emperor!"

The officers repeated the calls with fear-paralysed tongues. Fully sober, they could almost see Chen Sheng with their drink-inflamed eyes, see his poor peasant's face, slightly wrinkled and darkened by the sun. Because of his stature, he had been chosen from among the conscripts to be a camp leader. What if he had muscles of iron? He knew nothing of military lore.

The greatest danger lay not in Chen Sheng but in the rain. The rain prevented them from marching, it cut off their supplies. Another seven days of rain and all nine hundred of them would die of hunger. But even before then, was there anything the conscripts would not dare when they found themselves threatened with starvation?

*

It was still raining the next day. The two officers were reluctant to leave their tent and meet the glares of hatred. The men had been living on fish and prawns for some time now. Although it filled their bellies, the diet seemed to make them as crusty as the shellfish. The conscripts were no longer docile and obedient. They were full of angry complaints:

"What shall we do? We can't march, but if we stay here we'll all drown!"

"We'll get ill if we keep eating nothing but fish!"

"The firewood is finished. We can burn our pallets today, but how will we cook tomorrow? Must we eat raw fish? We're not otters!"

"They say it's nearly a thousand miles to Yuyang."

"We'll die anyhow when we get there!"

Their eyes were large with the fear of death. Why did they have to die in Yuyang? Because the military law prescribed execution for all who disobeyed orders. The law was not of their making, but they had to die! And even if there were no such law, after reaching Yuyang what good would they gain by defeating the Hsiung Nu tribesmen? The conscripts originally had been peasants in the six kingdoms conquered by the state of Chin. Although their own countries had given them nothing but wars and forced labour and had never shown them any kindness, at least they had been "free citizens." They deeply regretted that they had not fought for their countries when the troops of Chin invaded. They were slaves now, conscripts who had to plunder for the rich landowners, the "free citizens" of the powerful state of Chin. Weren't they going to Yuyang to protect these free citizens who held them in such contempt, to win booty for rich landowners like their officers? And weren't they going to pit their poor men's bones in mortal combat against the Hsiung Nus — nomads moving south in search of pastures — in order to turn them into slaves like themselves?

The conscripts had never really thought about their position before. But because they were held up so long by the rain, because they had to eat fish every day, because they were out of firewood, and especially because of the weird cries of the foxes in the night, these new thoughts seeped into their minds like a mist.

The written strip of cloth found in the belly of the fish, the fox that howled like a man in the middle of the night — these things the nine hundred conscripts considered uncanny. But that was as far as their ideas went. They had had more than their share of strife because this one or that one had wanted to be king. Their only desire was to be free again. And they had their superstitious reasons for believing that their day of deliverance was close at hand. Hadn't a stone fallen from the sky two years before inscribed with the words: "When the First Emperor dies, the land will be divided"? And hadn't the wizard who lives east of Hwashan Mountain and drives a chariot with a white horse predicted, "The Dragon Emperor will die next year"? Well, the First Emperor of Chin had died and been succeeded by the Second. Now was the time to realize the part of the prophecy about dividing the land!

It seemed to the nine hundred conscripts that the only thing worth risking their lives for was the joy of planting their own land. They were not interested in "Chen Sheng — Emperor." If they had to go on having emperors, they wanted one who would be different from the old Emperor, one who would give them land of their own to till.

\*

The wind continued to blow, the rain continued to beat down. But more tumultuous than the storm were the cries of the nine hundred conscripts. Wave after wave of their riotous shouts drove into the tent of the two officers.

The situation was getting out of hand. Slowly the officers strode from their tent. They would have to put their prestige to the test.

They walked as if making a routine inspection of the camp. Their unexpected appearance produced an unexpected effect. True, the clamour of the men ebbed bit by bit. But in place of using their mouths, the conscripts demonstrated with their eyes. They were not greeting their officers with any "eyes right" salute, however. There was hatred, ridicule in their stares, a "What are you going to do about it?" sort of look. The officers had been prepared to entertain requests, consider complaints. To end their isolation they would have welcomed even "insolence." Instead, they were met with coldness and made to feel more isolated than before. It was as if they were in a foreign country, in an enemy camp, in a wilderness of venomously flashing eyes.

They were separated from the men by a swirling Yellow River of hate. They had absolutely nothing in common with them. The conscripts were suffering, there were things they wanted. But they were not going to voice their wishes to these two officers.

Finally the officers halted on a small mound outside the camp and pretended to survey the terrain.

Great Marsh had indeed become one big marsh. Thatched huts seemed to rear abruptly through the white mist. The water

had risen so high that two or three villagers were casting their
nets almost in front of the doorways.  Weeping willows dab-
bled their trailing branches into the waves.  Reeds, covered up
to their white tassels, trembled above the water as if with irrepressible emotion.  The sky was leaden and rain fell in large
drops.  The scene was like a typical painting of a river village
in the mist and rain.

Watching uneasily, the officers were gripped by a strange
emotion — a feeling of desolation and tragedy!  Not necessarily stupid, they were convinced by the tour of the camp they
had just made that they were in an untenable position.  Fear
acted as a prod that sharply reminded them of the class character flowing in their veins with the blood of their forefathers.
They could not stand with folded hands on this desert island
of a mound and wait for the hatred of the slaves to rise and
drown them in the flood.  They would have to gamble everything on one stroke!

"You see it, don't you?  It's either them or us."

"Shall we kill the two camp leaders first?"

"If necessary, we'll finish off the whole nine hundred!"  The
first officer swung his right hand in a vigorous determined
gesture.  "We'll bury them alive!"

"Who will dig the pit for us?"  There was no surprise in
the other's voice.  He was only discussing procedure.  In his
cruel tones there was a deadly competence.

"Why can't this misty stretch of water be the pit?"  The
first officer smiled with satisfaction as he looked at the vast
watery expanse below them.  Then the smile faded and his
visage was darker than ever.  Angrily biting his lips, in a low
voice he asked his companion:

"How many of them are loyal to us?"

Hah!  Loyal?  Not a one!  These were not their own men.
There never were enough soldiers of the rich landowner class
even when Chin was conquering the other kingdoms, and then
so many of the best warriors had been lost with General Meng
Tien.  Even for camp leaders it was necessary to use slaves.

The danger of the situation confronting them was very apparent to the officers.

*

"The Emperor should not have conscripted slaves for soldiers!" said the second officer angrily. Suddenly he knew that the golden age of his forefathers was gone, never to return.

"Indeed he should not! Since the days of Lord Shang's reforms our ancestors protected our country with shield and spear. Soldiering is a glorious occupation. How can we let it be sullied by slaves! Since the First Emperor ascended to Heaven there is no more order. Giving weapons to slaves is the idea of that treacherous minister Chao Kao. His father and mother both were slaves!"

"Our new Emperor holds the sword by the blade and lets others grasp the hilt!"

The two officers dared speak so openly only because they were on a small mound far from the royal court. But even as they talked, their boldness diminished. The wind was blowing hard again. Wet cowhide armour is always cold, and now, aided by the wind, it chilled them to the bone. After looking at each other in silence, they raised their faces to let the cool rain soothe their helpless melancholy. How far were they from home? They could see only endless clouds and mountains stretching into the distance. Far to the west was Hsienyang, the capital. What was the situation there? The royal guards were all proven warriors of the previous emperor. But the flood of slaves was too great. Hsienyang would be inundated just like Great Marsh!

*

The officers returned to their tent as depressed as when they had set out. The shadow of the coming fall of their class covered their faces like a pall. There was no doubt but that they were in for a battle to the death. The only question was how to strike before the enemy was ready and inflict a mortal wound.

— First kill the two camp leaders?

— What about the other nine hundred?

— Probably we can browbeat or bribe half of them.

— We can collect all their weapons and put them in the fire.

These thoughts travelled between the two officers in their exchange of glances. Suddenly, they heard a booming voice shout:

"If we stay here, we'll starve. If we get to Yuyang — late — we'll die too. But if we act together we will all live. As for the officers — let them drink themselves to death!"

There was a roar of laughter followed by a clamour of many voices.

The officers paled and their lips trembled. Then their expressions changed again. Biting their lips and raising their brows, the two armed officers of the ruling class were filled with a murderous rage. But before they decided on a course of action, a gust of wind blew open the flaps of their tent and exposed them to the yelling mass. The clash could be delayed no longer. This was also evident to the conscripts, who shivered with excitement as they looked at the officers in the tent. The officers stood glaring, red-faced with fury. But after all there were only two of them!

"Shouting is forbidden in the camp! Leaders, arrest the rioters!" snarled an officer, drawing his sword. He rushed at Wu Kuang, one of the camp leaders.

The conscripts responded with a bellow of rage that shook the tent. Today the armed slaves were not taking any orders! Like a huge bear, Wu Kuang seized the officer's sword and hacked it into his waist. The maddened conscripts surged over the other officer and beat him to the ground before half a groan could escape his twisted mouth.

Like wildfire the crash of slaves breaking their chains spread from camp to camp. Every village, every county in the realm once ruled by the First Emperor of Chin was rocked by the explosion in Great Marsh.  Oppressed peasants rose throughout the land!  Like a great tide they swept away the corrupt officials, the cruel repressive laws!

The wind was the paean of victory, rain beat the war-drum for the attack, the autumn floods in Great Marsh were the proclamation of the revolt of the enslaved peasants.  Ranging from village to village, from county to county, the nine hundred, carrying out history's decree, freed the angry fire so long pent-up in every thatched hut!

The Emperor is dead!  The land will be divided!

*October 6, 1930*

# ABOUT THE AUTHOR

Shen Yen-ping, who writes under the pen-name Mao Tun, is one of the most outstanding exponents of revolutionary realism to appear in China since the New Literature Movement of 1919. He was born in 1896 in Tunghsiang County, Chekiang Province. Together with Cheng Chen-to, Yeh Sheng-tao and other writers, in November 1920 he founded the Literary Research Society, one of the first organizations to be formed in China to advocate a new outlook in literature. In 1921 he became editor of the *Fiction*, a literary monthly published by the Commercial Press in Shanghai. He completely overhauled this periodical and through it launched a fierce attack on feudal and comprador influences in current Chinese literature.

From 1926 to 1927 he edited the *Minkuo Jihpao*, a revolutionary daily in Hankow. When Chiang Kai-shek betrayed the revolution, and the Kuomintang became firmly anti-Communist, he left Hankow and returned to Shanghai.

From then on he used the pseudonym Mao Tun in his novel-writing, which served to expose the evils of the reactionary Kuomintang regime and to reflect the revolutionary struggle of the people. He wrote the novels *The Canker*, a trilogy, in 1927, *Rainbow* in 1930, *Three Companions* in 1931, and *Midnight* in 1933, as well as a number of short stories, essays and articles.

During the War of Resistance Against Japan (1937-45) Mao Tun kept up his literary activities by editing the periodical *The Literary Front* and writing the novels *Corrosion* (1941) and *Frosted Leaves as Red as Flowers in Spring* (1942), the play *Before and After the Chingming Festival* (1944), besides various short stories, essays and articles.

In 1949, after the founding of the People's Republic of China, Mao Tun was made Minister of Culture and continued to hold this portfolio until 1964. In 1954, he was elected a deputy to the First National People's Congress, and later re-elected to the successive National People's Congresses. He is now concurrently Vice-Chairman of the China Federation of Literary and Art Circles, Chairman of the Union of Chinese Writers and Vice-Chairman of the Fifth National Committee of the Chinese People's Political Consultative Conference.